Foreign & Domestic

The Price You Pay for Love 2

by

Destiny Skai

Lock Down Publications and Ca$h
Presents

The Price You Pay for Love 2
A Novel by *Destiny Skai*

Lock Down Publications
P.O. Box 944
Stockbridge, Ga 30281

Visit our site at
www.lockdownpublications.com

Copyright 2021 by Destiny Skai
The Price You Pay for Love 2

This is a work of fiction. Names, characters, places, and incidents either are products of the author's imagination or are used fictitiously. Any similarity to actual events or locales or persons, living or dead, is entirely coincidental.

Lock Down Publications
Like our page on Facebook: Lock Down Publications @
www.facebook.com/lockdownpublications.ldp
Cover design and layout by: **Dynasty Cover Me**
Book interior design by: **Shawn Walker**
Edited by: **Nuel Uyi**

Stay Connected with Us!

Text **LOCKDOWN** to 22828 to stay up-to-date with new releases, sneak peaks, contests and more…

Thank you!

Submission Guideline.

Submit the first three chapters of your completed manuscript to ldpsubmissions@gmail.com, subject line: Your book's title. The manuscript must be in a .doc file and sent as an attachment. Document should be in Times New Roman, double spaced and in size 12 font. Also, provide your synopsis and full contact information. If sending multiple submissions, they must each be in a separate email.

Have a story but no way to send it electronically? You can still submit to LDP/Ca$h Presents. Send in the first three chapters, written or typed, of your completed manuscript to:

LDP: Submissions Dept
P.O. Box 944
Stockbridge, Ga 30281

DO NOT send original manuscript. Must be a duplicate.

Provide your synopsis and a cover letter containing your full contact information.

Thanks for considering LDP and Ca$h Presents.

Destiny Skai

Previously from Part One...

The sun had just began to lower below the horizon, as I drove through the evening traffic. After discussing a few things with Demerius earlier, I had a new mission at hand. Ever since I'd discovered Keith's body in his home, my supervisor had been on my ass demanding answers. It looked very awkward that I had guided him upon his release from jail and not even a month later he'd ended up dead.

I had enough on my plate with Antwan, I needed my payday. A hundred grand didn't come easily. Neither did a conviction. All I had to do was keep the cards falling correctly and I would receive my end of the deal on both parts. Money and celebrity dick. It was all a plus.

A creepy feeling surfaced as I smiled turning down the next intersecting street. The luxurious homes were in need of a new face around the area, and I was about to be the first candidate. I had worked my ass off for the Tampa police department and still couldn't receive a promotion, a better pay grade. . . Nothing. After finding my flow in the streets of the dirty orange state, I started to apply my skills by pressing other people. If you didn't cut me in on the deal, you were going to get cut out. If you went behind me and continued to do the same thing, I would eliminate you from the streets until your death date.

Pulling inside the driveway, I holstered my weapon before killing the ignition. Stepping out, my heels clacked across the pavement with a sweet melody of happiness. This moment was surely one to remember. Ringing the doorbell of the elegant home, I waited patiently until she opened the door. When she looked into my face, her posture quickly changed.

Foreign . . .

Climbing out of my bed, I looked at the clock. It was nearly eight o'clock at night. The signs of the child was kicking hard. After my nasty session with Aaron last night, I passed out and didn't wake until this morning. I still didn't understand why I couldn't keep my eyes open, but sleeping my days away was not about to be my new objective.

Heading downstairs, I buttoned up my robe. I was craving for a fresh bowl of fruit and my stomach was turning circles just as I began to move. If Aaron kept the sex game straight like last night, he wouldn't have to worry about anything with the divorce. All in all, I still had time to straighten things out with Domestic.

The sound of my doorbell ringing grabbed my attention. Swiftly heading through the living room, I opened the door and paused when I saw the sheisty-ass cop chick.

"Can I help you?" I asked with sarcasm dripping from my tone. I wanted to know how the fuck the bitch got my address.

"Hey. Foreign, right?"

"Yeah. That's me. What do you need?"

"Well actually, I'm here to talk to you about your husband, Aaron. If it's not too much to ask, could I come in and have a second with you?" Her expression seemed like it could've been urgent.

Stepping to the side, I allowed her to enter. Leading her to the couch, I took a seat in the leather chair across from her. "Would you like anything to drink?"

"No, thank you. I didn't mean to just barge in, but I didn't know if you were alone or with him at the moment."

"What does it matter if I was? Is something wrong?" This bitch's vibe was definitely off key. She seemed a little too edgy.

"True indeed, it wouldn't have mattered whether he was here or not because I came to speak with you. Not him."

"What about? If this is about the football scandal with the little teen, I don't know anything. I'm only his wife."

"This isn't about the scandal. I've already gathered my evidence on that, and the truth will be revealed sooner or later. The trial date should be set. The reason I'm here tonight is more personal."

I had to look her up and down when she uttered *personal* from between her lips. I damn sure didn't have any smoke with her. Neither should Aaron. Regardless of the case approaching, the authorities had no reason to be snooping around our home.

"What is this about? I'm honestly not into the whole guessing game."

Emilia gave me a slight nod like she was about to expose my entire kindergarten history report. "Aaron has been cheating on you of course, and his affairs are starting to cause confusion in more than one home."

"Excuse me! What are you talking about?" Confusion in what home because this is the only crib Aaron lays his damn head in.

Her legs crossed hearing my remark. "Do you honestly feel that way?"

"So what the fuck are you saying? My husband is cheating with you. That's what you mean?"

9

"Not just me, plenty of other women too. I'm just the one he's spilling his seeds in. I know you may feel a certain type of way about this, but I felt like you deserved to know."

The pain of her statement left me with a scar so deep on my heart. Aaron was hanging on by a thread and out of nowhere this woman was telling me that he was playing house at another bitch's crib. Not just one, but numerous?

Leaning up in my chair, I eyed her with a devilish smirk. "This has to be a joke, right?"

"I'm afraid not," she replied with a straight face.

I laughed before standing to my feet. "Miss. You don't even know me or my husband, for that fact. I saw you snooping around at Demerius' carwash a few times. You sure that's not what this is about because it surely seems like he's close to you also."

"No, sweetie," she paused, "you and Demerius are close. I'm only doing my job when it comes down to you ever seeing me at that wash. You've been sneaking around on Aaron and it's quite obvious that you're in love with another man. Not to get off the subject, but I thought it may have been the reason for your husband's behavior."

This lady was calling out shit that no one else could possibly know. Her recent pop-ups at Demerius' business were sounding more like a spying mission. At the time, I didn't even know if I could trust the words coming out of her mouth.

"I don't know what you're talking about. I'm not cheating on my husband. I have a job at the carwash. It's the only reason you've ever laid your eyes on me. You've never seen me touch him so please don't speak on things you have no knowledge of."

Snickering, Emilia pulled out her phone and recited Aaron's number. "Do you think I'd be wrong if I could tell you what color your bedspreads are?"

I knew her bluffs were beyond accurate. The steam blowing inside my head told me to get up and beat this bitch to death. "It seems funny that you think you know anything about my husband. What if I beat your ass and called it self-defense due to you raging in my home?"

"What if I throw your ass in jail faster than a prostitute out of Dade County? I still have on a badge, sweetheart. Remain calm."

She was sitting like the Queen of England in my home and from the looks of it, she was beyond comfortable. Rocking my foot harder than a motor engine, I eased my tension. I should've made her stay on the other side of the door where I had all control of the situation. But things were about to fly off the handle once Aaron crossed the threshold of our home.

"Listen, Foreign, I didn't come to make you seem like the bad person here. I'm only making you aware of what's going on. You're sleeping with your enemy, baby. He's the one who's telling me a different story when he's at my house. I'm sure if you call him, he wouldn't be able to deny these accusations. You don't even have to mention me being here," she stated with confidence.

Testing her arrogance, I got up and grabbed my phone from the kitchen counter. Dialing Aaron's number, he answered after the fourth ring.

"Hey, baby?"

"Don't *hey baby* me, Aaron. Is there anything you need to tell me?"

"Foreign, I can't hear you. What did you say?"

"Oh, you heard me. I said is there anything you got to tell me?"

Hearing the phone beep, the call ended leaving me on the line alone.

"Maybe I should try back at another time," Emilia said before rising out of her seat. She headed for the door and left before I launched my phone into the wall. The tears that stained my eyes were for the last time. My mind was officially made up, I was leaving Aaron Young for good.

Aaron...
Twenty minutes earlier . . .

Today was going to make the twelfth session in my sex class and I felt excellent. I could honestly say it felt great to open my eyes and realize that my girl could've left but stayed. She was ready to abandon the vows we'd made because of my horrible deception. The more time I sat in this class it began to come clearer. Foreign was hurt and the only way she could heal herself was to step away from me. Learning that love wasn't easy was the hard part for me. Through it all I was able to smile because I still had the love of my life by my side.

After Ms. Anderson cleared the class to leave. I approached her desk. "Hey, Aaron. Did you gain anything from the class tonight?" she asked, giving me her undivided attention.

I flashed her a positive grin before nodding. "I enjoyed it. The classes have been going great and I want to thank you personally for all the help."

"No problem. It's what I do. To be honest, I feel that you had it under control the entire time. Your heart shows that you want to change. When you've accepted change, you gain more because of your acceptance to something different. If it pushes you forward, go for it."

"True. I just wanted you to know that me and my wife are doing great again. We mended our differences. I can't say we've fully rekindled from my painful mistakes but were rebuilding."

"That's great, Aaron. Remember, time heals everything. The scar may still be visible, but the pain will eventually subside, if you change."

Grabbing a piece of paper, she scribbled something down on it before passing it over to me. Taking it, I viewed the address to her main office in Miami. We're having a main event for the center next month. It would be delightful if you and the wife could come and show support."

Agreeing to her wishes, I placed the info into my pocket and shook her hand. Walking out of the treatment class, I held my head high as the rain poured down heavily over the building. It took a strong person to admit things that could possibly destroy their character, fame, or relationship. It's what separated the pure from the cold hearted. If you're willing to risk everything you have for the one person you love, make sure they're willing to do the same for you. Foreign was my heart and nothing compared to her worth in my eyes.

Getting outside, I jumped in my car and sped off quickly. My mind, body and soul were ready to get back to her. Last night was magical. It had been a while since we bonded that hard and she definitely had me feigning.

Dialing Lexi's number on the phone, I stopped at the red traffic light. The sound of a Mustang engine pulled up directly beside me. Cutting my eyes at the car, I admired the dark black paint and midnight tinted windows.

"Hello?" Lexi yelled through the phone.

"What are you doing, sis?"

"Trying to find out who I'm screwing tonight. What do you want, Aaron? If you lost Foreign again, I'm not helping," she laughed into the receiver.

"Shut up. I just called to let you know I finished my class. Thank you for helping me, for real. I love you."

The light turned green and I continued across the intersection. I could see the bad ass Mustang that mashed the gas smoothly behind me.

"You're my twin, Aaron. That's my duty. I love you too."

Hearing my phone beep, Foreign's name flashed across my screen. "Lexi, she's on the other line now. I'm gonna call you back, okay?"

"Yeah, yeah. Make it tomorrow. Bye, boy."

Clicking over, I noticed the Mustang's speed had slightly increased. "Hey, baby."

"Don't hey me." The rest of her words began to slightly break up.

"Foreign? I can't hear you. What did you say?" I asked talking louder into the receiver.

The sound of the Mustang engine was now accelerating heavily. I glanced to my side and watched the car pull directly next to me like it wasn't a one way street. I jerked my car over slightly just to be cautious. Foreign's voice was still cracking in the phone and she didn't sound happy. Before I could reply, the car rammed into me and I couldn't grip the steering wheel fast enough.

My car flipped recklessly over the curb and the slow spin caused my life to flash before my eyes. All I could feel was the hard catastrophe of my car flipping uncontrollably across the ground. My neck connected with the windshield knocking the feeling out of my body, before crashing into the tree in front of me.

The smoke from my vehicle began to thicken and the sound of the Mustang's motor decreased, while I silently begged for help. I could hear the thump of my heartbeat slowing down through my ears before I blacked out.

Chapter 1

Foreign

After Emilia left my heart in shambles, I wasn't able to get any sleep. All night I tossed and turned. It was difficult to sleep with a broken heart. When Aaron didn't bother to come home or answer his phone, it made me wonder if he was with that bitch. However, that was my confirmation that we were over. Domestic had been blowing up my phone, but I didn't bother answering. I had no energy to talk to him at that moment. My life was in shambles, and I needed to get away from Aaron. It was over, and I wanted a divorce immediately. There was no coming back from this, and I was going to be sure to deliver the news to his parents in person.

A few minutes away from my in-laws, I veered off of Oak Preserve Boulevard and into the Pebble Creek suburban neighborhood. Aaron thought it was a good idea to have them in the same neighborhood, so they could be close to one another. While that may have been a good idea back then, it wasn't now, and it was because I hated their son with a passion. His trifling ass had the audacity to not come home after his hoe came to our home and busted his ass out. The closer I got to the house, my stomach was in a thousand knots. However, something in my spirit wasn't happy.

Finally, I pulled into the driveway and put the car in *park*. There were a few vehicles in the driveway. A few of them were out of place. Curiosity took over me, so I grabbed my Birkin bag and rushed to the door. It wasn't locked, so I walked right inside. Mr. Young was sitting on the sofa, holding his wife in his arms, while my parents were sitting there with distraught looks on their faces. Lexi wasn't in the living room, but her car was outside. My eyes immediately fell upon that bitch—Emilia—standing in the living room. She was wearing a business suit.

"Hello," Emilia said.

My first instinct was to drop-kick that hoe. All I knew was that she'd better not be standing there looking for Aaron. These new side chicks were bold in the new millennium. First, the bitch showed up to my home, now she was at my in-laws' residence. When it came down to family, I was very territorial over what was mine.

"Mrs. Young, I need to speak to you. Please have a seat."

"Why are you here, Emilia?" Her presence was awkward since everyone was silent. That made me wonder what she said to them.

My father stood up and came towards me. "Come have a seat by your mother."

"I think I'd rather stand. So just please tell me what's going on." My bag hung heavily on my shoulder, but I let it fall to my hand to gain some comfort.

Detective Slut Bag turned in my direction. "Mrs. Young, there is no other way to say this, but your husband was involved in a fatal car crash."

Emilia's mouth continued to move, but I couldn't hear anything she was saying. The only sound I heard was the rapid, strong drum beat of my heart. A build-up of water flooded my vision, and slowly cascaded down my brown cheeks, smearing my make-up. For my own sanity, I took a few deep breaths because I wasn't sure about what she said.

"I'm sorry—say that again."

My father grabbed ahold of my waist and held me tight.

"Mr. Young was in a car accident. He lost control of his vehicle and crashed into a tree."

"Is he—Is he—" My brain wouldn't allow my mouth to speak those words.

"I'm sorry, Mrs. Young, but your husband didn't make it. He died at the scene."

"Nooo!" The loudest scream erupted from my diaphragm, and pierced the ears of every person sitting in the room. Every bone in my body lost its tone, allowing my body to collapse. My father's hands were still on me, but that was the last thing I remembered.

Domestic...

Hearing my phone sound off inside my pocket, I dug in to grab it with my eyes still closed. It was about ten in the morning, and I could feel the sun beaming against my eyelids. I didn't bother to check the caller ID, figuring that whoever was on the other side wanted something very important.

"Who is this?" I answered dryly.

"It's your favorite cop in the neighborhood. We have a problem."

Hearing Emilia's voice, I sat up on my king-size bed. "What do you want? It's too early for this nonsense."

"It's never too early when I'm involved."

Rubbing my eyes, I stood. "You must want me to take that shit again? I said it's too early, Emilia."

"Your little girlfriend is in the hospital."

"What?"

"Foreign. She found out that her husband died last night in a mysterious car crash. A crash that I have yet to understand. Funny thing is, he owed me a lot of money, but it seems that he had more of a personal problem with someone."

Glancing at the phone, I felt a slight chill crawl down my spine. Emilia's slick talk over the phone caused me to be a little more cautious, especially after hearing that the hit was a success. Regardless of her playing both sides, she still was not to be trusted under any circumstances.

"Listen, I'm sorry to hear all of that, but where is she? That's my only concern."

"They've already transported her to the hospital. I'm sure that you would have wanted to hear this. After all, you didn't want him around anymore."

"I don't know what the fuck you're talking about. I'm worried about Foreign, nothing else. Thanks for filling me in on her whereabouts."

"Today, you and I need to have a conversation—I'll be waiting, Demerius!" she ordered before hanging up in my ear.

The news of Foreign's husband wasn't shocking information to me. It was the way things worked. Foreign was becoming very important, and I never wrestled with people about anything that belonged to Demerius Payne. I couldn't help being addicted to her amazing body, beautiful face, and sweet persona. Foreign was meant to be my wife. She only needed me.

I grabbed my keys, then tossed on a pair of Jordan's and sweats. Heading for the door, I stopped at the kitchen to retrieve my gun before leaving my home. My mission was to bring Foreign home with me. After all, I was her husband now.

Foreign...

The sound of a machine constantly beeping caused me to slightly open my eyes. My tongue was dry, and the blurriness of my vision slowly dispersed for me to see clearer. My dad was standing over me with a worried expression. Likewise, Aaron's parents were there, and their faces were etched with concern. The remembrance of what Emilia told me earlier was the only thing slamming inside of my mind. The pain was unbearable. I couldn't wrap my head around the fact of Aaron being gone forever. As the tears escaped my eyelids, I tried to sit up in the bed.

"Please, baby girl, I think you need to relax. You passed out." My dad's words fell on deaf ears because all I wanted at that time was to see my husband.

"Where is Lexi?"

Aaron's mother approached me with a look of disappointment. Her expression was stern, but her tears showed the catastrophe she was experiencing at the time.

"Foreign, I just want to let you know that my son's legacy will not stop here. He will always be great. Aaron will live through me for the rest of my life. It's been brought to my attention that you were also seeing someone else while dealing with my son. I can't believe that you would express your pain to me about what he was doing to you and turn around to pull the same betrayal. That's something that I can never forgive. After the funeral, we will discuss what's yours, so you can move on."

Before I could reply to her disrespectful statement, she turned and exited the hospital room. Aaron's father squeezed my hand, with a look of empathy pumping through his face. My tears turned into loud sobs, as he pulled me in for a firm hug.

"She's a little hurt right now, Foreign. I know what you're going through. And regardless of her remark, you will always be my daughter. Just give her some time."

Planting a kiss on my forehead, he shook my father's hand before leaving behind his corny ass wife. I couldn't believe the way she was trying to handle me, when I was the one suffering about my husband. The audacity had me dropping tears of anger, instead of sadness. My eyes shifted to my daddy standing in front of me with a clueless face.

"Foreign, I know that I can't possibly understand what you're experiencing with this tragedy. I don't want to tell you the way you should feel because this is a predicament that I've never gone through for myself. All I can tell you is that Aaron loved you, and he wouldn't want anything but happiness for you."

"I can't believe he's gone, daddy. What am I supposed to do? My entire life was with him." I couldn't help but cry. My heart just wasn't able to settle down.

"All we can do is move on and hold firm, baby. We all have one life. The only thing I can be grateful for is, not losing the both of you. What if you were in that car? There would be double times the pain for everyone to take on today. I can bet you that Aaron feels the same way."

Nodding, I allowed his words to soothe my brain. They couldn't remove the pain, but they eased back my tears. Aaron was surely smiling down on me, and I knew that he was thanking our God that I wasn't beside him for that terrible moment. It was painful. The torment of losing your loved one was something that you could never take back.

"Do you want me to give you a ride home, baby? The doctor said that you needed some rest." He seemed so worried that I had to calm him. I couldn't even imagine losing my father.

"No, daddy. Go ahead. I'll call a ride."

"Are you sure?"

I replied before wiping my face. "Yes. I am. Go ahead and go home."

Rubbing my cheek, he grabbed his jacket and walked out. I sat in my own misery before a knock erupted on my door.

"Come in."

I watched Domestic stick his head inside of the room. He smiled after seeing me awake. Stepping inside, he held a vase full of beautiful white tulips and roses. The thought of him finding me at the hospital sent numerous red flags in my head. But of course, he could have received his info from Detective Suck and Fuck.

"Hey, baby. Are you okay?" He eased over to my side and placed the flowers on the small desk.

"Not really. My husband died in a car wreck. I'm just so lost right now."

Sitting beside me, Domestic placed a hand under my chin, so I could match his gaze. "I'm so, so sorry about your loss, baby. I know that losing your husband is a hard thing to soak in, but at the same time, it's the way this evil world works. My heart was in pieces when I heard about the trouble. I just wanted to make sure that you were safe and okay."

"Who told you?" I stared deeply into his eyes to see if he would lie. The question caused him to pause before he spoke.

"Detective Flores. She knows that you work for me at the carwash. It was a blessing that she was able to get in contact because I wouldn't have known anything."

He planted a kiss on my cheek. I inched backwards to place a little space in between me and him. "That bitch is dirty. I don't know what type of games she has up her sleeve, but she isn't right. I recently found out that my husband was having an affair with her. I don't think that's just a coincidence. Do you?"

"To me it is. I don't know anything about her personal business. She's investigating a recent robbery that happened with one of my co-workers a few months back. She's a little overbearing, but not to the point where I'm focused on whatever she has going on. My only concern is about you, Foreign."

Removing his hand from my leg, I began to gather my things. "I don't mean to be in my feelings right now, but I still can't deal with the fact of losing him. That can't be replaced. No matter who's here for me."

"What?"

My comment caused his face to screw up with anger. I realized that he was very persistent when it came to me, and I didn't want him to think that his credit was going unnoticed.

"Domestic, I don't want you to feel that I'm dissing you because you have shown me nothing but sincerity since I've been dealing with you. This is something that I have to deal with on my own. I don't want to push my problems on you. Let alone about something dealing with my husband."

Before I could move past him to call for the doctor, he blocked my path. His chest touched the tip of my nose and his arms flexed as if he wanted to grab me.

"Foreign, I love you. I know that I'm not Aaron and I know that you truly loved him, but I'm holding my position in your life for a reason. All I want to do is make you happy. You still have me, beautiful."

His hands were wrapped around my waist, and the hurtful face he wore was about to crumble my heart even more. There was already enough going on with my life, and I didn't need another man diving off the cliff for me because of his emotions.

Wrapping him in a tight hug, I rubbed his back to ensure him that all was going to be well. "Demerius, I'm not going anywhere. I just have to get past this. It's hard for me."

His expression said that he wanted to say more, but I could tell by the way he bit on his lip that nothing more was coming from our conversation.

"Can I at least drive you home?"

I waited before answering. I really didn't need him to be so close at the moment, but there was no other choice. All I wanted to do was, be in the comfort of my home.

"Sure."

As I gathered my things, we headed out to the counter where I signed myself out. I knew that things weren't going to be all sunny by tomorrow, but seeing Domestic by my side showed me that I wasn't alone.

Chapter 2

Foreign

The next day

Cracking my eyes to the direction of birds chirping, I glanced at the patio door. The sun was sneaking its way through the large blinds, alerting me that it was a new day. My head still rested gently against my pillow, and I could feel Aaron's hand slide around my waist, pulling me closer to him.

"Good morning, baby."

The sound of Domestic's voice forced my eyelids to grow wide in fear, and that's when it hit me. Rolling over, I realized that my current vision was only a dream. Aaron was still gone, and there was another man lying in his spot. My skin began to tingle with fear after Domestic rose up and looked at me.

"Are you okay, Foreign?"

"No." I jumped out of my bed, and quickly rushed towards my phone. "You're not supposed to be here, Domestic. Oh, my God! How did I let this happen?" I cursed myself while looking for all my clothes.

"Relax. It's not like your husband is coming home, baby."

That fuck ass comment nearly made me launch the lamp at his big fat head. The fact of my husband not coming home wasn't the point. It was still his crib. Not only that, his family was welcome to stop by at any time. The thought of Aaron looking down at my actions gave me chills. Last night, Domestic offered to drop me off after dragging me around the city for six hours. I had to admit, catching a great breather on the beach calmed my nerves. Not to mention the shots of liquor he gave to me in order to see my depression subside. All he asked for was a smile, and it kind of grasped my mind away from the thoughts of Aaron's death. One thing led to another, and he ended up inside my bed—falling asleep with me.

"It's not about that. It's respect, Domestic. My husband just died." I stood with a look of annoyance.

Standing up, he crossed the room swiftly. I could feel the breeze of his body frame rushing towards me. My instincts told me to flinch, but I glared into his eyes, as if I was daring him to try me.

"All I wanted to do was make sure you was okay, Foreign. So cut the smart talk. I understand that you're still grieving. I get it. But remember that

I'm the one who actually took the time to make sure you was okay before running off to do miscellaneous things. I don't see nobody else here right now."

Domestic said that shit like he was hurt to the core. His hand gently trailed the side of my cheek before flashing a nonchalant grin.

"I'ma give you time to bury your husband. I know you need a moment to get things in order. After this tragic moment passes by, I will be waiting to be here for you. Leaving is never an option. We work around differences and show each other support. That's why I'm here."

Grabbing his shirt, he placed it on and pecked the side of my lips. "Call me when you're ready to see me."

Walking him down the steps, I opened the front door to Lexi ringing the bell. When her eyes landed on Domestic, she frowned. My heart felt as if it crashed through the bottom of my stomach. *How could I explain a man leaving out my husband's home? A day after his death!* No statement could fix the guilty expression I wore at that moment.

"Uh—Who is this, Foreign?" She pointed to Domestic like he wasn't two feet away from her.

He moved past her with no comment, and climbed inside his car. Cranking up the engine, he pulled out of the driveway. I was still trying to catch my breath from being caught slipping with this crazy ass nigga. Lexi stared at me. Fire pumped through her pupils, as she stood with her arms crossed, silently demanding an answer.

"Lexi, calm down. It's not what it looks like." I lied quickly. Aaron's sister was far from gullible, but she had a large spot in her heart for trusting me.

Lexi walked right past me. I locked the door and followed her to the living room. She tossed her purse on the couch, and I sat directly across from her. Before I could open my mouth, she cut my throat with her first words.

"You're a liar, Foreign."

I instantly jumped on the offensive track. "Excuse me—I have no reason to lie to you, Alexis. Is that the way you feel about me? I'm your best friend, and you've never said that to me before."

"My brother is gone. As of yesterday, a piece of my soul was stripped away from me. I've been studying your behavior since this other mysterious guy stepped into your little life. You've changed. My brother didn't even know what his relationship was coming to with you. From my understanding, you asked for a divorce and he didn't give it to you. Then, all of a sudden, my brother ends up smashed into a tree while leaving a session with his counselor. No one knows about these classes but me and you."

The anger began to build in my system, and I couldn't allow her to continue. "Are you saying I had something to do with my husband dying, Alexis? If you are, I advise you to stop getting high on whatever drug you're taking. This is Aaron we're talking about."

Tears formed at the corners of her eyes. I could see that she was already prepared to give me this excruciating speech. Domestic bumped into my father and in-laws at the hospital. Instead of investigating his identity, they allowed him to enter. So, I knew that the story was sure to be remixed if Aaron's mother had any sight of another man in my presence.

"Lexi, we're only friends. He made sure I got home safe. That's all. You just so happened to pop up while he was here, that's all. What's your problem? You're acting like I had something to do with Aaron passing away. That's ridiculous. You know that I loved your brother with all my heart. He was cheating, so I started to step out because I felt that he wasn't being a husband to me. He created this wedge, Lexi. Not me. Still, after all of our differences, we decided to fix things. The problem was settled."

"One day of being dead, and I guess fixing it flew out of the window. How could you even be around another man after something like this, Foreign? What if he had something to do with this?"

"Lexi, that's absurd. He doesn't even know Aaron. This is way beyond his head."

Standing up, she grabbed her purse. "I'm never wrong when my mind tells me something. This is still my brother's home, so be sure not to get comfortable. I wanna know what happened to my brother, and I'm not going to stop until I find out."

"Lexi, he crashed his car. Accidents happen every day. How in the hell could you feel this way towards me? That's bullshit."

I was up on my feet now, because this bitch had me ready to box her ass in the throat for her stupidity. Lexi was thinking irrationally, and I knew that came from her being upset about the death of her twin. But to think that I was involved with him having a wreck made me feel highly disrespected.

"Foreign, Aaron wasn't in an accident. He was side-swiped off the road."

Her remark caught me off guard because I was never aware of him being hit by another car. Emilia only mentioned the wreck. "What are you saying? That there's a hit-and-run driver on the loose?"

"Aaron was murdered, Foreign. He was pushed off the road intention-ally. I hope whoever had something to do with it pray to their God because I'm not stopping until I have their head for what they did to him."

As she turned to leave, I remained in the same spot until she exited my home. The news about my husband was like a sharp knife to the back. The momentum of his death was still at the top of my heart. The thought of him being taken away by the hands of a sick, twisted person made my mind wonder. How were these people going to catch a murderer who caused my husband to lose everything we worked so hard to build? It surely wasn't just a mission for Lexi, because I was on a mission to watch this detective bitch and see exactly what she knew. That was a promise.

Emilia...

The moment I arrived at the scene of Aaron's car accident, my emotions scattered like roaches when the lights turned on. My body shook with not only disappointment, but pain as well. That month I spent with him, sexing daily while he and his wife were having problems. All I could picture was being with that man forever. Around that time, Foreign had a miscarriage and their marriage was slowly falling apart. They weren't getting along. Be-sides, Aaron was broken. Therefore, I provided him a shoulder to lean on, and a pussy to rest in peacefully every night without the bullshit. However, that didn't last much longer because he broke up with me through a fucking text message. *What type of bitch move was that?* The bastard didn't have the balls to face me like a man and do it in my face. That proved to me that a nigga would eat your ass and still play you.

Fast forward a month and a half later, I found out I was pregnant. That was the happiest moment of my life because I knew that a payday was going to happen right after that. My job was giving me grief about the rape case that ended in a suicide. While I was on leave, my bills fell behind because I wasn't being paid. Aaron tossed me money here and there, but not what I wanted. All because his precious little wife kept her eyes on his money! So, from that moment on, I started to plan and plot my next move. The funny thing about that situation was, I didn't know if it was from Aaron or his fellow athlete. Either way, I was getting paid.

Sliding my car into *park*, I exited the vehicle and walked up on the porch. Before I rang the doorbell, I unbuttoned my top to expose my breasts a little. The door opened, and my lustful eyes fell upon a muscular, sexy figure and landed on his dick print.

Licking my lips, I smirked. "So, is this how all the athletes answer their front door?"

"Maybe." Calvin grinned, while making his chest jump. We stood there for a few seconds longer, eyeing each other before he spoke again. "You gone stand out here or you coming in?"

"I was waiting on an invite." Stepping past the threshold, I walked inside and took a seat on the plush, white sofa. There was a half empty bottle of Patron sitting on the glass table. That would explain his demeanor.

"So, what brought you over, Emilia?"

"I came over to see how you were holding up."

Calvin sighed and picked up the bottle. Placing it to his mouth, he chugged quite a bit before taking a deep breath. "Not good. My best friend, my brother, is gone and I'm lost. None of this is making any sense to me."

"Yeah, this is so tragic. It pained me to deliver the news to his wife and parents." A flashback of the scene crossed my mind. "Seeing his lifeless body made me sick to my stomach. I'll never get that image out of my head."

"Please," Calvin held up his hand. "Spare me the details."

"I'm sorry. I know this has to be a tough time for you."

"You damn right it is. The fuckin' tabloids and every news station in the world has been tarnishing his name over that bullshit ass rape case. Then this happens." Calvin shook his head and took another sip. "They trying to make my boy go out bad. He didn't touch that bitch."

"I've been told that."

My response made him frown. "You didn't believe him?"

"Honestly, I don't know what to believe." I lied.

"That's fucked up. You know Aaron wouldn't do no shit like that."

Rubbing my hands against my thigh, I contemplated my next question. "Did you see Aaron with that girl at any point during your party?"

"No. His sister and his wife showed up. They had a fight and then he left." Calvin wiped his eyes. "You need to be talking to that nigga—Antwan. He the one who invited them hoes to the party."

"I already did. So, now I'm asking you since it was your party. Did you touch her?"

"Fuck no," he snapped.

"Chill. I'm just asking a question. This is still an open investigation."

"Well, you need to find the right muthafucka. My nigga just died and you over here with the bullshit. That's just like a snake ass, no good ass detective."

There was so much hostility in his voice. His dark eyes were narrowed into tiny slits, and his chest heaved up and down. I had never seen him so angry. Not even when I told him that there was a possibility that I was pregnant with his baby. Around my conception date, I had a threesome with him and Aaron. Therefore, I didn't know who the baby belonged to.

"Okay, now you're going overboard with your tongue and you need to chill the fuck out."

Calvin rose to his feet. "Bitch, this my fuckin' house. You don't tell me how to talk. As a matter of fact, get the fuck out. This conversation is over."

Now I was standing on my feet with an equally hard stare. The nice approach was out the window, and it was time to put the pressure on his hoe ass. Calvin thought he could talk to me any type of way just because we used to smash.

"This conversation about the case might be over, but not this one. Aaron owed me one hundred thousand dollars and I want it."

"Good luck getting that shit from a dead man."

Laughing, I put my hand on my hip. "That's where you're wrong. Since you concerned about his legacy, you need to clean it up. After all, he is your brother right? You're going to get me the money, and I'll make this go away. You can bury Aaron with his name intact, or I'll tarnish it forever. He'll no longer be known for taking the Buccaneers to the super bowl, but a pedophile instead. The one who raped a minor at your party."

"Fuck you. I'm not giving you shit. There's no proof that he did any of that."

"Just try me." Highly annoyed, I pushed past him and headed towards the front door. Before I let myself out, I turned to face him. "Oh, before I forget—If I don't get my money, I will tie you to this case and nail your ass to the cross. Now play with me if you want to."

Snatching the door open, I stood face to face with Aaron's twin sister, Alexis. She rolled her eyes so hard I thought they were going to fall out of the sockets.

"What the fuck you doing here? Haven't you delivered enough bad news for one day?"

"Not quite. I have one more stop to make." Ignoring her snide remarks, I looked her up and down. "Sorry for your loss."

"You lucky you wearing a badge bitch 'cause I'll beat your ass."

I allowed her threat to roll past my ears since she was mourning the loss of her brother. If Alexis kept that hood chick shit up, I was gone issue her ass a brand new set of bracelets and not the expensive ones that she's used to. Mark my words.

Chapter 3

Lexi

That bitch—Emilia—put a bad taste in my mouth. If she was at Calvin's place, it couldn't be good. My curiosity was about to be laid to rest, though. First, I was in need of a drink.

"What you got to drink in here?"

"Remy. You want that?"

"Yeah."

"Follow me."

Calvin and I walked into the kitchen. I stood beside him at the counter, while he placed two glasses on the granite countertop. My head was spinning. "So, what did that punk ass detective want?"

Filling both glasses half way, he handed me one. "She digging about that case your brother involved in."

Sipping the drink, I sat the glass down. "That hoe getting on my fuckin' nerves. I wanna kill that bitch."

"That bitch was talking real fuckin' greasy. I had to put her ass out. She talking about paying her a hundred grand to keep Aaron's name clean. What you know about Aaron owing her money?"

My eyes widened in the sockets. "I don't know shit about that. Her ass probably lying. She just trying to swindle you out some money. Don't pay that hoe shit."

"Fuck her. I ain't giving her ass shit."

"You better not."

Calvin and I ended up in his bedroom watching television. Drinks and laughter was exactly what I needed. We were watching *Four Brothers*, which so happened to be me and Aaron's favorite movie. The loss of my twin was really taking a toll on me. No matter how hard I tried to remain strong, I found myself breaking down.

"I can't believe he's gone." A steady flow of tears began to make a trail down my cheeks.

"Me too," Calvin replied.

Calvin scooted closer to me and wiped away my tears. "We're going to get through this together. I'm going to be right here with you every step of the way. I promise."

Nodding, I leaned against his shoulder and sobbed. My other half was gone. We were born together and now I had to live life without him. That felt damn near impossible because a part of me died when his soul left his body. On the inside I felt empty and I needed something to relax my mind and body. When I looked up at Calvin, he was looking into my eyes. As we moved closer to each other, our lips connected. Sex should've been the furthest thing from my mind, but I needed affection. Therefore, he would be my therapy in the meantime.

In the midst of foreplay, our clothes found their way to the floor, and Calvin found his way between my legs. The sensual movement of his tongue sent my body into euphoria, as his hand caressed my inner thigh. My eyes rolled to the back of my head when he latched onto my budding pearl. An orgasm was near, and my legs began to shake.

"Shit! I'm cumming!" I gasped.

Calvin continued to nibble and suck until my juices started to pour out. In the middle of my release, he climbed on top of me and pushed in every inch of him. My body wanted to collapse, but my pussy wanted attention. Taking it all in, I wrapped my legs around his waist and sucked on his neck.

Our chemistry was crazy. It had been that way since they were drafted. Antwan was just something to do in the meantime. Especially since I knew that no commitment was coming from Calvin. But that was cool with me because I didn't want that headache either. We were on the same page, and our arrangement was nothing short of amazing. Good dick was always attached to an 'ain't shit' nigga, and that was what kept me coming back.

I was hella wet and the squishy sound played throughout the room like an acappella. Every satisfying stroke, hitting deep into my guts, distracted me from the pain I felt in my heart. Calvin was really scrambling a bitch eggs without a doubt.

Unlocking my legs from his waistline, I planted both feet firmly on the mattress and threw my pussy back on him. Our strokes were in one accord every time we pulled away and met back in the middle with a powerful thrust. The shaft of his thick rod rubbed against my clit, triggering another orgasm. I wasn't ready to bust yet, so I did all I could to stop that from happening.

Calvin placed both hands on my knees, pushing them apart. Applying pressure, he pressed them against the mattress until they were damn near touching. Slowly, he thrusted in and out until he caught his rhythm. Once he was comfortable, Calvin increased the pace of his strokes, while plunging in and out swiftly. Intense pressure filled the bottom of my stomach, which caused me to sound off.

"Shit! Yeah. Beat this pussy."

"Um. Hmm. Um. Hmm."

Calvin laid the pipe down for what felt like forever. My thigh muscles grew numb, and he was still pounding away. My mouth was even dry from all that damn moaning. I knew he was about to cum when he raised one of my legs above his shoulder and went crazy in the box. Sweat drops fell from his forehead and splashed onto my skin. However, I didn't mind. Calvin let out a slight growl, as he reached his peak and spilled his little seeds into my tummy. On his last stroke, he freed my leg and kissed me in the mouth.

Both of us laid side by side in silence. There was no telling what we were thinking about, but I was almost one hundred percent sure that we were both thinking about Aaron. After listening to each other breathe for roughly fifteen minutes, Calvin decided to open his mouth.

"What are we going to do about this bitch Emilia? I refuse to let her ruin my best friend's legacy behind some bullshit."

Rolling onto my side, I looked deep into Calvin's eyes. "Tell me the truth. Did Aaron have something going on with Emilia?"

Calvin was such a terrible liar. Every time he told a lie, his eyes revealed the truth. He had a hard time keeping eye contact when he wasn't being truthful. Therefore, I knew the answer before he said anything.

"Nah."

"Calvin, don't lie to me. You of all people know what he did on a daily basis." Pausing for a moment, I took a deep breath. "I'm not going to tell Foreign, but I need to know for my own sanity. This bitch wasn't barking around Aaron for no reason."

"Yeah, you right." He sighed. "Her and Aaron used to fuck around. It lasted for about a month and then he broke things off with her. Of course she wasn't happy about it, but she didn't have a choice."

"See. Now it all makes sense. It's all good. I got something for that slimy ass bitch. She just wait."

"What are you going to do?" Calvin's alert expression made me aware that he was concerned about my plan. One of his brows was up, and one was down.

"You mean what are *we* going to do? I have a solid plan to clear all of this up. I just need your help."

"I'm down for whatever."

"Good. Let me use the bathroom first and I'll tell you all about it."

"Okay."

Exiting the bedroom, I went inside the bathroom and sat down on the toilet. The plan that I had in mind would clear my brother's name without a shadow of a doubt.

Domestic...

After ending my conversation with my guest, he got in his vehicle and pulled away. Foreign passed directly by the black Mustang and turned inside of the car wash. Stopping the car, she climbed out of her Bentley and stepped in front of me.

"I think we need to talk."

Leaning my head to the side, I looked at her with an arrogant grin. Our last encounter was awkward. Being pushed out of her mini mansion showed me that I wasn't meant to be seen. If I couldn't cuff one to be mine only, then I wasn't cuffing at all.

"What is it that you wanna talk about, Foreign? I know that you have a lot going on with your loss and all. I don't want to make you feel uncomfortable by being around. Some of his family may be watching." I made sure the tone of my voice sounded sarcastic.

I could see the mug forming on her face before she spoke. "Domestic, stop doing that!" Her voice allowed me to lock in on her beautiful face. Foreign possessed a natural attraction in my heart, and I adored when she was angry. Envisioning her throwing back against my manhood, I stepped in her grill.

"Who you talking to, girl? You better remember that I'm here for you. Don't try to make me go against you. You see I love you. Stop playing games with me." Grabbing her lower back, I pulled her closer to my body. Her perky breasts were pressed against me, and I could feel her stomach tighten in fear.

"It's not that. You know that I care for you, Domestic. I just don't need you to be in your feelings right now. This isn't a process that's going to take me forever to get past. I don't want to leave a bad taste in your mouth about me getting some space to bury Aaron. It's my only struggle, and I know that it has nothing to do with you. But in order to defeat the demons I'm fighting right now, I just have to get this funeral over and done."

"Walk with me to my office!" I ordered before entering the building. I knew that she would follow, from the way her tone softened. My touch—my aggressiveness—was all I needed to show Foreign who was in charge.

The only husband she needed to think about was me, and I was going to force that in her head every chance I got.

Maneuvering past the register and counter, we entered my office and I locked the door behind us. Closing my blinds, I removed my shirt and tossed it to the floor. Hovering over her small frame, a whisper escaped my lips. "I know how to make you feel better and you ain't leaving here until I fix it."

"Domestic, sex is not my problem. I just have tons of pressure right now. It's not you."

My finger pressed against her lips, demanding silence. Removing her jeans, I gently lifted her into my arms. "Wrap your legs around me."

Foreign huffed with sadness before obliging to my wishes. I knew that face. The one she always made when I got her body to quake from my delicate touch. My hands caressed her soft bottom, enjoying the feel of her smooth skin. Licking the tip of my fingers, I rubbed her clit, causing her to fidget in my arms. After my hand rotated a few times, the sound of her moistness began to match my wrist.

"Sss. No. Please, let's just wait." Her eyes were closed, and the way she ground against my hand told me that I was the one in charge.

Pressing my rock-hard dick against her pussy lips, I eased inside and kissed her lips before she was able to release that loud moan. Foreign's walls felt like they tightened against my piece, and I could see that rebellious side of her fading away, as she locked into our connection.

Straightening my back, I started to deliver firm strokes. My entire rod disappeared in her warm goodness. Her mouth hung open in satisfaction, as we listened to the sounds of our breathing erupt with every thrust.

"Domestic." She called my name with a hint of ecstasy. I knew that she was already coming from the powerful motions of my body.

"When I say tighten up, that's what I mean. You hear me!" I spoke with a deep low voice inside of her ear.

"Yes, daddy. I hear you." She panted with her hands moving to different parts of my back.

Her pussy farted with every stroke, and I could tell my sex game had her mind wrapped in a bind. Spreading her legs further apart, I pounded away as if she was never coming back.

"Shit. *Domessticc!*"

I watched her juices spill to the floor, as I had my way with her watery goodness. I held my position on her, while beating out her back for ten minutes until I nutted deep in her belly. Kissing her lips, I eased her back to the floor. "Do you feel better?" I asked, as she held on to me for dear life. All she could do was, nod.

"If you would like to, we can head to my house and shower. Maybe catch a little dinner."

I watched her take a deep breath before collecting her clothes. "Domestic, I have something I need to tell you." She was now standing back in front of me like a woman who didn't know how to break it off with a man.

"That depends on what you have to say, Foreign. I'm not really trying to hear no more bad news—if you know what I mean." Buttoning up my pants, I leaned back against my desk. I was prepared for her to try and tear down our small dose of chemistry as if it meant nothing. Things were surely not going her way. Just as I thought she was about to make her move, the sweetest words I ever heard slipped out of her gorgeous lips.

"I'm pregnant."

Her eyes studied me, but I couldn't let the excitement spill out too much. Walking over to her, I grabbed her chin. "With whose child?" I asked like a lawyer for a cheating scandal. I continued to follow her pupils until she pointed at my chest with a sturdy finger.

"Are you sure?"

She sat with a positive expression to let me know her seriousness. I smiled before pulling her in for a giant kiss and hug. My mission was a success, and now she was giving me another trophy to strike off my goal list.

"Are you really happy with this? I didn't want you to feel that I was telling you this now that my husband is gone. It's the only reason I kept it to myself for so long. You have a family already and I didn't want to step on your toes with that." There was an edge of disappointment in her voice.

While rubbing her stomach, I spoke. "Don't ever say nothing like that to me. You are my family, Foreign. We are a family."

"What about your son and Casey?"

"You just let me worry about that. You need to be at my place tonight. No exceptions. I understand what you have to do with this funeral process. But after that, I need you to let me build this relationship to its highest peak. It's the only way we can love each other wholeheartedly. Just let me be here for you. That's all I want."

"Thank you."

Kissing my lips, Foreign opened the door to my office. Tonight, her words trailed off perfectly and left me with a smile before she left me to myself. My grin spread wide as she dispersed out of the front door. Psychology was easy when it came to reversing it on a female. No power was able to stand against a man with the knowledge of a woman's heart. Aaron was only a substitute for the moment. It was time to switch her life around and make the new changes fit my standards. After all, it was my way or the hard way. Either one was fine with me.

Chapter 4

Foreign

After I left the car wash, I headed to my in-laws' house. When I pulled up, Lexi's car was in the driveway, along with Aaron's coach's car. Things were awkward between me and his family at the moment, so that made it difficult to show up. However, my husband still needed to be buried, and I wasn't about to let his mom or Lexi stop me from doing that.

As usual, the front door was open; so, I walked in and proceeded to the living room. The chatter in the room subsided the moment they saw me. Lexi and Calvin were sitting close together like they were booed up. Ignoring them, I sat my purse down in the empty seat.

"Good afternoon." Everyone greeted me except for Aaron's mother. She had no problem with letting it be known she wasn't fucking with me. Lexi even said something.

Aaron's coach approached me with a faint smile. "Mrs. Young, I'm so sorry for your loss."

"Thank you."

"If you ever need anything, I'm only a phone call away."

Fighting back the tears, I held my breath for a few seconds and nodded. "I appreciate that."

"No problem," he replied.

The coach then stood in the middle of the room and cleared his throat. That was my cue to sit down. The open seat was beside Aaron's dad. I was thankful for that. He reached over and grabbed my hand.

"How are you holding up?"

"Not too good." The question alone made me break out into tears. "I'm still trying to make sense of it all. It's like once we decided to fix things and get back on track, this happens."

"It's going to be hard, but I'll be here for you. I don't care what time of the day or night it is, you can call me."

"Thanks, dad. I—"

"Harold!" The first Mrs. Young shouted. "We have a guest here that would like to speak. You can talk to *her* later."

Swiftly, he turned his head in her direction. "Don't be rude. You think you're the only one affected by this tragedy?" Instead of replying, she folded her arms and sat back on the sofa.

"I'm sorry, Foreign. I don't know what's gotten into her."

If I didn't have respect for Mr. Young, I would've snapped on her for being disrespectful. "It's okay."

"Go ahead, coach." Mr. Young nodded, giving him the floor.

"As you all know, Aaron was special to our team. He was special to the league in general. This tragedy has affected us in ways we would've never imagined. We were a family, and it hurts that we've lost one of our own. Aaron was like a son to me, and I'm going to miss him tremendously."

He stopped for a moment to collect his thoughts, and to dry his wet eyes. "On behalf of the Tampa Bay Buccaneers, we will be paying for all funeral expenses. I'm assuming that you will be making the arrangements since you're his wife."

"Yes," I replied.

"I'm making the arrangements. That's my son." Aaron's mom shouted like an angry woman.

"Phyllis, you need to calm down," Mr. Young replied. "This is his wife and she has that right. I'm sure the both of you can put this together nicely."

"Why?" Phyllis stood up and put her hands on her hips. "She running around gallivanting around town like a loose teenager, when she was supposed to be a wife to my only son."

The gloves were off at that point. His mammy disrespected me for the last time. Rising to my feet, I looked her dead in the eyes. I wanted her to feel every word out my mouth.

"Let me tell you something, Phyllis. For the past three years, I have been a doting wife to your son. Aaron has been cheating on me since the day he went pro—with every bitch that would spread her legs for bragging rights and few measly ass dollars. Your son has been in the news for the past few weeks for a viral sex tape and having sex with an underage girl. Do you know how that made me feel? No. Because you don't give a fuck. You thought your son was so innocent, a goddamn saint? Well, he wasn't. I bet he didn't tell you that I had a miscarriage a few weeks ago because of him. And why? Because he was at a party engaging in sexual activities when he was supposed to be a married man."

The room was completely silent. Lexi and Calvin sat with blank stares. To my surprise, she didn't say anything. The coach stood in place with a shocked expression on his face. This had to be a surprise to him. Especially since he knew how close I was to his family.

"Well, you knew that came with the territory of being with a professional athlete. There will always be women throwing themselves at those types of men. Women can't do what men do."

"Oh, so it's fine that he's cheated on me repeatedly?" Tears were streaming down my face, as I chuckled. Not 'cause it was funny. But because I was hurt. I loved Aaron with every fiber in my body, but that wasn't enough to stop him from cheating.

"You know I'm truly surprised at your behavior. You're the same shoulder I cried on when Aaron cheated right before our wedding and in our house for that matter. You convinced me to take him back."

"That's because I knew that you were a good woman for my son. I knew that you truly loved him. You deserved the lifestyle he provided for you. But I guess that changed you along the way."

"Do you really think I give a fuck about his money? I had a career. He wanted me to quit. Did you forget that too?"

Lexi finally came to life and opened her mouth. "Foreign, you need to chill out. That's my mama you talking to. She's just upset that you were cheating on my brother. You had to know we weren't going to be happy about hearing that."

"Lexi, are you serious? You're the same person that told me to cheat back on your brother, so don't try to switch up now. Out of all people, you knew what was going on in my household."

Lexi shook her head when her mother looked at her. "You told her to cheat on your brother?"

"Ma, chill out—It ain't like that," Lexi replied.

My blood was boiling and I wanted to dash across that room and lay hands on her old ass. For the sake of Aaron, Lexi and their father, I grabbed my purse and began to walk away.

"Don't leave, Foreign!" Mr. Young called out. "You are his wife and you should be here to make the arrangements," he added.

Stopping in my tracks, I turned back to face him. "I'm sorry for my outburst, Mr. Young, but that's how I feel. Everybody wants to point the blame at me for getting tired of putting up with Aaron's infidelity. No one cared when I sat in that house crying because of random females sending me messages and videos of my husband. How much can a woman take?"

"I understand," he replied.

"You do, but your wife doesn't. Therefore, I'm done with all of this. Make the arrangements and I'll show up to the funeral, but I don't want any parts of this."

Phyllis was mumbling and shaking her leg. Whatever she was saying, it was obvious she didn't want me to hear. And at that point I didn't give a fuck what she had to say. We locked eyes once more.

"For the record, mommy dearest, before I started gallivanting, as you so eloquently called it, I asked Aaron for a divorce. I told him that I wasn't happy and that I was moving on with my life. When I packed my things to leave him, he unpacked them so I would stay. As you can see, I'm nothing like your son, I told him that I didn't want him anymore. That was the moment I moved on."

With that being said, I turned on my heels and walked out their house. In the car all I could do was cry. It was funny how things were unraveling right before my eyes. They had completely turned on me like it was my fault. As if Aaron was some goddamn saint! I couldn't wait for his funeral to be over with so I could carry on with my life.

Domestic gave me the one thing that I always wanted. Therefore, I was invested into our relationship. That disastrous meeting had me mentally and emotionally drained. All I wanted to do was, lay in Domestic's arms and sleep. He made me feel safe, so I had no worries about starting over with him. According to him, he was in love. I wasn't there yet, but I knew I would eventually be in that state.

One hour later, I was sitting in Domestic's driveway, awaiting his arrival. The headlights beamed through my back window, signaling his presence. Wiping my face, I looked into the mirror to see how bad I looked. My eyes were red and puffy from all of that crying, so there wasn't anything I could do about that. Seconds later, my door became ajar; the smell of Domestic's cologne filled my nose.

"Hey, baby. You ready to go out and get something to eat?"

Before I replied, I stepped out the car so he could see my face and answer his own question. "I'm not up to it. I just want to lay down."

The disappointment showed in his face, but he didn't reply. Domestic simply grabbed my handbag and escorted me into the house.

Lexi...

After all the soap opera commotion was over, I dismissed Calvin to handle the situation with my grieving mother. Obviously, she didn't like the fact that I told Foreign to handle her problems with another man. Truth be told, she needed to give Aaron a taste of his own medicine. She was my friend, and the respect my brother showed was little to none. I never expected her to step outside of our family boundaries to have a full relationship with another spouse. The objective was to relieve some frustration with some side sex. What Aaron didn't know wouldn't hurt him, especially when he was a being a freak of nature.

Hearing my father call my name from the living room, I prepared myself for the nagging that was about to take place. I grabbed my cell and quickly dialed Foreign's number to see if she would clean up her statement. After ringing twice, she sent me to voicemail. Instead of hanging up, I left her a quick message.

"I like how you threw that trash ass statement on my name in front of my mother when I only tried to help you. I treated you like a sister and always stood by your side. You're making me feel that this is personal, Foreign. Maybe it's just a mistake and you were hurt at the moment. You need to correct this or never speak to me again. And that's a promise, Foreign. Don't test me!" I warned before ending the call.

By the time I decided to head into the family room, my dad was standing to his feet as if he were coming to retrieve me. Flopping down on the couch, I crossed my legs. My mother shifted in her chair before speaking.

"Lexi, what would possess you to tell this woman to cheat on your brother? We're family, and that was your twin. I'm having a hard time trying to understand this."

"Just be humble, baby," my daddy said, while shrugging.

"I don't get what the big deal is with you and Aaron's personal life, mama. He was a cheater. He deliberately defiled his relationship status after jumping in every ocean he spotted. That's not something I can be the judge of. Prayer couldn't help Aaron. Neither could I. Foreign took what I said out of proportion to make me look like the idiot. She asked for my advice, and I told her to treat his ass the same way."

"Watch your mouth, Alexis. I'm your mother! This is my son you're criticizing, and I will not allow it under my roof."

She was raising her voice louder than a preacher on Sunday morning. I knew from that point, things were about to be blown up because of personal anger. Her emotions about losing her only son was a devastation that most couldn't deal with. She didn't realize that everyone else was also affected by the same tragedy. Being married and miserable in her own marriage was the liable purpose for her actions. That shit wasn't about to fly with me, whether she was my mother or not.

"I don't care about this being your house, Ma. You need to cut this act. Aaron isn't just your family, old lady. He's my brother and also my father's son. We love him the same way. Don't make it seem like I was against my family when he chose to play himself with this situation. He didn't even have the decency to hide it correctly."

"How dare you speak to me like that? I took care of you, Alexis. You're being a selfish little pig. My son is gone and you guys are moving around as if this isn't a priority."

"A priority? Priority about what, Ma? Is this about burying your son? Or is it about that forty million dollar insurance policy for his contract? You want control, right?"

My dad cut his eyes at her. Obviously, the news was a shocker to him also. "Phyllis, what is she talking about? What policy?"

Judging from her stuttering, I knew that I struck a secret nerve. Aaron's payback from the N.F.L was no longer a lingering insurance paper. It was worth millions. Not just that, Foreign was entitled to every penny. She didn't know, but Aaron left half of his empire to her. My mother was now creating a vendetta to slime Foreign completely out of his will.

"Aaron's policy has nothing to do with the way she disrespected this family's name. A valid proof in court of that will destroy her chances of getting anything that belongs to my boy. I can promise you that."

Standing to my feet, I moved towards my father and placed a delicate kiss on his cheek. "I'm sorry, daddy, but I can't do this. I'll see you at the funeral."

"If you walk away from this conversation, you can exit your way out of this family also. We're not tolerating disrespect!"

Ignoring her outburst, I walked out of the home, leaving her with my ass to kiss. I was too established within my life to watch her tear me down, as if my pockets were hurting for my brother's money. The humbleness of our family was about to decrease. The money was in everyone's vision, and Aaron was surely gonna turn in his grave after seeing the stunt his mother was about to pull.

Foreign...

After settling with Domestic for the past few hours, my mind felt more at ease. The drama Aaron's mama had on her mind at the time was beyond foolish. Within days, my entire life flipped upside down. My husband was gone. Family was turning on me like I was being a true slut to their superstar.

I'd settled and dealt with so much pain with Aaron that it turned me rock-hard solid.

"What you thinking about?" Domestic whispered before kissing my left shoulder. I was snuggled in his arms with my ass pressed against his steel frame. His eyes demanded an answer, but I knew that he only wanted to know for his own sake.

"Life. It's like everything just happened so quick. It's the reason I'm beefing with my husband's family. I don't mean to sound like it's your fault, because this is definitely what I want. I don't know. I guess it's just bad luck."

"You know that we all can't have the same vision, Foreign. I hate that your husband left so soon. Even for his family's sake, I wouldn't know what I would do if I didn't have a chance to prove my love to you. I can't help that we gained a bond throughout these few months. But I'm none of their concern. Only yours." His voice was stern.

"You're right, but they still deserve closure on this. I tried to be supportive through the mishaps and I'm still labeled as the traitor. It's like I was never even a part of the family."

"Well, guess what?" Domestic said before leaning up to look down at me. "I respect your mind, heart and decisions as a grown woman. It doesn't matter who likes it because they aren't in your shoes. You're holding my child right now and I know that God don't make mistakes. We're family now and that counts for a lot. I'm prepared to go against them in every way if they proceed to do these disrespectful things to you."

The thought of Domestic paying Aaron's family a visit never crossed my mind, but I could see that he meant business. They were still my family. So, of course, I wouldn't allow him to disrespect them. The fact of me moving on was the only thing they needed to get understood.

Moving the strands of hair from my face, he glared into my eyes with a look so severe I could feel goose bumps crawling over my body like a scary movie on a rainy night.

"You know that I'm your husband now, right?"

I wanted to reject the statement just from his approach. It was creepy with a hint of love added in between. Instead of disagreeing, I nodded with a phony smile.

"Good."

Clicking off the lamp, he cuddled up with me. His strong arms caressed my waist. Domestic was surely on the psycho passion path, but I knew that his affection was purely from the heart. That was all I needed. After I buried

Aaron within the next few days, my focus was going to see what level I could grow if I worried about my man and child. It hurt deeply, but it was just the way life worked.

Chapter 5

Domestic

The strong sounds of sobbing woke me from my slumber. Foreign's side of the bed was empty and cold. That led me to believe that she had been up for a while now. When I looked at the clock, it was a quarter to eight and time for me to get up and head to work. Planting my feet on the floor, I stretched long and hard before getting up to follow the noise. As I made my way downstairs, I found Foreign sitting on the sofa with her head buried in her hands. Proceeding with caution, I placed my hand on her shoulder.

"Are you okay? I heard you from the bedroom." Foreign didn't move at all. She continued to cry like I wasn't standing there. Figuring she didn't hear me the first time, I kneeled down in front of her. "Baby, I'm asking if you are okay. Don't ignore me."

Foreign raised her head slowly. The look on her face was pure evil. The bloodshot in the corner of her eye confirmed my suspicions of her crying for hours. Funny thing is, I never felt her get out of bed. Looking me in my eyes, she shook her head.

"No. Domestic, I am not okay. I just lost my husband for God's sake. How do you expect me to feel?" Her words were laced with snappiness.

"I expect you to grieve. But what I don't expect is for you to be walking around depressed like your man isn't standing right here. I mean—damn, I'm catering to your needs, and all I'm getting is attitude in return. That shit ain't cool. It's not like you and Aaron were together when this happened. You moved on, remember?"

Foreign's eyes grew dark. The tears flowing freely from her eyes increased drastically. "That's where you're wrong. The night I met up with my father, I agreed that we would make our marriage work one more time. But I never got the chance to tell you."

It took me a minute to digest her words. Then I thought back to that night when I was blowing up her phone and she wasn't answering me. If she wasn't in such a fragile state, I would've smacked the shit out of her for insulting me like that. Especially after I poured my heart out to her!

"That's funny because I remember that night clear as day. I called you dozens of times and you didn't pick up. You even turned your phone off." Standing up, I scratched my head. "You and that nigga was fucking, huh?"

Foreign shook her head. "Domestic, don't do that."

"Don't do what? You boldly stated that you were about to work out your marriage, so let's be honest. Did you fuck him that night?"

"No. I didn't."

That was a boldface lie. If she thought I was going for that, she was sadly mistaking me for a damn fool. "You know I don't believe that? But anyway, I'm curious to know something. If you were willing to work out your marriage, what did you think was going to happen once you told me you pregnant with my child?"

Foreign took a deep breath. "I don't know what I would've done. That was the reason I didn't say anything in the first place. I was trying to figure out my next move."

Silently, I prayed that I was able to remain calm. My inner beast was begging to come out and knock some sense into her brain, but I had to keep him caged. The last thing I wanted to do was scare her off. Then again, she saw what happened to Casey and she stayed.

"Your next move, huh? That's quite selfish, don't you think? You must've forgotten who was there for you when pretty boy was slinging dick off the field to every groupie that came his way. It was me who loved you past your pain."

"No. I didn't forget, but that's not important right now. My husband is dead, Domestic. Have some compassion for what I'm going through. This is hard for me. I've been with Aaron for years, and things weren't all bad."

Now I was furious. The fact that she continued to disrespect me made me snap. "Stop calling him your husband! I'm your husband now. Once this is over, we're making it official."

Foreign's eyes were now expanded and stricken with fear. She removed herself from the sofa and faced me. "I can't do this right now. I think its best that I go home and grieve in peace. We clearly have different views on this situation. I'm not about to argue with you because you don't understand the fact that I still love my husband." Spinning on her heels, Foreign stormed off while continuing to mumble.

If Foreign thought she was leaving me, she had another thing coming. Swiftly, I took giant steps behind her until we reached my bedroom. She began to gather her items and place them on the bed.

"What are you doing?"

Foreign didn't bother to give me any sort of eye contact. "What does it look like? I'm going home."

"That's not your home. This is your home!"

She paused and looked up at me. "No. This is your home. Not mine."

45

"You don't mean that."

"Yeah, I do."

"Why are you making things so difficult for me? From day one I've showed you nothing but love and respect. Do you know how many men would've dogged a female for fucking on the same night at random? I didn't do that because I knew that you were something special. Someone that I could be with."

"You didn't do me any favors, Domestic. We didn't even know each other."

"That's what I'm saying. I still treated you with the upmost respect, but I don't get credit for that. You were married and didn't get the respect that I gave you. That's crazy."

"What's crazy is this damn conversation." Foreign snatched up her bag and keys and pivoted from the opposite side of the room. Once she was close enough, I blocked her exit.

"Foreign, please don't leave. We both said things we shouldn't have. I'm sorry."

"Well, I'm not sorry. I meant every word I said. Now if you would please get out of my way, I would like to go home."

"I'm not letting you leave, so you might as well put your things down and get back in bed. It's obvious you need some rest."

"Yeah, I do. Sadly, I won't be getting that here." Foreign tried to step around me, but I grabbed her wrist and removed her car keys.

"You're not going anywhere, and I mean that."

"Domestic, give me my keys."

"Why? You don't want to be here with me?"

"No. I just want to go home." Foreign tried to snatch the keys out of my hand, but I raised my arm in the air so she couldn't reach it.

"Go lay down. You're upsetting my baby."

"And you're upsetting me."

Foreign was trying her best to retrieve her keys, but that wasn't happening. Quickly, she grew tired and backed up. "Keep the keys. I'll call me a Lyft."

"You ain't calling shit."

"Yes, the fuck I am. I'm getting away from you. I'm tired of this shit." Foreign tried to rush past me once more. Frankly, I was tired of going back and forth with her. She needed to understand who the man was in this relationship. That was when I reached out and grabbed her by the hair, pulling her towards me. "Let go of my hair!" she screamed.

"Shut the fuck up!" Dropping her keys to the floor, I put her in the chokehold. "Listen to me, I love you and I'm not letting go."

"Domestic, stop," she clawed at my arm, in hopes that I would free her.

"I'm trying my best to not put my hands on you, but you making that so hard to do. You're my lifeline." I placed a kiss on her right cheek. "You belong to me now, so get that through your head."

Releasing her, I grabbed her by the arm, pulled her towards the bed and I shoved her onto the mattress. Foreign placed her hand at the base of her throat and caressed it. "Stop playing with me before I hurt you. No one loves you like I do. Not even Aaron's punk ass."

"Aaron never put his hands on me," she sniffled.

Rushing her, I smacked her in the face and grabbed her throat. The force I placed against her body caused her to fall backwards on the bed. "You made me do this. All you had to do was, be compliant. I love you too much to hurt you."

"No, you don't," she mumbled. "If you did, you wouldn't have slapped me.

"Yes, I do. I'm sorry about that. I'm going to make it up to you. I promise."

Leaning closer, I placed my lips onto hers. Foreign was too upset to kiss me back, but I didn't care. My left hand made a trail up her thigh. The dress she was wearing provided easy access to her middle. My erection rose, so I slipped it from my boxers and slid up in her.

"Domestic, stop," she whimpered.

"Just let me love you. Stop being so damn combative."

Slowly, I stroked her pussy with ease. Foreign didn't fight it. She just laid there like a dead fish with her eyes closed. That didn't bother me one bit because it still felt good sliding in and out of that wet shit. My hand was still on her throat. Applying pressure, I went deep in her guts until I caught a nut and fed my seed. Kissing her on the lips, I pulled out and headed for the shower.

After spending all of fifteen minutes cleaning myself, I entered the bedroom to find Foreign lying in bed. The pillow she clutched covered her face, but I knew she wasn't asleep. Stepping inside the closet, I pulled out a dress shirt and some slacks. The time on the clock forced me to move a bit faster. Tracy had a key to open up, so I wasn't too pressed on being late.

Once I was dressed, I sprayed on some cologne and walked over to the bed. Foreign's eyes were closed when I moved the pillow. "Baby, I'm truly sorry for my actions a while ago. I have a bad temper and sometimes I blow things out of proportion. Be patient with me please, and I want you here when I get back." Placing one last kiss on her cheek, I left the house and made my way to the car wash.

Twenty minutes later, I was pulling up and my mood instantly changed. Parked in the lot was Emilia. That was the last face I wanted to see at the start of my morning. Whenever she showed up, bullshit was sure to follow. In the back of my mind I knew what she wanted, but I ain't have shit to say about the situation. And if Emilia wasn't careful, I was gonna apply the same pressure I did with Foreign an hour ago. So, that bitch better tread lightly.

Stepping inside the building, Emilia wasn't directly in sight. That only meant one thing: she was waiting inside my office.

"Good morning, Tracy."

"Morning, boss. That crazy ass detective is here." Tracy blew a bubble with her gum and popped it.

"Yeah, I know."

"Is Foreign coming in today?"

"No."

"Hmm," she snickered. "Let me find out you back boning that crazy ass lady."

"Let me find out you minding my business again."

Tracy held her hands up. "Hey, I'm just looking out for you."

"I'm good."

Taking quick, short steps down the hall, I reached my office in less than five seconds. As expected, she was sitting her pesky ass behind my desk, smiling. Closing the door behind me, I secured the bottom lock and turned to face her with an evil glare.

"Emilia, why the fuck are you sitting at my desk?"

"Hello to you too, Demerius." Emilia removed herself from my chair and positioned herself in front of my desk. "It looks like someone didn't get their morning dose of ass on this fine morning."

"Fuck you!"

"What's wrong, Domestic? You couldn't manhandle her and take what you wanted the way you did me the other night."

Emilia just didn't know that she was a zebra in a lion's den. I could visualize me snapping that hoe neck in three seconds if she didn't skate her ass up out of my office. "Don't you have some crime to fight or some shit?"

"As a matter of fact, I do," she smirked.

Walking past Emilia, I sat down at my desk and turned on the computer. It was about to be a long ass day. The women in my life were giving me hell. Casey kicked the shit off by taking my son away, but I had something for her ass. Then Foreign had the nerve to be in my damn house crying over her punk ass husband. I couldn't wait for his funeral to be over with so she could bury her feelings along with that ungrateful ass nigga.

"Well, you need to go handle that. I have work to do."

"That's why I'm here."

Raising my head, we locked eyes. "What is this about?"

"Do you mind if I have a seat?"

"Actually, I do."

Emilia sat down anyway. "I know you don't really mean that. You're just grumpy right now." Folding her hands, she placed them in her lap and crossed her legs. "Now, if you don't mind, I would like to get down to the reason of my visit."

"Please do."

"Where were you on the day Aaron Young was killed?"

"I had nothing to do with that, so you not about to sit up here and blame me for some shit I know nothing about." I had a strong feeling that was the reason for visit.

Emilia didn't blink as she looked into my venomous eyes. "Then answer the question, Domestic. Where were you?"

All I wanted was for her to leave. I had a business to run, and I didn't need the law running off my customers. Leaning back in my chair, I exhaled harshly. "I was at work."

"Are you sure?"

"That's what I said."

"Domestic, I'm going to be honest with you. This has your name all over it. You are the only person that would benefit from his death. I mean after all, you are sleeping with his wife."

The attachment she placed between Foreign and Aaron was starting to piss me off again. She was starting to sound just like Foreign. "If you must know, they were in the middle of a divorce. Therefore, I had no reason to get rid of him. Foreign was already in my possession."

"Possession!" Emilia sat straight up in the chair. "That's what she is to you? A piece of property!"

"Call it what you want, but that's my woman." Standing, I adjusted my blazer and approached Emilia. Calmly, I grabbed her arm and escorted her to the door. "Now, if you don't mind, I have a real job to do."

"So do I," she snatched away from my grip.

49

"I'm offering a service to the community. Not harassing tax- paying and law-abiding citizens like you're doing right now."

"Isn't that cute?" she said with sarcasm. "But we both know that's not true."

"I also know that if you were sure I had something to do with this, you would've arrested me by now. Have a blessed day, Emilia."

Emilia pulled her dress down. "You do the same and I'll be seeing you sooner than later."

"I'm looking forward to it. Bye!" Slamming the door in her face, I went back to my desk to start my day.

Destiny Skai

Chapter 6

Lexi

Miami, FL

The warm breeze blew through my hair, as Calvin flushed the topless Camaro down on I-95 blasting rap music. Shielding my eyes from the sun, I rocked a pair of oversized Versace shades, while taking in the view. South Beach was a popular spot to hang out and enjoy the beautiful sight of the ocean.

On occasion, I would frequent the area for spring break and Memorial Day when I wanted to get in touch with my ratchet side, but the circumstances of the trip were for business purposes only.

Aaron's funeral was only a week away, and his image needed to be squeaky clean before the celebration of his life occurred. I refused to bury my twin with a dirty ass legacy based off the lies of two thirsty ass prostitutes and Antwan's hating ass.

When we arrived at the Richmond Pines Apartment, we went up to the third floor as instructed. That was my type of area because all the hood niggas could be found. Tampa had too many lame niggas for my taste. Antwan was the perfect example.

With a firm fist, I hit the door three times and waited. Calvin stood directly behind me. I could feel his hand on my ass, so I smacked it away. "Aye, keep it in your pants, okay?"

Calvin laughed. "Chill out."

"Who is it?" A female called out from the other side of the door.

"Lexi," I replied.

The door swung open. From her girly features, I knew that was exactly who I was looking for. "Lexi?"

"Yes. Are you Samantha?" I watched, as she looked back and forth between me and Calvin. She was a pretty mixed girl, and I could see how she gained access to an exclusive party.

"Yes." Samantha opened the door wider. "Come in."

Calvin and I walked inside and stopped. Samantha led us into the living room. To my surprise, the apartment was nice and neat. To be honest, I didn't know what to expect upon our arrival.

"How was the drive?"

"It was good—Thanks for asking," I replied before jumping directly into business. "Okay, Samantha, we both know why I'm here, but I have some questions that I need you to answer."

"Okay."

"I also need to record you."

"Okay," she agreed.

Once I received the confirmation, I pulled out my cellphone and pressed record. Before I committed to anything, I needed proof just in case she tried to recant her story. If she knew better, she wouldn't try me. I would hate to come back to Miami and beat her ass for playing with my money. "Can you state your name for the record, please?"

"Samantha Hawkins."

"Samantha, when you were invited to the party, was there a particular reason you came? I mean, with you being underage and all—"

"Yes," she nodded. "I was personally invited to the party by Antwan. He wanted me to come."

"So, you know him personally?"

"Yes. We've been talking for three months."

"Does he know how old you are?"

"Yes."

"That night at the party, did you have sex with my brother—Aaron Young?"

Samantha sat with her hands in her lap, twirling her fingers. Then we could hear the voice of a woman coming from the back. "Samantha!" she shouted.

"Yes, Ma."

"Come here."

"Give me a minute, Ma. I'm talking to someone!" Samantha shouted over her shoulder. She then turned her attention back to me, but not for long.

"Come here, now!" her mother demanded.

"I'll be right back. I have to check on her to make sure she's okay." Samantha left us alone in the living room.

Calvin and I sat quietly and waited on her return. My phone started to ring and when I looked down at the screen, I could see Foreign's name. I didn't want to talk to her, so I sent her to the voicemail. The same way she did my ass after throwing me under the bus at my parent's house.

"You still not talking to your best friend, huh?" Calvin had his eyes locked in on my phone screen with his nosey ass.

"I'm busy and I don't feel like talking to her." I hated when he was all up in my business like that. That shit was mad annoying.

"Don't you think you being too hard on her?"

"No, I don't."

"Lexi, you know that's not right. Aaron did that girl dirty and she well within her rights to cheat back or move on for that matter. Don't you think she was tired of being in a one-way committed marriage?"

"Calvin, I don't care what she was tired of. She should've gotten a divorce. And it's not like he wasn't trying. Aaron was going to classes to make his marriage work."

"Yeah, at the last minute."

"Well, whose side you on?"

"Come on, now. Aaron was my best friend, my brother, and you know that. I know him better than anybody."

"Not me," I rolled my eyes.

"Wait until we leave here. Watch I teach you a lesson about rolling them damn eyes at me," Calvin smirked.

"Well, if you want to continue to get this pussy, then you better get on the right team. I don't care how good the dick is." She snickered. Calvin didn't get a chance to respond because Samantha was finally coming down the hallway.

"I'm sorry about that. My mom is on dialysis, so I have to take care of her."

"You good."

Samantha sat down and looked at me, as I started the recording again. "What was the question again?"

"Did you have sex with my brother—Aaron Young?"

"No."

"Who did you have sex with?"

"Antwan."

"Was there anyone else you had sex with?"

"No. It was just him."

After she answered the most important question, I stopped the recording. "Thanks for agreeing to do this."

"Thank you for helping me. Things are really hard around here with my mom being unable to go to work. This money will really help us."

"I'm glad I could help." Opening up my purse, I removed the envelope and passed it to Samantha.

In exchange for her testimony, I agreed to pay her twenty thousand dollars to get rid of my little Antwan problem. When it came down to my brother, I would break any and every law to help him. That's what siblings were for. Calvin and I left the apartment and checked into a hotel for the remainder of the day.

Casey...

A pair of soft lips pulled me from my slumber. My eyes struggled to open against the bright light that beamed against my lids. "What time is it?" I yawned when I was finally able to focus on Shawn's handsome face.

"Seven. We need to get up and get on the road. We have a long drive ahead of us."

"I'm tired."

"That's because you wanted to be fast and stay up all night." Shawn slapped me on my ass and crawled from the bed. "Get up so you can take a shower."

"I'm getting up," I whined, while hitting the pillow with my hand.

It took me an additional ten minutes to finally get up and go into the bedroom where DP was sleeping. To my surprise, he was awake when I walked through the door.

"Good morning, sunshine," I smiled.

"Hey, Ma." His main focus was on his cellphone.

"How long have you been up?"

"Not that long. Shawn woke me up, like, twenty minutes ago."

"Okay. Well I'm about to get dressed. Make sure you have everything packed and ready to go."

"Okay."

Once I left DP, I took a shower and got dressed. Shawn was outside, talking to his brothers—Tim and Craig. Meanwhile, I was sitting in the room, staring at old pics of me and Domestic in my cellphone. It hurt me to my soul to pack up and leave Florida because of Domestic. A man that I loved beyond the end of the earth. A man I would've laid down and died for. For years, I've tried to live up to his expectations and be the woman he wanted me to be.

Our love was like a fairytale in the beginning. He was my modern day savior. I was a waitress at IHOP, and a student when we first met. Seven months later, I found myself pregnant with DP. Domestic didn't waste any time moving me into his home and taking care of me. My waitress days were over, and it felt good to be taken care of by a man. That was something I never experienced.

In my mind, I knew that I would be Mrs. Payne once I gave him his first child and son. That never happened. One month after living under his roof, I got my ass beat for hanging out with my friends and coming home late. Domestic was waiting for me at the front door. As soon as I walked in, he hit me in the mouth. That was the first time I wore a busted lip in my life.

Over the next few months, Domestic was out doing his own thing while I was stuck in the house pregnant with his son. He alienated me from my family and friends, claiming he was all that I needed. That left me all alone. I had no one but him.

There had been rumors of him cheating. My homegirl even confirmed it after catching him with another female. That shit broke my heart. Tired of crying and being depressed, I cried on my male friend's shoulder, and I ended up in his bed with him planted deep between my legs. That was the one and only time I cheated, but Domestic would never live that down, no matter what I did to make things right. When it was all said and done, he showed me that every attempt that I made wasn't good enough to mend our broken family.

"Baby, you ready?"

Shaking the thoughts from my head, I looked up to find Shawn standing at the door. Smiling, I replied. "Yes."

DP was sitting on the sofa when we walked out the room. The sadness in his eyes made my heart sink. Something was telling me that our conversation was about to go wrong. My heart raced as I sat down by him. "Are you okay, baby?"

"Yes."

"Are you sure?" DP nodded, but I didn't believe a word he was saying. After all, he was my child and I knew him like a book. "Are you having second thought about leaving with me? If so, you can stay here with your father. I won't be upset."

"Mom, I want to go. I'm not staying here without you."

A two-parent home was all DP was used to. Therefore, I needed reassurance that my son was okay. Gently, I placed my hand on his face as I kneeled down in front of him.

"Baby, I want you to know that I do not want you to choose sides. That's not why I'm doing this. I'm leaving because this is the best and safest thing

56

for me to do. The relationship that I have with your father has nothing to do with you. I would never put you in a position to where you feel you have to choose."

DP placed his hand on my shoulder. "Ma, I get it. I'm not a kid anymore. I know the things you went through with dad and it's okay for you to get away from him. He's happy and you should be happy too."

The words delivered from my son's mature lips to my ears made me realize that he had been paying attention for a long time. I was happy to receive his blessing. All I could do was, nod and smile.

DP then stood up to face Shawn. Extending his hand, he reached out to my new man and they shook hands. "Thanks, Shawn, for taking care of my mom."

"No problem, man—I love your mom and you—I'll be here for the both of you," Shawn reassured him.

Outside, we stood on the porch to say our farewells. We placed our final items in the truck before pulling off. I stared out the side mirror and watched the house shrink as we drove further away. This was my start to a new beginning with a man that loved me more than I loved him. My future was looking brighter already, and we weren't out of the sunshine state as of yet.

Chapter 7

Foreign

The coldness from the hard tile chilled my thighs. Heavy, uncontrollable tears dripped from my swollen eyes onto my chest. For the past hour, I had been barricaded in the bathroom on the floor. Domestic was sound asleep, and I didn't want him to hear me crying.

The day I had been dreading had finally arrived, and I was sick as a dog. My chest was tight, and I was having a hard time breathing regularly. Aaron's funeral was a few hours away, and I wasn't ready to say goodbye. Despite everything that was going on right before his demise, I still loved him with all of my heart. I wanted a divorce, not become a widow. Aaron still had a full life ahead of him. There were mistakes he needed to correct and more growing as a man. Sadly, he was robbed of that. I guess God had other plans for his life.

A sad and awkward life lay before me and I didn't know what to expect. The last time I spoke with anyone in the Young family was the day me and Aaron's mom had a big blow-up in their living room. The worst part of it all was, not speaking to my best friend— Lexi. Not once had she reached out to make sure I was okay. Our friendship was more like a sisterhood. Which was why I thought things would've been better than they are now, but I guess I was wrong.

The trials and tribulations I went through in my marriage—no one knew them better than Lexi. That's why it hurt when she suddenly turned her back on me. Out of all people, I expected her to be the one standing in the paint with me. In our case, blood was thicker than water.

"Foreign," he paused. "Baby, are you okay? What are you doing in there?" Domestic shouted.

The sound of his overbearing voice sent an unwelcoming chill over my body. The last time he saw me crying, he abused me mentally and physically for grieving my dead husband. That was my chance to get away from him, but I stayed. My loyalty ran deep when I was in a relationship. The desperation I felt about being a mother kept me in a situation that common sense should've taken me out of. Domestic promised he wouldn't hit me again, but in my heart I knew that was a lie. It was only a matter of time before he laid hands on me again.

The bathroom door finally eased open, and Domestic walked in. I didn't even bother to look up, and I was certain that he could hear my heart pounding like a drum within the shallow walls. I was too torn to argue and fight about displaying my feelings. Nevertheless, I was prepared for whatever was about to happen.

Domestic stood in front of me and grabbed my chin. Slowly, he tilted my head upwards so I could look at him. *Here we go*, was my first thought. "Are you okay? You've been out of bed for a while now."

The fact that he knew how long I was out of bed was downright crazy. That meant he was awake, but pretended to be asleep. Domestic's current behavior had become quite baffling, to say the least. His obsession with control was more than I could handle. It was scary, but now it was too late. I was pregnant with his child, and I knew he would never let me go. Intense pressure started to build up in my chest. I could feel a fight brewing, but I didn't care. My other half was killed right after I cursed him out. I was not okay.

"No," I replied, while shaking my head. Anxiously, I awaited a snide remark to fly from his mouth.

Domestic took a deep breath. I could see his nostrils flare. Then he released a slight grunt. "Baby, I'm sorry for your loss and I want to apologize for the way I've been acting. The situation with Casey has taken me out of character."

That was so typical—to blame Casey for the way he'd been treating me. There was no way she had that much control over him, and I wasn't about to believe that. Therefore, I didn't respond.

"Are you listening to me?"

I nodded, but I didn't open my mouth.

"You don't have anything to say?"

"No."

Domestic's eyes grew a shade darker than usual. "Humph, I guess you want to leave me too and take my child away from me?"

Now he was trying to flip this around and make it about me. As if I was the one that changed overnight. "No. I would never do that."

"What's the problem then?"

I could feel myself about to cry. Sniffling, I rubbed my nose with the back of my hand. "You're not the man that I've grown to know and love. I miss the old Domestic."

"I'm still here. That's why I'm apologizing." Domestic kissed my hand. "I overreacted and I need you to know that."

"Overreacting is an intense argument or saying things you can't take back, not putting your hands on me. That was not okay. You really hurt me."

Domestic released my hand and walked over to the bathtub. He turned on the water and came back over to me. Fear immediately took over, and I was about to get up and run until he grabbed my arms.

"Are you about to drown me?" I panicked. It sounded crazy, but I was dead ass serious.

"I'm not a monster, Foreign. I made a mistake. Let me take care of you."

The water was hot, yet soothing. My body relaxed instantly, and a sense of calmness was present. Domestic used a washcloth to clean my face. "Foreign, I want you to know that I love you and I'm not going anywhere. Neither are you. I'm going to be here to support you and my child until the day I leave this earth and in the afterlife. To start, I will be accompanying you to the funeral."

That serene moment quickly disappeared. It was now replaced with a sudden thunderstorm. My brain slid on brakes and came to a complete stop. Domestic's presence at Aaron's funeral was a terrible idea. That was like throwing a match on the ground at the gas station. To keep him calm, I had to be as sweet as possible.

"Baby, I appreciate you wanting to be here for me, but I don't think that's a good idea. I'm already going through the motions with my in-laws, and the last thing I need is a battle at his homegoing service."

A faint smile crossed Domestic's lips before he opened his mouth. "I wasn't asking permission, sweetie. I'm telling you that I will be in attendance. You think I'm going to let you face them alone? I don't think so."

Domestic washed my body thoroughly, using my shower glove. The way his strong hands massaged my body weakened my flesh. It was ironic how the same hands that made me feel good, caused pain during my assault last week. After my bath, Domestic and I got dressed and headed out to the auditorium where the service was being held.

The parking lot was beyond crowded. There were stretch limos, hummers and every luxury car you could think of. Domestic brought his Maserati to a complete stop in front of the entrance and put it in *park*. "Go inside and find your parents. I'm about to park the car." Grabbing my hand, he stroked it gently. "Don't worry, I'll keep my distance."

"Thank you."

Domestic got out of the car and came around to the passenger side and opened the door for me. As I stepped out, I could feel a million eyes staring at me, like I was naked. No one knew who I was at the moment, thanks to my oversized shades and big black hat. That was guaranteed to change once I was inside and the service started. The camera crew was also outside, and I definitely didn't want them filming me. So, as I walked up the steps, I made sure not to make any eye contact with the media.

Inside, my parents were seated on the first row in the third section. That was where I sat as well. Sitting in the middle section on the first row with his mother was out of the question.

Aaron's casket remained opened throughout the entire service. My eyes were wet the entire time. It was so hard to see him lying there lifeless. I just wanted to lay down beside him and tell him that I'm sorry for not acknowledging his illness when he was trying to make it work.

Once the choir was done singing, we read the obituary silently, and his closest friends and family members were allowed to go up and speak. I didn't have the strength to do that. I was too broken on the inside to speak publicly. My father placed his arm around me as I sobbed uncontrollably. My heart was gone forever.

Next up on the mic was Calvin. Lexi stood beside him as if they were a couple. He was dressed in all black and wore a pair of dark shades to cover his eyes. "Good morning, everyone."

"Good morning," the crowd responded.

"God is good all the time," he continued.

"And all the time God is good," the crowd finished his sentence.

"This is a hard day for me as it is for everyone in this room."

"Amen," a few people in the church replied.

"Aaron and I were best friends. I loved him like a brother." Calvin sniffled. "Let me rephrase that. We are brothers, we just have different parents. Aaron and I met in high school. We played on the same football team and we both wanted to be captain of the junior varsity squad. We didn't get along for shit at first," Calvin chuckled and looked into the crowd.

"I apologize for my language, but that's a fact. One day we were at practice and the coach was tired of the two of us bickering, so he put us in teams of two and said whoever scores the first touchdown will be the captain. We accepted the challenge because we wanted that spot so bad. Me and Aaron got on that field and showed out. We couldn't score for nothing in the world." Calvin stopped to dry his eyes with the handkerchief Lexi handed to him.

"There was a minute left on the clock. We only had five minutes in total. Aaron caught the ball at the sixty yard line and smoked me. He ran until he made that touchdown and I was on his heels. When he did that signature dance that he did when we won the Super Bowl this year, I was heated. I was so mad that I tackled him and we started to fight. The coach made us do forty hours of community service together and that's how our brotherhood started."

Calvin wiped his eyes again. "I love you, Aaron. We're brothers always and forever. It's gon' be lonely out here, but I'll see you on the other side, my good brother." Calvin locked eyes with me. "Foreign, my brother loved you until his last breath and I know you love him the same way. Keep your head up, sis. I'm only a phone call away if you need anything."

My tears flowed harder, as I mouthed the words *thank you*.

Calvin passed the microphone to Lexi. The moment she started to talk, I laid my head on my father's shoulder and closed my eyes. I couldn't stand to look in her face because of the way she had been treating me. The church listened and laughed at the childhood story she shared. When she told everyone about the love she had for her brother, my heart broke for her. They were closer than close, and I understood her pain. However, I wasn't expecting her to mention how she served as a counselor to me and her brother.

"Me, Aaron and Foreign have some wild memories and there's so much that people would never understand about my brother and that's okay. What I do know is that Foreign loved my brother throughout everything and she can explain that better than me. Come on up Foreign." Lexi looked down at me and flashed a smile.

I couldn't believe she put me on the spot like that, but I graced the crowd with my presence like a wife is supposed to. Lexi handed me the microphone and kissed me on the cheek. Speaking at his funeral was not on my list of things to do, but I no longer had that choice. My father stood by my side, as I cleared my throat and told them about the way we met. It felt like I was on the stage for an hour, but it had only been a few minutes.

"In closing I just want to thank everyone that showed up to honor my husband and his legacy. I appreciate the calls and flowers that I have been receiving. I haven't gotten back to everyone, but your deeds have not gone unnoticed." Glancing down at Aaron, I felt light-headed. My father grabbed me, as I held on to the podium for dear life. "Aaron, words will never express the way I feel about you. I just wish I had another century, another decade, another year, another day, and another second to spend with you. We were supposed to grow old and gray together, but God had other plans for you. You'll always be in my heart. I'll love you forever, Aaron."

The cemetery was just as crowded as the auditorium. Twenty- five doves were released to represent his age of death. When the pallbearers lowered his casket into the ground, loud screams could be heard by me, Lexi and his mother. No one was ready to let Aaron go. It was finally over, and I would never see his face again.

From the gravesite, I could see Domestic standing by the side of his car. In a zone, I staggered towards him as my heels kept sinking into the dirt. Out of the blue, I could feel a hand grab my arm. When I turned around, I was standing face to face with Lexi.

"You are one evil and treacherous bitch!"

Snatching away from her, we faced off. "What the fuck are you talking about, Lexi?"

"How dare you bring another nigga to my brother's funeral!" she screamed directly in my face.

"Excuse me!"

"You heard what the fuck I said. My brother hasn't been dead two weeks and you ready to forget about him like he was shit at the bottom of those expensive ass shoes he bought you."

Looking around, I checked to see who was watching us. The last thing I wanted to do was make a scene, but Lexi tried it. "First of all, you know that I wanted a divorce from Aaron. I moved on. I've forgiven him repeatedly. What more do you expect me to do?" I snapped.

"To show my brother the respect you didn't show him when you was staying out all night and getting fucked by that new nigga. Do you know how many times he called me early in the morning crying, looking for you? I covered for you when I knew you were doing him wrong." Lexi's eyes had tears formed in them.

"I guess your mother has rubbed off on you." I pointed my finger in her face. "Do you know how many times I've cried over his infidelity? Your brother cheated on me numerous times and I stayed because I love him. I lost babies because of him, but no one cared about that. He hurt me to my core. He damaged me."

Lexi's eyes grew into tiny slits. Her chest heaved up and down, as the tears flowed freely from her eyes. "My brother was in counseling because he wanted to make that marriage work. So, give him some fuckin' credit. He may have cheated, but he was never attached to none of them hoes. Every night he came home to you out of respect, but did you do the same. No! Aaron would've never flaunted any one of those in your face the way you doing right now."

I was not about to argue with her. Aaron's death was hard enough, so I decided to let it go. "For the record, he only came to be supportive while I grieve. He knows everything that's going on right now and didn't want me to face it alone."

"So you pillow talking with that nigga about me and my family? You barely know that nigga." Lexi shot daggers in Domestic's direction. "He's probably responsible for my brother's death. So you plan on living off my brother with this nigga?"

"Money?" I chuckled. "He has his money and multiple businesses, in case you didn't know." It took everything in me to keep from flying off the handle at that cemetery. Lexi was really tripping and adding insult to injury, making those false accusations. "I'm going to walk off now before we say things that we're going to regret. It's obvious we both need time to cool off."

Lexi smirked through her tears. "It's a little too late for that. Besides, everything I said, I meant. And as far as our friendship, it's over. I never want to see or hear from you again. My brother is dead and so are you." Lexi pointed her long nail in my direction. "If I find out he had anything to do with it, there will be a problem."

Lexi stomped off and left me in my thoughts. I didn't want to believe that our friendship was really over. When I turned around, Domestic was standing beside the passenger door, waiting on me. To my surprise, he didn't mention what he'd just witnessed. Instead, he drove us away in silence. In the back of my mind, something told me this wasn't the last of it.

Back at the house, Domestic sat downstairs drinking Vodka straight out the bottle, while I remained upstairs. He wanted us to watch a movie, but I wasn't up for it. All I wanted to do was, lie in bed. After staring into space for two hours and thinking about Aaron, my eye lids finally grew heavy and I began to drift off into a light sleep. That only lasted for a few minutes before I was greeted by a sharp pain to my face. When I opened my eyes, I was staring at the devil, better known as Domestic.

"Bitch, you got me looking stupid out here in these streets. You still love that nigga. What the fuck wrong with you, hoe?" Domestic's fist landed hard against my jaw.

His actions caught me off guard, and my first reaction was to protect my best asset—my face. "Domestic, stop!" I wailed in pain, while putting my arms up.

"Fuck you! I just watched you on national news crying for a nigga that didn't treat you right, professing your love and shit. All the while I'm standing around looking like a duck ass nigga." Domestic delivered another punch, but to my thigh that time. The pain shot straight through my body.

Swinging my arms, I managed to hit him in the face. I just wanted his two hundred plus pound frame off of me. Domestic straddled my body and placed his large, heavy hands around my throat and started to strangle me. My life flashed before my eyes. I begged and pleaded, but he was too volatile to hear my cries.

"Domestic, I love you," I pleaded for mercy.

"No, you don't!" he screamed. "That's not what you told his sister. You let that hoe disrespect me for the last time."

"You're going to kill our baby!" I screamed, hoping he would stop his vicious attack on me.

When that didn't work, survival mode kicked in and I had to fight back. Aaron was the reason I didn't carry a baby full term, and I wasn't about to let Domestic do the same thing to me. Using all of the strength I had in my body, I threw wild punches and scratched his face in the process. Blood appeared on his flesh, and he stopped hitting me. Just when I thought the fight was over, Domestic snatched me off the bed. The rug burned my skin as he dragged me into the closet. My body was sore, as I laid there weeping. Domestic slammed the door, and I could hear a click. Pulling my weak body up, I reached for the handle but it was locked.

"Domestic, let me out!" I screamed.

Through the door, I could see him go to the bed and lie down. Domestic left me in the closet, and all I could do was cry until I fell asleep.

Chapter 8

Lexi

"I can't believe this bitch tried me and my brother like that," I shouted, while kicking off my shoes and flopping down on the bed. "She brought the nigga she was cheating with to his damn funeral. It doesn't get more disrespectful than that." Foreign had me hotter than Arizona in the summer.

"I know this is stressful, but I need you to stop worrying about that. It's over with. Just relax and let me take your mind off of things." Calvin made himself comfortable at my side and massaged my shoulders. He could be caring at times. But I also knew that was his way of trying to loosen me up so I could give up the nookie easily.

"You think you so slick."

"What I did?" He cut his eyes and flashed a devious, freaky smirk.

"You trying to trick me out my panties," I placed my finger on his soft, edible lips. "But you ain't getting none of sweet, gushy pussy tonight, baby, so tell your boy to stand down." I noticed his boy was trying to rise on the low.

"I been getting this for too long." Calvin caressed me by the nape of my neck and made a slow trail downwards to my lower back.

Rolling my neck in a circular motion, I closed my eyes and allowed my muscles to relax. Calvin pushed me back onto the bed, while using his large hands to instruct me to lay on my stomach. I obeyed his silent command. Calvin's hands were big and strong. He wasn't a running back for nothing.

My body was beginning to react to the sensual touch of his fingertips caressing my flesh. With my arms resting at my sides, I was able to get comfortable immediately. I could feel the zipper to my dress sliding down until it rested against my butt.

"Ooh shit, you wearing these lace panties I love." Calvin's warms lips were pressed against my cheeks.

My ass was completely naked when Calvin added the oil to my massage. Straddling my thighs, he pressed his knuckles against my skin and applied pressure to my tense muscles. It felt so good to be catered to by a man. My boy toys weren't capable of being affectionate, but that didn't bother me one bit. I wasn't about feelings and all that mushy shit, but with Calvin it was different. True enough, he was the average professional NFL whore, but when it came down to me he always showed me a different side to him. In the present moment, it was needed. My twin left the world, leaving me all alone. The rest of my life on earth was destined to be lonely without his aggravating ass calling me, begging for advice. At that point I would do anything to hear his voice again. My heart was hurting, and the tears started to flow.

Calvin saw my tears and kissed my cheek, as he rubbed my shoulders gently. His affection and attentiveness was so important for my sanity.

"This is hard for the both of us, but even harder for you. I know what Aaron meant to you. He meant a lot to me too. Y'all shared blood, but Aaron was my brother too. I would've done anything for him."

"I know," I whispered in between sniffles.

"I know I can't take his place, but you have me for life. I'm going to be here by your side until I join my brother in the sky."

I could hear the sincerity in his voice. He genuinely loved my brother, and I could never deny that. Calvin was never a fake friend to Aaron, and that was one of the reasons I fucked with him so hard. True enough, Aaron didn't want us sleeping together, but shit—I'm a grown ass woman. He couldn't tell me who I couldn't sleep with. Especially when he was laying wherever and whenever!

Calvin kissed me once more. His warm tongue traced my ear and neck. "Let me take your mind off of things for a little while."

Against my wishes, he had me ready to release a Tsunami on his king-sized bed. Rolling over onto my back, Calvin hovered over my body and looked into my soul. There was always a twinkle in his eyes when he looked at me. If I didn't know any better, I would think he was soft for the kid. We locked lips as if it was the last time.

Since I lost my virginity, I had always been a sexual person. However, relationships weren't my thing. After my first heartbreak, I decided that I would never let another nigga play me. I had no problem with fucking and leaving them. That's what set me aside from all the females they were used to smashing. I was always the nigga in our situation, and I kept them in the friend zone.

Calvin planted soft kisses on my flat belly and thighs. When he reached the treasure he was so desperately looking for, Calvin used his tongue to part my lips and nibble on my budding flower. Caught up in his rapture, I placed my hands on the top of his head and enjoyed the pleasure. For the next hour, Calvin made love to my mind and body. When it was all over, I slept peacefully in his arms.

Calvin...

The sound of the doorbell sent me downstairs in a hurry. Thanks to the cameras outside of the house, I already knew who was standing on my front porch ringing the doorbell. Dressed in nothing but a pair of boxers and tank top, I opened the door and stood face to face with Emilia.

"What are you doing here?" I huffed with aggravation.

"Good morning to you too." Emilia barged into my home without an invitation.

"I didn't invite you in." Slamming the door, I turned to face her with a mean scowl. "What do you want? It's too early for this bullshit and I don't have the time or the energy to deal with this."

She laughed and placed her hands on her hip. "I came by to deliver some good and bad news. Which one you want to hear first?"

"If it's coming from you, neither could be good. So, stop bullshitting and tell me why you at my crib this early in the damn morning."

Emilia looked around the house. "Where is Alexis? I know she's not too far away."

Shrugging, I replied nastily. "I don't know. Why you asking about her?"

Emilia rocked on her heels. "She's always here, that's why. Is that your girlfriend or some shit?"

"I don't think that's any of your business."

"Hmm, aren't we feisty this morning?"

"I prefer the term, *pissed the fuck off.* Now why the fuck are you here? Damn," I huffed with irritation.

Emilia flipped her hair behind her ear and grinned. "Well, I just want you to bring up the fact that Aaron was laid to rest with his dignity intact. As you can see, his reputation is stellar, but all of that can change in the matter of seconds, if you don't give me what I want."

"And what would that be?" I sat down on the sofa.

"One hundred thousand dollars. Aaron was supposed to pay me, but unfortunately he's no longer with us."

"For what?" I asked curiously.

"He's no longer under investigation for having sex with an underage girl."

"That's because he was innocent of that."

"If that's what you say."

"It's what I know."

"Hear me and hear me well." Emilia moved closer towards me with her hand on her holster. "If you want to make this go away, I suggest you cough up that hundred grand and I'm not playing."

Immediately, I felt like I was being threatened. Leaning forward, I folded my hands and ground my teeth. It was something I did when a person had me fucked up. "I don't know who the fuck you think you talking to, but quit trying me. I'm not about to pay yo' ass shit for telling the truth. You must've smoked that dope from the department's narcotic department." As I stood up, I pointed towards the door. "It's time for you to roll up outta here, Emilia."

Rolling her neck, Emilia pointed at me. "I'm going to leave right now, but you better believe I'll be back." Seductively, she swished her hips while walking towards the entrance. Stopping at the door, Emilia turned to face me with a crooked smile on her face and ran her pointer finger down the center of my chest. "Next time, offer a bitch some dick or something."

Aggressively, I pushed her hand away. "Bye, Emilia!"

Emilia crossed the threshold, as the door slammed behind her. When I turned around, Lexi was standing by the sofa with a bright, evil smile on her face. In her hand, she held up her cellphone. "We got that bitch now."

"You recorded everything?"

"Just as sure as I'm standing here looking, handsome." Lexi sat the phone down on the table and stretched. "Even the part where she was push-ing up on you for some dick. From the sounds of things, she's had it before."

There was nothing left to say. I just stood there with a puzzling look on my face. Lexi folded her arms across her chest. My silence was confirmation enough. Aaron always replied in the same dumb ass way whenever he was guilty and didn't want to admit it. All she could do was, shake her head and laugh.

"That's that same dumb ass expression my brother had whenever he was guilty. I know that look all too well."

Finally, I decided to respond. There was no telling what Aaron told Lexi, so I might as well be honest. "It wasn't like that. Me and Aaron had a threesome with her. That was it. I swear."

Lexi giggled. There was no reason for her to be upset because she al-ready knew what time it was with us. That was the reason she refused to give a nigga like me her heart.

"You good. I know how y'all operate. That's why I never give y'all my heart. That shit dead as that hoe's career after I put her ass on blast."

Lexi smiled at the thought of getting Emilia fired from the force. That served her right, after trying to sabotage her brother's career and threatening her cutty buddy. If anybody threatened Calvin, it was going to be her and no one else.

Chapter 9

Domestic

After dealing with the emotions of the funeral and Foreign, I decided to take a day off and deal with my future wife. Without thinking, I snapped and laid hands on her. I even locked her in the closet when it was over. Foreign was my world, but I needed her to know that I was in charge. My word trumped everything, so whatever I say goes.

For thirty minutes, I listened to her beg and bang on the door until I finally fell asleep. Foreign had to learn not to disobey or embarrass me. Those consequences would never end up well. Picking up the phone, I called the car wash.

"Thank you for calling Supreme Touch. This is Tracy speaking, how may I assist you?" she shouted cheerfully into the phone.

Loudly, I cleared my throat and stroked my chin. "It's nice to see that someone has customer service skills."

"Sometimes!—You just caught me on a good day," Tracy joked.

"Every day better be a good day if you wanna keep your job."

Judging by the deep breath Tracy took, I could picture her rolling those big ass eyes in that dome of hers, while popping her bubblegum in my damn ear.

"Stop being so sensitive. You know I love working here. Nothing makes me happier than waking up and knowing that I'll be serving you for eight hours a day."

"I bet you do." I sat up on the side of the bed and planted my feet firmly on the floor. "I need you to run the office for me today."

Opening the camera app on my phone, I observed Tracy sitting her fingernail file down on the counter and admiring her nails. "I got you, boss."

"I'll be back tomorrow and I'll throw in some overtime for you doing me this solid."

"It's all good. I promise to keep these niggas in check while you're away."

"A'ight. See you tomorrow and find you some work to do. You work at a car wash, not a nail shop." Tracy rolled her neck and looked into the camera. Before she could respond, I ended the call and sat the phone down on the bed. I walked over to the closet where my woman was held captive for the night.

Unlocking the door, I glared down at Foreign, who was curled up on the floor, draped in one of my winter coats. I kneeled down beside Foreign and tapped her shoulder. "Foreign. Foreign. Get up." At first she didn't move, so I repeated the same steps until she started to squirm around.

Foreign cracked her eyes open slightly and yawned. As her eyes roamed around the closed in space, I could tell she was slightly confused. The slight touch of my hand caused her to shiver. That was a feeling I knew all too well.

Foreign resisted my touch by creating a larger space between us. That was the reaction I was expecting. It was confirmation that she was afraid of me, which meant I could control her without a doubt. Raising my hand, I reached out and helped Foreign off the floor. My threatening nature caused her to flinch and block her face from a blow she thought was on the way.

"Get up. I'm not about to hit you." Those words rolled smoothly off my tongue, as if I never laid hands on my baby in the first place.

"I got it." Foreign attempted to get up on her own. With very little force, I grabbed her by the arm, so she could see that I wasn't a threat. We stood face to face for a few seconds before Foreign looked away with sadness in her eyes.

"I know you're upset with me." Using my right hand, I pushed the loose strands of hair from her face, before forcing her to look at me. Gently, I ran my finger across the bruises on her smooth skin. Guilt gripped me by the balls for damaging such a delicate flower, my queen and the mother of my child.

"You have every right to be. I just need you to understand that I don't appreciate being humiliated. I'm a man. I'm your man. And you will treat me with respect. The last thing I want is a combative wife."

Foreign's eyebrows heightened with surprise, like she didn't know marriage was in our future. Then she started to rock on her heels.

"What's wrong with you?"

"Nothing." Foreign shuffled towards the door. Before she could make a clean break, I grabbed her arm.

"I'm talking to you."

"If it's okay with you, I would like to use the bathroom."

"Go ahead." The second I released her arm, Foreign darted into the direction of the master bathroom.

When I made it to the door, Foreign was sitting on the toilet with her hands covering her face. Just the thought of the pain I inflicted on her broke my heart. Never had I thought our situation would be a repeat of Casey. Her silent cries hurt the most. It made me walk away because I wasn't sure if she was crying about the bruises or punk ass Aaron. Either way, I felt trouble brewing in my spirit.

The love of my life appeared and stopped a few feet away from me. "Take off your clothes."

"What?"

"Take off your clothes."

Slowly she removed her clothing and stood in front of me naked as the day she was born. Extending my arms, I grabbed her hands and pulled her closer to me. There was hesitation at first, but she followed my lead. With saddened eyes, I locked in on the dark circle on her cheekbone. It was ugly, and I was the reason behind it. Gently, I rubbed her belly. My seed was growing inside of the womb of the woman I loved, and I was making shit difficult. Softly, I spoke directly to Foreign.

"I'm sorry. I didn't mean to hurt you this bad." It was the truth. "Last night I lost it. I'm not good with controlling my emotions or anger. The thought of you trying to leave me made me snap. All I want is a family with a wife. Is that too much to ask?" Foreign shook her head, but she didn't open her mouth. "I need a woman that balances me. That woman is you. Just be patient with me, please, baby. I need help."

Foreign shed a few tears before parting her lips. "Domestic, what do you need help with? I've been the woman you needed me to be. I'm here with you, but you act like you don't know that by now."

"Maybe physically, but not mentally. For me to see you expressing your feelings for another man infuriated me. You messed with my pride, and I didn't appreciate that. I've been in your corner all this time. That nigga didn't appreciate you. I did." My emotions quickly got the best of me, and I found myself yelling. To my surprise, she didn't flinch.

"I need you to understand something." Foreign's eyes sparkled when she spoke to me softly. "Aaron was my husband and we were together for a very long time. Despite the drama I went through with him, we were still married. Do I love him? Yes. Does that make me love you any less? No. We are together and Aaron has gone to his final resting place. I'm about to have your baby. I want to build a family with you, but I don't want to be beaten in the process. I can't live like that, Domestic."

"I love you, Foreign, and I'll do anything to keep you."

"But this is not the way. All you're doing is pushing me further away from you."

74

Hearing those words rattled me to the core. It was like she didn't understand a damn thing I just said. To insinuate that she had a thought about
leaving would prove to be fatal. Those thoughts definitely needed to be
erased from her brain. Standing, I grabbed Foreign and pushed her onto the
bed. My body was longing to feel her soft skin against mine. Once I stripped
out of my clothes, I climbed on top of her small frame and took what belonged to me.

Foreign closed her eyes while I made slow, passionate love to her. Sexy
moans escaped her lips as I laid down the pipe. She was sprung. There was
no denying that. My sex game and aggressiveness was what attracted her to
me in the first place. The lame she was married to ain't have shit on me. For
the next hour, I made my baby cry, skeet and scream my name. When it was
all over, the only thing she could do was go to sleep.

After my job was done, I left the room with my phone clutched tightly
in my hand. In the kitchen, I scrolled through my call log and pressed *send*.

"Wassup, bro?" Carlos answered on the third ring.

"Aye, I need you to come by the wash tomorrow so we can chop it up."

"Say less. I'll be there." After a few sentences, I ended the call and decided to hit up my son. I hadn't spoken to him since his evil ass mammie
snatched him from within my grip.

"Hey, Dad."

"Wassup, son? How you doing?"

"I'm good. How you doing?"

"I'll be better if my only son hit his pops up. Wassup with that?"

DP sighed into the phone. "I wanted to call you, but I thought you were
mad at me."

Taking a seat on the living room sofa, I ran my hand across my face. "I
could never be mad at you. That's on your mama. She placed the distance
between us. It's not your fault."

"I know what was going on between you and my mom." There was a
long-drawn-out pause. Immediately, I felt like Casey was standing at his
side coaching him. "You really hurt her, dad and that was the reason I left
with her. I hope you understand that."

Truthfully, I was livid. Not at DP, but his stankin' ass mama for trying
to stain my image. "Son, I want you to understand something. Me and your
mother had a tumultuous relationship. It wasn't all bad, but it wasn't all
good either. Neither one of us are innocent about the outcome of our relationship. We are both to blame. I'm not asking you to pick sides. All I'm

saying is, don't get in between something your young mind have no knowledge about."

"See, that's the thing, pops. I know all about it. Mom told me everything. What I don't understand is why wouldn't you let her be happy with Shawn? You have Foreign. Why couldn't she have someone? And don't say because you were taking care of her. Shawn is a good man and he treats me good. He makes my mama happy."

To hear my son give the next man props fucked with me. How in the fuck could he say that when that nigga Shawn's money wasn't even close to mine! That shit was bogus as fuck, and it was his mammy fault with her nasty trifling ass. My blood pressure was high and I was ready to snap, but for the sake of my son's feelings I remained calm.

"DP, from the sound of things, your mother has tainted your thinking, and I don't appreciate that. Our situation is deeper than rap, and you'll never understand that until you've walked a mile in my shoes with the mother of your own child. You and I need to have a face-to-face conversation. Where are you?"

"I'm out of state."

The second he replied, I could hear Casey screaming into the phone. "Listen here, motherfucker, I'm being courteous enough to let my child talk to you. Don't start asking him a million questions about our whereabouts because he not gone tell your abusive ass shit. You got that?" Casey snapped.

In that moment, I lost it. "You a silly ass bitch if you think I'm going to sit back and allow you to brainwash my muthafuckin' son. Bitch, I'll bury yo' ass alive and do a death sentence before I let that shit happen. Fuck wrong with you, ho'!"

"I hope you know that your son heard your stupid ass," Casey shouted with a sinister laugh.

All I could see was a devastating look on my son's face. I allowed Casey to pull out the monster in his presence. "DP, son, listen to me, please."

"Goodbye, Dad!"

"DP," I shouted.

"He walked away. See, I didn't have to tell him anything about your psychotic ass. You just proved everything he suspected of you, dumb ass."

Those were the last words I heard from him. I was furious. All I could see was fire-red blood flooding my vision. Casey was a dead bitch walking, and I put that on my mama. Through gritted teeth and a puffed up chest, I spoke harshly. "You bottom of the barrel bitch, when I catch you, its lights out, ho'. You purposely turned my son against me and now you gotta go. Watch your back, bitch!" I ended the call. No more words needed to be spoken because Casey's days on earth were limited, and I meant that shit.

My heart was in a tangled web. The one person I lived for and would die for wanted nothing to do with me. It made me furious. All I could do was drink, cry and punch every item in sight. After tainting my bloodstream with alcohol for two hours, I returned to my bedroom in rare form. Foreign was sleeping peacefully until I straddled her legs and wrapped my hands around her throat, startling her.

"Domestic, what are you doing?" she screeched at the top of her lungs, while gripping my wrists with the little bit of strength she had.

"I'll kill you if you take my child away from me."

"I'm not," she screamed in fear. "Why are you doing this to me? Domestic, I love you. Please don't hurt our baby."

The sound of her sweet, soft voice pleading with agony, made the demon in me disappear. I don't know how she did it, but I instantly turned into a gentle giant. Tears cascaded down my face. "I'm sorry, baby." My hands loosened from around her neck. I was now holding her in my muscular arms. "I never meant to hurt you."

"You keep saying that, but you don't mean that. You keep apologizing, yet you continue to abuse me. That's not love, Domestic. That's called manipulation." There was a fear-stricken look in Foreign's eyes, as she expressed her pain. "I'm not your punching bag. What did I do to deserve this type of treatment from you?" she sobbed through tears. "And I've never been through this with—"

I cut her off expeditiously and snapped. "You better not say shit about that nigga. I don't want to hear that muthafucka's name." To get my point across, I caressed her jawline firmly. My breathing was heavy. "I've never disrespected you. Not once. I expect the same thing from you."

Foreign nodded, but didn't part those luscious lips that I loved to see wrapped around my wood. Instead, she closed her eyes. Affectionately, I kissed her eyelids.

"You belong to me now. The only way out is death." The sweet scent of her skin was tantalizing, as it filled my nostrils. "I'll never let you leave me. I would rather spend the rest of my life in a six-by-nine cold, dusty cell before I live without you."

Foreign had a spell on me. The warmth of her flesh calmed me when I lay down beside my woman and caressed her belly until I fell asleep.

The loud slam from the front door startled me. My mother, Veronica, better known as the evil witch, had returned home, and I knew all hell was about to break loose.

"Demerius! Demerius! Get your ass in here right now," she screamed at the top of her lungs.

When I walked into the living room, Veronica was standing beside the sofa with a tennis racquet in her right hand. The left hand clutched her brief-case.

"Yes. Yes, ma'am," I stammered with sweat dripping on my forehead.

"Who the fuck told you to call your daddy?"

My scrawny ass couldn't think of a single vowel to say, because the evil bitch had me shaking like a leaf. My teeth chattered. Hot liquid ran down my leg. It was embarrassing, but there wasn't shit I could do at such a young age.

Veronica stared at me with the most terrifying glance. The white in her eyes vanished, and all I could see was black. I knew she was gon' beat my ass, but I wasn't prepared for the brutal attack brewing. With one swift move, Veronica raised her right arm and struck me across the head with the tennis racquet. Instantly, I was dazed, and everything went pitch black.

The next morning, I woke up on the cold tile floor. My body ached terribly. I just knew I had broken bones. Black and blue bruises covered my skin like a Dalmatian puppy.

Chapter 10

Foreign

A strong, succulent aroma whiffed through my nostrils, tickling my senses. Domestic's side of the bed was cool when I rolled over and touched it. That let me know he had been up for a while. With sleep still in my eyes, I managed to pull myself from the bed and go the bathroom to handle my hygiene. Once I was fresh, I headed downstairs. The one thing that played in my mind was the way he pleaded for my help. For that very reason, I decided to play by his rules. Especially, if that was going to ensure the beatings would stop.

Domestic was in the kitchen, shirtless, standing sexy in all that delicious chocolate. The sight of his muscular back made my knees buckle. I wanted to jump his bones on sight. Tiptoeing behind him, I wrapped my arms around his waist and rested my head against his back. "Good morning."

"Good morning, beautiful," he replied.

There were some movements with the pans, but I didn't budge until I felt him attempting to turn around. Domestic hugged me tight and kissed my forehead. "I love you so much, baby. I'm going to make you the happiest wife. I promise."

"I would appreciate that very much."

"Are you ready to eat?"

"Yes, we are," I smiled, while taking a seat and rubbing my belly. "What did you make?" Whomever I was carrying was hungry. There were little movements in my belly. It made me smile. All I ever wanted was to be a mother, and it was finally happening.

"Fresh biscuits from scratch, salmon patties and eggs. Do you want orange juice or water?"

"Orange juice."

Domestic fixed me a plate and sat it in front of me. "This looks so good, babe. It tastes good too."

"I'll be the judge of that." I flashed him a warm smile.

Consumed by hunger, I opened the biscuit and sat it back on the plate. Fresh steam rose from the middle and filled my nostrils. The Alaga syrup was sweet, and the biscuit was mouthwatering. "Babe, this is so good. Who taught you how to cook like this? Your mother?"

Domestic took a seat at the table across from me. After opening up his cloth napkin, he sat it in his lap and looked into my eyes. "Nah. She ain't teach me shit. She was too busy working and yelling at me and my brother,

80

instead of being a mother." He sighed. "I learned how to cook on my own. Veronica wasn't interested in being a parent. That woman doesn't have one maternal instinct in her body."

That was the last thing I was expecting to hear from him, but that would explain a lot. Including his disdain for the woman that gave him life. "I'm sorry to hear that, babe. Nonetheless, you turned out to be a decent man."

"Oh really?" he smirked.

"Yes," I nodded, while scooping a forkful of eggs into my mouth. Domestic's dark eyes were locked in on me, as I sipped my orange juice. It was evident I needed to clean up my comment. "You have your flaws and so do I, but we're human. I love you, Domestic. Flaws and all."

"I love you more."

Domestic nodded and sipped on a dark colored liquid in his glass. It was definitely liquor in his cup. After breakfast, I excused myself and went by my house to check the mailbox. Upon my arrival, I was surprised to see an unknown vehicle in my yard. There was a man standing on the porch, so I greeted him politely.

"Hello, how can I help you?"

"Yes." He looked down at the envelope he was holding. "I'm looking for a Foreign Young."

"That's me."

He passed me the envelope. "You've been served."

"What?" I gasped.

"Have a good day, ma'am."

I stood there with my jaw on the ground until he exited the driveway. Inside the house, I ripped it open and snatched the papers out. "This better not be another Aaron scandal."

My eyes scanned the first paragraph, and I automatically lost my breath. "This bitch didn't let the dust settle on his grave before pulling this stunt on me."

Tossing the papers onto the sofa, I removed my cellphone from my bag. Lexi's phone rang until the voicemail picked up. "Come on, Lexi pick up." I dialed her number two more times and still no answer.

My mind was discombobulated. Out of all the shit I put up with in my marriage to Aaron, I couldn't believe she would cross me like that. If I wasn't pregnant, I would go to that house and slap her teeth down that filthy ass throat of hers. Snatching my keys and bag up, I stormed out of the house. The adrenaline in my body caused me to hurry to the car wash. My ass was a wreck, and I needed Domestic to talk me down before I did something I wouldn't regret.

Lexi...

The time had finally come for me to bring down the guttersnipe that was trying to extort my brother. Emilia was about to be out on her ass faster than she could run to the border for some Mexican cheese.

My heart tightened, as I stared at the selfie of me and my other half, my twin. "I miss you so much, Aaron. Things aren't the same without you. I swear that I'm going to make sure every single person that came for you in some way is going to pay." Clutching my phone tight, I held it to my chest. "I love you, twin."

When I opened my eyes, Calvin was standing in front of me with sadness in his eyes. "I miss him too. That was my brother." Calvin knelt down and put his arms around me. "I'm here for you, Lex, I promise you that."

I nodded.

"You ready to take this bitch down?"

"I am."

Calvin wiped my tears away. "Let's go handle this bitch."

The ride to the precinct was fairly quiet. We made small talk here and there, but my main focus circled around my brother and everyone that crossed him. And yes, that included Foreign. She called me a few times, but I ignored all of her calls. We had nothing to discuss. She betrayed my family when she brought her side nigga to my brother's funeral. So, as far as I was concerned, our sisterly bond was buried the day I put my flesh and blood into the ground.

"Come on." Calvin opened the passenger door, so I could exit.

"Aren't you quite the gentleman?"

"I just love your sarcasm, baby."

"That's not all you love."

"You got that right."

Confidently, I swished my hips and made my way through the double doors of the Tampa Bay Precinct. Calvin followed my steps closely like my guard dog. Purposely, I slammed my purse down on the counter to interrupt the cackling between the chatty co-workers.

"Excuse me," I snapped rudely.

The woman sitting rolled her eyes before looking at me. "How can I help you?"

"We can start by you getting rid of that attitude," I hissed. "I would like to speak to the captain now."

"What is this in regards to? I'm sure I can assist you."

A slight chuckle escaped my lips. "I'm afraid my needs are above your pay grade, sweetie. Now get the captain out here."

The receptionist turned and looked at her co-worker. "I'll talk to you later. Let me help her." She then picked up the phone and made a call. "He'll be right out."

"That wasn't so hard. Now was it?"

Swiftly, I turned on my heels in an about face. Directly in front of me stood a handsome, older man. Definitely easy on the eye. "I'm Captain Fuller. How can I help you?"

"I'm Alexis and I would prefer to speak to you in private."

Captain Fuller shoved his hands into his slack pockets. "In regards to?"

"Detective Emilia Flores. My family has been harassed by this woman and I would like to file a report, in private and in your office." My voice heightened, causing stares from the other patrons. The tight look on the captain's face displayed his discomfort with the situation.

Stroking his beard, the captain extended his left arm. "Right this way."

My heels click-clacked against the tiles, as I followed him down the hall and into his office. Captain Fuller closed the door and sat behind his desk. Adjusting his coat, he cut his eyes in my direction. "So, what has Detective Flores gotten herself into?"

"Well," I crossed my legs. "For starters, she's trying to extort my fiancé for one hundred thousand dollars."

Captain Fuller's eyebrow heightened in surprise. "Do you have proof of that?"

"As a matter of fact, I do." The smile on my face was wide as the sun.

My cellphone was already in hand and ready to go. I opened the gallery, hit *play* and held it in his direction. The look on his face was priceless, as he watched his good ole girl in blue attempt to extort money from Calvin. When the video was over, I shoved it into my bag.

Captain Fuller stroked his temple with both hands and sighed. "Is that video real?"

"Just as sure as I'm sitting here."

"What is it that you want me to do?"

"I want her badge."

"There's going to be an investigation into her behavior. I can't just take her badge without proof that she actually did it."

That was not the response I was looking for. Something needed to be done, and it needed to happen right away. "Listen here, Captain Fuller. As a black woman, I know your kind. I know you love to protect your own, but guess what? So do I?" Standing, I clutched my bag in my hand tightly. "You have no idea who you are messing with. Aaron Young was my brother."

"Aaron Young, who played for the Buccaneers?"

"The one and only."

"So, your father is Adrian Young?"

"Yes, indeed, and he knows some powerful people in very high places. Now—" I leaned forward to get closer to his face—"Are you going to help me or should I call my father to get involved?"

After the daunting question, he was standing at attention. "No. I've met your father and I don't need him to be involved in this. We can handle this on our own."

Lowering my eyes, I gave him a serious, no-nonsense look to ensure that I wasn't playing. "Are you sure about that?"

"Yes, I am. You have my word."

"Are you going to put your dog on a leash?"

"Consider her handled."

"Okay," I nodded. "You have forty-eight hours to get back with me. If not, this video will hit every news outlet in the country. Don't test me." I reached inside my pocket and removed a business card. "Call me once everything has been resolved."

"Will do."

Calvin grabbed my hand and escorted me out of the office. Smoothly, he gripped my ass. "Fiancé, huh? I think I like the sound of that."

Smacking his hand away, I giggled. "Calvin, please. I'm not enough for you and we both know that. You need a bus load of hoes to satisfy your sexual appetite."

"See, that's where you're wrong at. You're enough woman for me."

"We'll see about that." Not believing a word he said, I laughed it off and walked out the precinct.

Chapter 11

Foreign

All I wanted was a perfect marriage, a perfect life, and to be the best wife that I could be. However, the universe had a funny way of throwing a monkey wrench into my plans. My life was everything except perfect. Almost every day under Aaron's roof was hell on earth. Many nights I laid around, not eating or sleeping because I didn't know the whereabouts of my husband. That shit drove me insane. The one thing that hurt the most was my inability to carry a baby in my womb.

My favorite parking spot was empty, as expected. From my first day on the premises, it had become my designated spot. Dressed in a boyfriend tee, joggers and crisp white Adidas, I strolled towards the entrance. Based on my appearance, it looked like I was about to beat someone's ass.

Tony greeted me on my way through the door. To my surprise, Tracy wasn't at the front desk. In steady, quick steps, I walked towards his office. Domestic was sitting behind his desk, tapping away at the computer. When the door slammed, he looked up at me.

"Hey, beautiful. What's going on?"

"I just want to kill this bitch," I screamed, while grabbing my hair.

Domestic jumped from his chair and took me into his big, beefy arms. "Who, baby? What happened?"

"Aaron's mother." A river of tears ran from my eyes.

"What did she do?"

"When—I—got—home—" I sobbed between words. "There was an officer at my door. He served me papers. Aaron's low down trifling ass mama is petitioning everything he left behind."

Domestic grabbed my shoulders. "What? She can't do that."

"Apparently, she can."

"Nah," he stroked his beard. "This shit ain't going down like that. Where do they live? We need to go and pay them a visit."

Shaking my head, I sniffled. "I can't let you do that."

"I can't let anyone hurt you like this. I'm your man and it's my job to protect you." Domestic raised my chin so I could look into his dark, brown eyes. "Tell me where they live and I'll go there."

"I can't face them right now."

"You're not in this alone. I'll be right there and I dare a muthafucka to say a word to you."

Snot dripped from my nose. I used the back of my hand to catch it. "Please," I shook my head. "I can't do this right now. I just want you to hold me. Can we go home?"

"Not yet. I have a few things that I need to wrap up and then we can leave. Lay down on the sofa until I'm done."

"Okay."

Domestic's phone rang. He looked down at the screen before retrieving it from the desk and placing it to his ear. "I'll be right out." Then he looked at me. "I'll be right back."

"Okay."

My eyes closed briefly. All I wanted to do was, forget about everything wrong in my life at that moment. The sound of a loud motor grabbed my attention. Moving closely towards the window, I could see Domestic getting inside of a shiny, black Mustang with midnight tinted windows. For the next few minutes, I stood there hoping to see who was inside the vehicle. When I saw Domestic emerge from the sports car, it pulled off quickly. So much for knowing who was behind the wheel.

Tracy walked into the office, smiling. "Hey, boss lady, where have you been?" She sat down in the chair, popping her gum loudly. "Don't tell me you done quit on us."

"No. I'm just taking some time away. I'll be back once I feel better."

Tracy leaned forward with her elbows planted on her thighs. A wide grin spread across her lips. "Mm. Mm. Mm. You done let that man get you pregnant."

"I don't know what you're talking about."

"Girl, I have three kids of my own. I can see right through that glowing, sad face of yours. And you look different from when you started to come around. You even put on a few pounds."

"It's that obvious, huh?"

"Girl, Ray Charles can see that. So, are you happy about becoming a mommy?"

That question came with a Catch-22 answer. In all honesty, I wasn't happy. But that wasn't something I cared to share with his worker. Tracy had been there a while, and there was no doubt in my mind that she wouldn't repeat what I said to Domestic.

Saved by the bell, my child's father walked into the office with slanted eyes and a hint of aggravation. "Ghetto hoochie, why you in here? This is not what I pay you for. Get out my office. You have work to do."

Tracy's smile instantly turned into a frown. It was almost like she wanted to cry. Domestic could be very harsh with his words, so I had to intervene.

"Baby." My voice was soft, yet loud. "You don't have to talk to her that way. She was only checking on me. That's all. Be a little nicer."

Domestic scratched his head and blinked several times, as if he was confused. The room was dead silent for several seconds until he sighed long and hard. "I'm sorry. Tracy, can you get back to work! You have customers out front waiting on you."

Tracy rose to her feet slowly. "No problem, boss."

Shaking my head, I sat up on the sofa and planted my feet on the floor. "Tracy, I'll be right out."

"Okay," she replied softly and exited the office as quickly as she came.

Domestic and I made eye contact once we were alone. He needed to know that his reaction wasn't necessary. "Domestic, that was very mean. Why did you talk to her like that? You shouldn't talk down to your employees."

Domestic slammed the door. *Boom!*

When he turned back to face me, there was fire in his eyes. A look that I was all too familiar with. In three swift steps, Domestic snatched me up by the collar. It truly caught me off guard.

"Domestic," I panted. "What are you doing?"

"Don't you ever fix your lips to check me in front of my workers. What the fuck wrong with you? This is my business and I'll talk to these muthafuckas how I damn well please."

I nodded through sniffles that I understood.

"You better be lucky that we're at my place of business. 'Cause otherwise, I'll show you better than I could tell you."

"Please let me go," I begged.

Domestic released me, but not before pushing me backwards. My back slammed against the arm of the chair. Then he walked away casually as if he did nothing wrong.

For the next two hours I sat in silence until he packed up his duffle bag. "Let's go. I'm going to follow you."

"Where are we going?"

"To pay a visit to your in-laws."

"Domestic, that's not a good idea. Let me handle this on my own."

He growled: "I got this, let's go. They not about to keep trying you like this. I'm not having that shit!"

He was so adamant about confronting people he didn't know. The last thing I wanted to do was, start more unnecessary drama. My life was already collapsing beneath my feet. I just wanted this nightmare to be over with.

Domestic stopped at the desk and placed his keys on the counter. "Drive my car home. I'll pick it up later."

"Okay," Tracy replied, while grabbing the keys and eyeing me.

"I'll call you later." My smile was as phony as a three dollar bill. Not because of Tracy, but due to Domestic's actions.

Emilia...

The sun beamed hard on the back of my neck. I could feel the sweat trickle down my spine. My feet moved quickly across the pavement with Marshall on my heels. I was excited to serve the warrant and make an arrest. It had been a long time coming, and the evidence didn't lie. We jumped into my unmarked squad car. I pulled out the parking lot and did a mad dash to the perpetrator's house, doing sixty miles per hour all the way there.

"When we get here, follow my lead," I informed him.

"It's just an arrest warrant. I'm sure he won't put up a fight, Emilia. You acting like we're running down on the cartel or some shit. He's an athlete for God's sake." He chuckled.

"Ha! Ha! You heard what I said. Follow my lead. This guy can get a little rowdy. Just have my back and keep quiet."

"Whatever you say, boss."

"Sarcasm isn't cute on you, Marshall."

"Babies are cute. I'm a grown ass man." Marshall stroked his beard and looked in the mirror attached to the sun visor. "Admit it. I'm one handsome motherfucker."

"If you say so."

"What's wrong? Am I not dark enough for you?" he smirked.

"Not at all. I like my men how I like my coffee, dark and strong."

"Don't knock it until you try it."

"Yeah, whatever." I brushed him off and focused on the road.

Upon our arrival to the residence, I immediately noticed the unfamiliar car in the driveway. Out of my patrol car, I peeped inside the car. That was when I saw the rental car sticker in the window.

"Hmm. Who you got up in here fucking with your nasty ass?" I mumbled, moving closer to the door.

"And that's your business how?" Marshall was standing right behind me.

"I thought I asked you to be quiet when we got here."

Marshall stood beside me, while I knocked on the double French doors. After standing there for damn near a minute, the doors swung open. Antwan cut his eyes at me before glancing at my partner. My eyes were stuck on the bulging print in his Polo boxer briefs. A bitch almost drooled.

"How can I help you?" he asked.

"Mr. Williams, I have an arrest warrant for you." The piece of paper I was holding was now in his face.

"For what?" he frowned.

"You're being arrested for statutory rape against the little girl you let into this party. Samantha, I'm sure you remember her."

Antwan's eyes were the size of two baseballs. "Man, you got that all wrong. I didn't rape that girl."

"Yeah, yeah. Tell that to the judge. In the meantime, I need you to go and put some clothes on." Antwan folded his arms like I was joking. Not once did he look at the paper. "I mean, unless you want to go down to the station with nothing on."

Marshall jumped in. "Sir, we need you to go and get dressed so we can leave today, not tomorrow."

"This some bullshit!" he shouted and walked away.

Marshall and I walked inside. Just like I thought, he was in there entertaining not one, but two women. They were waiting on him by the staircase.

"What's going on, daddy?" a female with pink hair asked.

"I'm being arrested on some bullshit!" Antwan blurted out in anger.

Both women looked familiar, so I moved closer to get a better look. All I could do was laugh. "Hmm. Pink and Cherry. Just the hoodrats I wanted to see."

"Excuse you!" Pink rolled her eyes. Cherry sucked her teeth and put her hand on her hip. They both were dressed in next to nothing.

"You heard me. What's wrong? Did I interrupt a threesome?"

"I guess you know!" Cherry snapped.

"You sound jealous." Pink laughed.

"Not at all. But you two chicken heads are about to come down to the station with him."

"For what?" Cherry rolled her neck.

"Extortion."

"Extortion? What the hell you talking about?" Cherry questioned.

"Extortion. You know blackmail. That thing you tried to do with Aaron for that sex tape. Remember that?"

"Nope." Pink had an attitude, and she wasn't afraid to show it.

"Don't worry, I'll let you hear the recording once we get down to the station. Now let's go."

"This is bullshit!" Cherry squealed and stomped her feet.

"Yeah, I know." Marshall was still standing in the middle of the living room floor. "Come put the cuffs on this one, while I call for backup." I pointed directly at little *Miss Attitude*, better known as Pink. Marshall walked over and gave our detainee a new set of bracelets.

Antwan finally joined us back downstairs and stood in front of me. "You know this is wrong. I didn't do this. It was Aaron, and you know it."

"I don't know shit. I wasn't in attendance, remember?"

"We already been through this, Emilia. What's the problem?"

"The problem is, the victim gave her statement and verified that you two were indeed having sex. Aaron never touched that girl, and how dare you try to tarnish his legacy."

Antwan chuckled. "Now you care about his legacy. That's funny, yet convenient, don't you think?"

"Not at all. I'm just here to get justice for the victim. Now turn around and put your hands behind your back." Without another word, Antwan did exactly what he was told. "Antwan Williams, you have the right to remain silent. Anything you say can and will be used against you in the court of law. If you cannot afford an attorney, one will be appointed to you."

"You know I can afford one. My attorney is on standby and I have nothing to say when we get to the station. Just make sure I'm booked, so I can bond out and get back to my threesome you interrupted."

"Arrogant, aren't we?" Leaning closer, I whispered in his ear. "You do know that I can bury you, so save your sarcasm for someone else and not me."

"I said what I said. Now take me to the station," he demanded.

Cherry was cuffed when backup arrived. All three were escorted outside and placed in separate patrol cars. Back at the station they were placed in different interrogation rooms. The first stop for me was none other than Antwan Williams. He made it very clear that he wouldn't be confessing, but I had a trick or two up my sleeve that said otherwise.

"Mr. Williams," I smiled, as I entered the cold room. "Are you ready to talk to me now?"

"I see you don't comprehend English very well. As I stated at my residence, I will not be speaking to you or any other clown that walks through that door fishing for incriminating evidence."

"My, my! Somebody has been reading a few law books." Pulling out a chair, I sat down and looked him dead in those guilty ass eyes. "So, you're refusing to talk to me? I can help you, but you have to give me something to go on. An incentive will be nice."

"I'm not answering shit unless my attorney is present. Now can I get my phone call?"

"Not yet. It's a line for that."

"Emilia," he leaned forward with slanted eyes. "Stop playing games with me and let me make a phone call. If not, I'll be sure to tell your superior that you are trying to extort money from me."

"You wouldn't dare."

"I would. Now try me!" He spoke through gritted teeth.

Before I could chomp him off at the knees, the door swung open. It was the captain. "Detective Flores, may I have a word with you now, please?"

"Sure thing." The captain walked me into a spare room and closed the door. His face was beet-red. "Something wrong, Captain?"

"That's an understatement."

"What's going on?"

"There was a complaint made against you by Alexis Young. The sister of the late Aaron Young."

"I'm not surprised. She doesn't like the fact that I arrested her brother and now she's out to get me."

The captain nodded. "Unfortunately, that's not the case. Do you know that she has a video of you trying to extort one hundred thousand dollars from Calvin, Aaron's teammate?"

Every word he spoke slammed against my head like a bowling ball. That bitch! I was speechless.

"Yeah, she recorded you when you were at Calvin's house."

"Captain, I can explain."

He held his hand up. "There's no need to. You were given strict instructions on going by the book. What you did was unethical and I cannot tolerate any more infractions from you. I allowed you back into the field, and all you did was abuse your authority."

My heart was racing. I couldn't believe what I was hearing. Being a detective was my life. There was no me without it. "What? What are you saying?"

"I need you to give me your badge and gun."

"You're firing me?"

"Yes. I mean unless you want to be brought up on extortion charges."

"That's not fair. What happened to an investigation?" My knees felt weak.

"Is that what you really want? An investigation. Ms. Young agreed to not press charges, as long as you were not on the force."

I was still speechless. That evil little bitch got me fired.

"Their father knows some very powerful people and the last thing we need around here is public scrutiny. I caught hell fixing your last mess."

"Fine. I'll go pack my things." I removed my gun and badge. Softly, I sat them down on the table and approached the door.

"I'll pack them for you. I don't want a scene."

My life was over. Everything I had worked so hard for was up in smoke, thanks to that spoiled rotten bitch. Quickly, I exited the building unnoticed and got into my car. That was the moment the dam broke, and heavy tears fell from my eyes. In frustration, I punched the steering wheel repeatedly.

Chapter 12

Foreign

Domestic took my keys from my hand and opened the passenger door for me. Chivalry wasn't dead after all. Putting on my seatbelt, I rested my head against the headrest and closed my eyes. Something told me this was about to be a long ride. Domestic got into the driver seat and started the car. When I didn't feel it move, I opened my eyes. He was staring directly at me.

"What?"

"Why do you feel the need to disrespect me? You know how I get, but it's like you enjoy making me mad."

"That is not what I'm trying to do."

"Then what exactly are you trying to do?"

"The only thing I'm guilty of is, defending your worker. I know she can't say too much to you because she works for you, but I can."

Domestic turned his body towards me. "Is that what you think? You can say anything to me and get away with it."

"That's not what I'm saying."

"Then say what you mean because that's my understanding of things."

"Did you see the look on her face when you spoke to her in such a rude manner? That girl was embarrassed."

"Let's get one thing straight. Tracy works for me. She has worked for me for years, so she knows how I am. Therefore, she'll get over it. That's the problem with you women now. We give you an inch and you want the whole damn football field. I pay Tracy to do a job and that's to work the front desk, not keep my woman company in my office."

Clearly, our conversation was going nowhere. There was no need to debate the situation because he had his mind made up that he was correct. Talking to him at times was like talking to a rebellious toddler. No comprehension whatsoever. "Fine, Domestic. Continue to do and say things your way. But let me say this—a woman will only put up with so much before she's had enough."

Domestic grinned. Then chuckled. "I guess that's a reference to you too, huh?"

I wasn't about to dignify his question with a response, so I just looked away.

"I tell you what. If you think you leaving me, you have another thing coming, so you can get that out your head right now. Me and you stuck until one of us take our last breath, baby." Domestic leaned in close to me and kissed me on the cheek. Then he placed his palm on my belly. "We're a family now and don't you forget it."

"How can I possibly forget it, Demerius? You only remind me every day."

Domestic's nostrils flared when he stared me down. "Watch your tongue before you lose it."

Silence.

"Now we're about to go handle this little situation with punk ass Aaron's parents. When we get there, don't be doing all that crying either. Your old life has perished, and you have a new one with me."

"Domestic, none of this is necessary. I can handle this on my own."

"So what you saying is that you don't want me to go over there? What? You embarrassed by me or something?"

"No. I'm not, but how does that look for me to bring my boyfriend to my in-laws' house? That will only make things worse. She already thinks I left Aaron for you in the first place."

"You did?" he replied snappily.

"I wanted to leave Aaron because he wasn't treating me right. All the cheating and scandals wore me out mentally and physically. That's why I wanted the divorce. When Aaron snuck to my parent's house, my father convinced me to stay and work on my marriage."

"That was the night I kept getting your voicemail, huh?"

"Yes," I nodded.

"You fucked that nigga that night too, didn't you?" His forehead held multiple wrinkles.

"We already had that discussion."

"A simple yes or no would suffice."

"What difference would it make, Domestic? Aaron is dead and gone. There's nothing else you need to worry about."

"If you say so." Domestic finally pulled out the parking lot. His nonchalant attitude told me that conversation was far from over, and the question would resurface. "Where am I going?"

"Davis Islands."

Dealing with my pain-in-the-ass mother-in-law was not something I wanted to handle with Domestic at my side. That would only make matters worse. The evil bitch was two minutes from me getting on her ass. All I needed was five minutes alone with her, and I would beat her ass the same way I did with Aaron's whores. However, there was someone that I needed to talk to.

It hurt to know that she would kick me when I was already down. My husband's death had truly taken a toll on my mental state. Aaron was everything to me, until he wasn't.

The psychopath that I was with didn't make it any better. I was still in pain and hadn't grieved properly, thanks to the angry man on my left. He was far too jealous for me. In reality, he had me second guessing on being in a relationship with him. I may have been inexperienced with dating different men, but I was smart enough to know this shit wasn't healthy by a long shot.

Domestic drove us to the community without any directions from me. That was when I instructed him on where to go. Now that we were sitting in the driveway, my stomach grew knots in them. It was the moment I dreaded, but it had to be done.

Grabbing my purse from the floor, I placed my hand on the door handle. "Wait." Domestic grabbed my left hand. "I know you're upset with me about earlier and I apologize. I'm going through some shit. It's a lot on my mind and I overreacted. It won't happen again." He planted a kiss on my hand.

"Yeah." That was a boldface lie. If I knew better, it would definitely happen again.

"All you have to say is *yeah*?"

And that was the moment I snatched my hand away. "What else do you want me to say, Domestic?"

"I mean shit, Foreign. The least you can do is accept my apology. I'm going through some heavy shit and a little support from my woman would help."

"I'm going through some heavy shit too. But you don't see me taking my frustration and anger out on you." The conversation was getting hot like fire, but I wasn't about to continue to fan the flame. He can have that.

Frustration laced his tone when he said my name. "Foreign, baby, listen to me. Now is not the time to pick a fight with me. You and I both know how bad this can get. I'm aggravated. I miss my fuckin' son and you not making it any better."

"Don't worry because I have nothing else to say."

"Just stop being combative all the time. Be the woman that I know you can be. Be the sweet and passive woman that I fell in love with. Not some rambunctious teenager."

That was all I needed to hear. It was time to exit the vehicle before a fight started. Being passive didn't get me anywhere in my marriage, and I was certain it wouldn't get me anything, but ran the fuck over. I was tired of being seen as a doormat in the eyes of the man that claimed to love me beyond the end of the earth.

Clutching my purse, I exited the vehicle quickly. Domestic followed. Before I could knock, the door swung open. My father stood there with a bright smile when he saw me. "Hey, my baby. I'm so happy you decided to come by."

"Hey, daddy."

The spark in his eye quickly faded when he realized I had a guest. "And who do you have with you?"

"Umm. Daddy, this is Demerius." Looking over my shoulder, I acknowledged my crazy ass dude. "Demerius, this is my father—Mr. Hamilton."

"Nice to meet you, sir." Domestic was all polite and shit, but my father was not having it. He didn't even reply.

"Who is he to you?" My father spoke as if Domestic wasn't standing behind me.

"That's what I'm here to talk to you about." He had me feeling like I was a teenager all over again. A girl who needed approval and permission to date.

"Come inside."

Domestic followed me into the living room area and sat down beside me. To my surprise, my mother was nowhere in the room. My father sat in his reclining chair across from us. The tension in the room was at an all-time high, and my secret wasn't out in the open yet.

My father sat back and crossed his legs. Old men loved to sit that way right before a lecture. "Foreign Young, do you care to tell me what's going on or do I have pull it out of you?"

"Where is mom?"

"Upstairs. She'll be down in a minute."

"Well, I would rather wait on her so I don't have to repeat myself."

"Fine."

For three long minutes, we sat in eerie silence, waiting on my mom to join us. When she made her grand appearance, I stood up and greeted her with a tight hug. "Hey, mommy."

"How's my baby doing?" she smiled.

"I'm okay." My mother released me and stepped in front of Domestic. "Aren't you handsome?"

"Thank you," he smiled.

"Mom, this is Demerius. Demerius this is my mother—Vivian Hamilton."

"It's nice to meet you, Mrs. Hamilton."

"The pleasure is all mine." My mom sat on the sofa positioned to the right of us.

"Okay," I sighed, while rubbing my hands nervously across my thighs. "The reason I'm here is to share some news with the both of you." A lump in my throat formed from the nervousness I felt. As a grown woman, I was sitting there afraid of what their reaction would be. Even though I knew they loved me unconditionally.

"I'm pregnant."

"That's wonderful news," my mom said sweetly.

"Is it Aaron's baby?" my father asked.

"Sadly, no. It's not." Looking my dad in the eyes, I admitted to the truth like I was in a confessional. "That's why Demerius is here. It's his baby."

There was a hint of disappointment in my father's eyes. I could tell by the way he shook his head. "So the rumors were true? You were cheating on Aaron all this time."

His response caught me off guard. "All this time?" I repeated. "What exactly do you mean by that? Because the last time I checked, I was the one being cheated on."

"Foreign, I understand that, but we didn't raise you to be this way. We taught you the value of marriage. The sacrifices that you had to make."

Tears pricked my eyes. "Are you defending his actions?"

"No, sweetheart. I'm not. All I'm saying is, he was a young, rich athlete. He wasn't perfect, but he loved you. The night we had a counseling session here, he apologized for his wrongdoings and you agreed to forgive him and start fresh. What happened?"

"Dad, I don't want to talk about that."

"Just answer the question. Did you or did you not agree to make your marriage work?"

There was no getting around the question. "Yes."

"Okay. So, how did this happen?"

"I was already pregnant at that time."

"Foreign." He shook his head slowly. Then his eyes rolled over in Domestic's direction. "Demerius, right?"

"Yes, sir," Domestic replied.

"I'm going to be frank with you. This little situation you have going on with my daughter has me truly bothered. For one, she was a married woman when you two met. Did it not bother you that she had a husband at home?"

"Don't be so harsh, honey. We don't know the full story." One thing about my mom, she needed to hear all the facts before placing judgment in the situation.

Domestic eased up in his seat, and I knew the conversation was about to take a left turn. "With all due respect, sir, no. Aaron was not treating your daughter with the love and respect that she deserved. She's a queen and should be treated as such."

"And how would you know that?" My dad waited for confirmation.

"The whole world knows that, but unlike them she's confided in me. I provided a shoulder for her to cry on."

"Apparently, you provided a bed for her to lay in too."

"Daddy! Stop please," I screeched. "I'm an adult and that means I can do what I want to do. You may not like it, but it's my decision. Aaron cheated throughout our entire marriage and I never cheated back until now. It wasn't my intention. It just happened."

Suddenly, his eyes softened and his eyes grew lighter. "I'm sorry, baby. It's my job to protect you. After all you're still my baby girl."

"Dad." My emotions started to kick in. "All I need is your support right now. I've lost so much and I don't know how much more I could take."

"Demerius, right?"

"Yes, sir."

"I have some questions for you."

"Okay."

"Are you prepared to be there for my daughter and this child she is carrying?"

"Yes, sir, I am."

"Are you sure because raising a child is a big responsibility? I don't want my daughter to be a single mother. Kids these days need a two-parent home."

Domestic reached for my hand. Our fingers intertwined. "Mr. Hamilton, trust me when I say that I love your daughter very much. I'm not going to do anything to hurt her."

"That's what my son-in-law promised me. We see how that turned out." My father tilted his head in our direction. "With all due respect, I don't know you or your intentions with my daughter. For all I know, you can be using her because she's vulnerable. I mean she did just lose her husband."

"Sir, let me help you understand something. When I met your daughter, I did not know who she was married to. All I knew was that she was unhappy. I don't want or need anything from Foreign. I am a successful business owner of three upscale car washes. I own two houses in the suburban part of town and two luxury cars that cost me a half a million dollars. So, as you can see, I have my own money."

"That's good to know."

It was time for me to step in and take over the conversation. "I need to tell the two of you something."

"What is it, sweetheart?" my mother asked sweetly.

"Today I was served papers that Aaron's mother is petitioning my stay at the house. Can you believe she's taking me to court for what's rightfully mine?"

"She did what?" my father shouted.

Removing the papers from my purse, I passed them over. "I can't believe she would pull some shit like this after everything I went through with her son."

My mother jumped to her feet. Storming towards my father, she snatched the papers from his hand. "Let me see this." Her chest heaved up and down as she read the contents of the letter. When she was done, she handed them back. "I ought to go over there and whoop her old ass."

Deep down inside I wanted to laugh, but the pain was too great. Later on down the line, it could be funny. All I could do was cry. Domestic was gentle when he wiped away my tears.

"Don't cry, sweetheart. I'm going to get in contact with our attorney and he'll take care of this little problem." My father planted a kiss on my cheek. "Be careful with my daughter—I have eyes and ears everywhere," he warned.

Domestic and I walked out into the dark night and went home. We barely spoke, and sex was not an option. I lay down and closed my eyes. The baby and I needed all the rest we could get. Especially after the fucked up day we had.

The Price You Pay For Love 2

Chapter 13

Unknown

It was after midnight, and the streets were eerily quiet. The only sounds that could be heard were the loud pipes on my Mustang. Bending the corner, I raised my foot off the gas and let it cruise up the block. There was an abandoned house five hundred feet from where my target laid his head. That's where I parked.

In my profession, patience was a virtue. My marks were studied carefully. I knew who their visitors were, their movements, if they had kids and girlfriends. Women and children were off limits, but a nigga could get it at any given moment. If the price was right, I'll run down on them like a quarterback.

Patiently, I watched the house from a short distance. In between my fingers rested a Newport cigarette. I pulled on it slowly and blew the smoke out my mouth. Weed was my go-to drug, but not when I was on a mission. I had to be focused.

On my lap sat a sub-machine Uzi. Before I left, it was going to be bloodbath. My client paid me a pretty penny to take this nigga out, and I was gon' do just that. There was about to be slow singing and flower bringing for the victim's family.

Cracking the window just a little bit, I flicked the cigarette butt out the window, and continued to lay on my prey. Minutes had turned into an hour before two dudes walked outside and sat on the porch.

"Showtime!"

Grabbing the Uzi, I rolled the window all the way down and hit the gas lightly. The engine growled, as I crept towards the house. Neither man knew what was unfolding until they heard a vicious bark pierce the silent night. Victim number one caught a few rounds to the chest and hit the ground. The second one ducked and fired a few shots in my direction. One of the bullets slammed against the frame of my car. That was my cue to get out of dodge. Slamming my foot down on the gas, the Mustang's tires screeched and raced off the block.

Casey...

Memphis, TN

Leaving Domestic was the best decision that I made in a very long time. Ever since we relocated, my life had been like a walk through the clouds. Shawn helped me find a job as a receptionist at a chiropractor's office. It had been years since I had a job, and it felt good to be back in the field. We lived in a nice three-bedroom home in a good neighborhood. Most importantly, DP seemed to adjust well under the circumstances. The only time I grew aggravated was when Domestic would call and question my son. He knew how to get underneath my skin.

Shawn was a different breed. One could easily tell that he came from a good, upstanding family. The way he cared for me and my son made my heart smile. His gentleness made me realize what I'd been missing out on during the time I was confined to Domestic. So far, every day I spent with him was a great day.

My body rocked with pleasure as Shawn held my legs up on his shoulders and slid back and forth inside my warm nookie. With every stroke, my girl released a gushy sound. Sexy moans escaped my lips every time he hit that spot in the bottom of my stomach. Placing a hand on top of my incision on the bikini line, I panted in between heavy breaths.

"Shit. Shit. Damn, Shawn." My left hand was now on the back of his neck, pulling him in for a kiss. Heavily engaged, I sucked on his tongue and rocked my hips.

The lovemaking was magical. Our feelings were mutual. Sex didn't feel like a chore. That was the way it felt with Domestic. His touch was tender. Sometimes it was rough, but I never wanted it to end.

Sweat from Shawn's face dripped onto my face. "Bae, you better cum 'cause I'm about to."

"No. Not yet," I moaned.

"You better put them fingers to work. I'm tired," he grunted, as if he was about to bust.

"Oh, my God, really!" He didn't have to tell me twice. My fingers found my clitoris and went to work.

An unexpected ring from Shawn's cellphone caused him to stop in the middle of our session. "What you doing? I was almost there."

"It's my brother and he never calls me this late." Shawn dropped my legs and picked up his phone. "What's going on, bro?"

"Bro! Bro! It's bad, man. It's bad," Tim babbled, while yelling into the phone.

"Bro, slow down."

"They shot him."

"Shot who?" Shawn asked, trying to remain calm.

"Craig. They shot Craig." Tim could be heard sobbing. "Craig, wake up. Help is on the way. Don't leave me, bro. Come on, bro, you gotta pull through."

Shawn panicked. "Is he breathing?" Then we heard the sirens in the background.

"Save my brother!" Tim shouted. "Nooo! Nooo!" Then the phone went silent. The call had ended abruptly.

Shawn called back.

"Hello."

"Who is this?"

"This is Officer Bryant."

"Is my brother okay?"

"I'm sorry, but he didn't make it."

Shawn's phone slipped from his hand and hit the floor with a loud thump. "He's dead. My fuckin' brother is dead."

"Baby, I'm so sorry." Pulling him close to me, I cradled his head against my chest.

"They killed my brother," he sobbed.

It broke my heart to see Shawn in such a fragile state. I knew this wasn't going to end well. The bond they shared was real. They were extremely close. Whoever committed the murder was in for a rude awakening. Everyone on the streets of the Tampa Bay area was in danger because Tim's crew was going to scorch the earth.

Emilia...

All night I tossed and turned. Reality had finally settled in. My life of being a detective was finally snatched away. The blood, sweat and tears that I put into my career didn't matter. He just dismissed me as if I wasn't great at my job. *What happened to a suspension?* Apparently, I wasn't good enough for that.

Suddenly, my start of the day was different. Dressed in my robe, I walked into the kitchen and fixed myself a cup of dark coffee. Opening up my laptop, I logged into my bank account. *Depressed* was the perfect word to describe the way I was feeling. My savings looked like shit, and my checking account looked even worse. These bills weren't going to stop, and I needed enough money to be comfortable for a while.

"If only I had gotten that money from Aaron or Calvin, none of this shit would be happening. Fuck!" I screamed, slamming my fist against the table.

The hot cup of coffee fell over and splashed directly onto my laptop. "Shit. Shit. No." Scuffling, I grabbed a dish towel and wiped off the keyboard.

For good measure, I held it upside down and shook it. "Please don't mess up. Please."

By the grace of God, my laptop was still working. It was such a relief. I had no money to waste at that point. After I fixed a second cup of coffee, I sat back to the table and checked my emails.

Boom! Boom!

The loud pounding on the door startled me. "Who the hell is that?"

Easing up from the table, I made my way to the front door. Tip toeing to see through the peephole, I spotted a familiar face. It was the last person I expected to see on my doorstep.

"Marshall, what are you doing here?"

"I need to talk to you. Can I come in?"

"Sure." I moved to the side so he could enter. "Come on in." We sat down on the sofa. "So, what do you want to talk about?"

Marshall passed me a folder and a plastic bag.

"What's this?" The contents in the folder had my full attention. Now, my eyes were on him.

"I know how important it is for you to figure out what happened to Aaron. The tow company found a tracking device on his car, so I picked it up. Take a picture of it, so I can put it into evidence. I'm sorry that you got fired. Hopefully, you can solve this case and the captain will give you back your job."

"A tracker." That just took the entire investigation into a new direction.

The wheels in my head started to spin. I had to get to the bottom of it and I needed to do it now. "Thanks, Marshall, I appreciate you stopping by. I'm about to get to work. He was a good friend of mine, and I just want to know what happened to him."

"If you need anything, let me know. I'm just a phone call away." Marshall walked out the door as quickly as he came.

For the next three hours, I spent my time investigating Aaron's car accident. When I was done, I revisited the crime scene. Slowly, I scoured the ground to see if there was any type of evidence left behind. It was a reach, but it was worth a try. The skid marks in the grass were still present. Vividly, in a flashback, I could see Aaron's car wrapped around that tree. Leaning against it, I placed my arms around it and cried.

"Aaron, I'm so sorry. I wish we could've made things right before you passed away. All I wanted was to be with you, but you wouldn't get rid of that bitch of a wife. You were so in love with her, but not enough to stop cheating. I've been plotting on your wife for months. Just when I had her out the way, this happened to you. Don't you worry. I'm going to get justice for you."

My face was drenched with tears.

A high pitched scream from my diaphragm came out of my mouth. "AARON!" My heart shattered all over again. He was the love of my life. I had to make it right. Jumping into my car, I made my way to suspect number one.

During the drive, so many thoughts crossed my mind. If I could manage to blackmail this one person in particular, I could take the money and flee. A fresh start would do me great justice. The west coast was always a place I wanted to live, and there was no time better than the present.

Pulling up into the parking lot, I stepped out the car dressed in a royal blue bodycon dress. My ass and curves were poking out from every angle. The whistles, stares and cat calls boosted my confidence level higher than ever before. Lately, the scumbag men I came across made me feel as if I wasn't a true prize. Arrogantly, I waved like I was in a pageant, as I approached his place of business. His real prize was about to enter.

Just as I opened the door, I came face to face with Domestic. He looked me up and down with pure seduction. Thirst was written all over his face. Rolling my tongue across my lips, I grinned. "Can we talk?"

"Sure." Domestic backed up so I could enter.

His little helper—Tracy—watched me closely. "Take a picture, it'll last longer."

"You wish." Tracy rolled her eyes.

Inside his office, I sat on top of his desk with my legs slightly open. I needed his full attention. Domestic closed the door and locked it. "Emilia, what do I owe the pleasure of this visit?"

"I'm doing just fine, Domestic. How about you?"

"I'm fine," he smirked. "But you can see that already."

"Don't flatter yourself."

"What do you want?" he huffed with slight irritation.

Leaning back on the desk, I crossed my legs. Well, since we are being so formal, let me get to the point."

106

"Please do."

"Somebody is in a rush."

"Unlike you, I have work to do."

There was no way he could've known I was fired, so I let it slide off my smooth back as sarcasm. "I need help getting out of dodge. It's time for me to leave this place."

"Why do you need to leave all of sudden? You must've did something that went against the ethics in your employee handbook." Domestic chuckled like I was telling a damn joke.

"Domestic, please. Don't start with me right now. There is too much going on, and I need a fresh start."

Domestic stroked his chin and nodded. "I get that, but what I don't understand is why are you coming to me? Me and you not smashing."

"If I'm not mistaken, you had a sample of *this* against my wishes not too long ago." Now I had his attention. "Anyway, I need you to help me out financially with some start-up cash. After all, you still owe me for saving your life."

Domestic now had a frown on his face. His arms were now folded across his buffed chest. "How many times do you think you can keep cashing in the same get-out-of-jail free card? Or should I say, voucher? It's not like I didn't pay you or help the little muthafucka that stole from me."

In an effort to sway him, I cracked my legs open a little bit. "I'm hoping, as much as I need it. I mean we do have an extended history Domestic. I've been keeping you abreast about everything going on in the department when it came down to your side business."

Domestic ran his hand down his handsome face and sighed. "How much do you need?"

"A hundred thousand."

"That's a lot of money. What the hell have you been doing with the extra cash I used to shoot you for your extra services? You spent all that shit?"

"I'm sorry, but I don't make six figures at the precinct or make money the way you do. So excuse me for not being loaded out the ass."

"Why do you think you deserve that type of money from me?" he asked rudely.

"I've never asked you for much and right now I'm in need," I purred, while rubbing my hands up and down my thighs. "Can you please help me?"

Domestic shook his head from side to side. "The last time I helped you out, I lost forty thousand dollars. When I told you about it, you wouldn't even help me get it back."

"I'm sorry, Domestic. I really am. He was having a hard time adjusting in the free world and started back using."

"Is that supposed to make me feel better? Because it doesn't. I give zero fucks about the habits that nigga had."

"You're not hurting from losing that money. You make millions, and I know that for a fact."

"You don't get it. It's about the principle. I took care of that nigga during his bid, placed money in his hand when he made it home and against my wishes gave him a job. That was to keep him out of trouble, and he stole from me. It's like he spit in my face, but in the end I spit on his grave."

"Wow! I knew you killed him all along." Domestic walked up to me and aggressively pulled the front of my dress down. "What are you doing?"

"You know I have a hard time trusting you when you talk crazy."

"You think I'm wearing a wire?"

"Smart girl," he grinned.

"I'm not here for that. You think I would wear a wire and ask you for money to get away?"

"All things are possible."

"I understand that you live by a code and I'm sorry that he stole from you, but I didn't know that he would do that."

"Emilia, you've been in law enforcement for how long? How much do you really know a thief? You don't." Domestic huffed and walked past me.

My sexual antics were not working, so I hopped down from the desk. "So what are you saying to me?"

"Are you not comprehending?" Domestic leaned forward with his elbows on his desk and hands underneath his chin. "Everything I said is cut-and-dry and straight to the point. But just in case it's not registering in your brain, I'll say it to you in layman's terms. I'm not giving you a hundred stacks. You must be crazy."

The faint smile on my face turned into a cold, furious stare. He had the audacity to tell me no. Where they do that at? Considering all the shit I did for him, the nigga should've been more than willing to run through a fire and save me. "That's your final answer?"

"What other language do you need me to say it in?"

Pissed at the way he was trying me, it was time to take the gloves off. Domestic really thought he was above the law, and I needed to bring him back to reality. "I bet if Foreign needed the money, you would've gave it to her."

Domestic smiled. "Without a drop of hesitation."

My blood was boiling like hot grits. "Is that right?"

"That's a fact."

"What has she done for you that I haven't?"

"Not that I owe you an explanation, but she's my fiancée and soon to be the mother of my child in the next few months. She can have everything I own."

"She's pregnant?"

"Yes."

Domestic took great pleasure in making me feel like shit on the bottom of his expensive shoes. All of that was about to change. "I guess congratulations are in order."

"True, but I know it's not genuine coming from you," he smirked, while typing on his phone.

"You know I thought I could come by here and ask for a favor from someone I considered a friend, but I was wrong." Both of my hands were now on his desk, as I leaned towards him. He needed to hear me loud and clear. "So, let me put it to you this way. In the next forty-eight hours you will give me one hundred thousand dollars in cash."

"Or what?" Domestic sat his phone and looked at me with an evil stare.

"All of your dirty little secrets will start to spill out so fast, that it will make your head spin."

"Is that a threat?"

"It's a promise and that's what I know. If Foreign finds out that we were plotting on her since day one, she will have everything you own."

"That's where you're wrong," he stated with arrogance. "Foreign will never leave me."

Domestic was so cocky that it made me sick. He needed to know that I could destroy him without me being on the force. "Oh, she will definitely leave you once I tell her everything. The same way she was ready to leave Aaron."

"Tell her. I don't give a fuck. Foreign stuck with me for life now. And your broke ass will still be here working for minimum wage." He laughed.

"You're so confident for someone who will be in prison for life." His nostrils began to flare when he heard the word *prison*. "See, I know that you killed Aaron. You did that to get him out the way. So you could have his wife all to yourself."

"I didn't do shit."

"You might not have done it yourself, but you are definitely involved." My brow shifted with curiosity. "Who did you pay to do your dirty work?"

Domestic's laugh was sinister. "Emilia, you know me better than that. If I had something to do with that, you really think I would tell on myself. You must be sipping on stupid juice."

"The plan was for you to get her out of my way, so I could be with Aaron. You were not supposed to kill him. How could you fall in love with her so fast? We dealt with each other longer than that and you didn't feel that way about me."

"And I never will. Now get the fuck out of my office," he spat nastily.

"Forty eight hours and all is forgotten. I'll collect my money and Foreign will never know anything about our business arrangement." I turned on my heels and left his office. If I didn't know anything else, Domestic was going to give me that money for the sake of staying free.

Chapter 14

Domestic

That hoe had a lot of nerves coming into my place of business and threatening me. Emilia forgot who she was fucking with. I didn't take being threatened lightly. Just when I thought everything was smooth-sailing, she waltzed her happy ass in here trying to blow shit up. Grabbing my phone, I sent out a quick text. 'Slide through. She's gone.'

Sitting back in my leather chair, I placed both hands on the back of my head. I thought back to the day Emilia approached me with the business deal that turned into a ghetto love story.

Emilia and I stopped beside my car and locked eyes. Clearly, something was on her mind besides business. "Why you keep looking at me like that? Something on your mind."

"Who's the woman in your life now?"

And there it goes. In the back of my mind I knew that was her main concern. "Nobody right now. I'm focused on business."

"I don't believe you."

Now I was offended. "Since when have you known me to be a liar?" Stroking my chin, I chuckled. "Oh, I get it."

"Get what?"

"I haven't pushed up on you, so you assume it's because I have a woman."

"See, you know exactly what I'm talking about."

"Emilia, I haven't seen you in almost a year. Then you pop up out the blue and you think the first thing on my mind is sex. I'm more interested in what you got going on. You didn't grace me with your presence just because you wanted some dick."

"You're correct, but I already told you that I have a job for you."

"But yet and still you haven't filled me in on what you want me to do. That's what I'm waiting on."

"Unlock your doors so we can talk inside." Emilia walked to the passenger side and sat down.

Taking my seat on the driver's side, I brought the car to life. Leaning over to where she was seated, I unfastened the buttons on her shirt. Emilia's eyes were struck with seduction. Opening her shirt, I glanced at her full breasts before I sat back in my seat.

"Really?"

"No offense, but you popped up out the blue and it ain't because you missed me."

"You think I'm wearing a wire?"

"I just needed to be sure. Now fill me in on this plan of yours."

For the next twenty minutes I listened to a supposedly foolproof plan. The entire time she talked, I scratched my head and gave her the side eye a few times. It amazed me. The lengths women would go to seek and destroy a man due to a broken heart was unbelievable. The tongue was lethal, but sex was a powerful weapon and deadly if it wasn't used properly.

Emilia took a photo from her pocket and handed it to me. "Do you think you can pull this off?"

Staring at the picture, I nodded. There wasn't a shadow of a doubt that I couldn't do it. My mind just couldn't wrap around the fact that she was actually going through with such a foolish plan. Under any other circumstances I would've said no, but I was curious to see how it would play out. And even more curious about the person I was staring at.

"Yeah, I got you. Just make sure you come through with my money."

"Oh, I most certainly will. Thanks. I'll be in touch."

"No problem."

When Emilia got out the car, I folded the picture and placed it inside of my wallet. Operation Crazy Bitch was in full effect. "And she wonder why I don't fuck with her."

Sitting up, I took my wallet from my back pocket and took out the photo she gave me. Foreign's eyes were so big and innocent. Our meet up was supposed to be about business, but it turned out to be something far more beautiful. Fate was a powerful force. We were meant to be together. The night she stumbled into my car wash after the meet up with Emilia confirmed that. My intention was only to get her hooked and dip out once Emilia snatched her husband. Once I fell in love with her, I couldn't let go.

"Get your head out the clouds!" a male voice shouted.

When I looked up, it was exactly who I was waiting on. I shoved Foreign's picture back into my wallet and put it in my pocket. "Close the door."

Carlos closed the door and sat down. The hoodie he rocked made it hard to see his face. "I handled that business. Both of them niggas was on the porch when I ran down on them. One dead. One alive."

"Good." Opening up the drawer, I removed a stack of hundreds and handed them over. "That nigga brother should be back any day now. Switch up vehicles and ride by there. Keep me posted on when they touch down. Casey gone try to sneak in and out with my son, and I'm not having that shit."

"That's fucked up, bro. I can't believe she snatched lil' man up like that. She knows you'll scorch the world behind your jit."

"Facts. This new nigga she got done pumped her with a bunch of empty promises about keeping her safe. I told her there is no place on earth that she could hide and me not find her. She about to find out how ruthless I can be."

"I don't blame you. I'll show out behind my jit too."

"We have another issue. You have to handle it before it gets out of hand."

"Damn!" Carlos exhaled hard. "Who else fucking up?"

"Emilia."

"We knew that was coming, but I'll handle her."

"Let me know when you do."

"Fa sho." Carlos stood up. "Let me get out of here before someone recognizes me. I'm supposed to be incognito." He chuckled.

"Yeah, do that." We dapped it up, and he disappeared quickly.

Veronica...

Sitting down at the table, I opened my napkin and placed it on my lap. "Dinner looks lovely, dear."

"Not as lovely as you, my love," my husband replied with a huge smile on his face.

"You're up to something. What is it?"

"You got me," Hugo smiled, showing off his pearly white teeth. Then he handed me a medium-sized leather box.

Excitement was only one of the emotions I felt. We had been married for twenty years, and each year was better than the last. When we met, Hugo had just relocated to Florida from New York. Our mutual friend set us up. He embraced me and my children, and we've been together ever since.

Being married to Hugo certainly had its perks. It came with protection, riches and power. The life of a mob wife was more than I ever dreamed of.

"The necklace is beautiful. I love it."

"I knew you would," he smiled. "That's only part of your surprise."

"There's more?" I beamed.

"Of course, there's more. What type of husband would I be if I didn't give you the best?" Hugo passed me a colorful brochure. "Happy birthday, my love."

My eyes widened in surprise when I noticed he planned me a trip to Thailand. "Oh, my God!" I jumped from my seat and planted the biggest, wettest kisses all over his face. "I'm so happy right now."

"That was the plan."

"You've been listening to me."

"With the help of your sister."

"She told you?"

"I told her to fish for information. She did a fabulous job. I will make sure all of you have a great time."

"All of who?" I asked curiously.

"You and all the wives are going. The men are staying here. So think of it as a girls' trip," he chuckled.

To hear that he wasn't going saddened me a little. Nonetheless, I was still happy. "You're not going?"

"No. You deserve time alone. We spend every waking moment together. Allow me to miss you," he cheesed. "Besides, I can't abandon the business for two weeks. That's far too long."

"Two weeks," I repeated.

"Yes. I've paid for spa days and excursions. All you have to do is show up."

Finally closing the brochure, I sat it on the table. "What's going on with the business, babe? And don't say it's nothing because I know you better than I know my menstrual cycle."

Hugo chuckled. "That I know."

"So tell me."

"We've had a few issues for the past few weeks. We retaliated, of course. I'm sure they won't clap back, but I'd rather be safe than sorry."

"Okay." Sipping the glass of wine, I decided to not ask for details. The less I knew the better. "Well, I'm happy with both gifts, and I can't wait to go shopping."

"I love you, sweetheart."

"I love you more."

"Now let's eat before our food gets cold."

On both plates were a few of my favorite foods. My birthday dinner included shrimp Alfredo, sauteed shrimp on the side, a well- done, juicy steak and a Caesar salad. My husband knew exactly what I loved the most.

The door slammed. Loud talking and scuffling could be heard coming towards the kitchen. Hugo sat his fork down and rose to his feet. In walked Demetri and three of our workers. One of them was being dragged in. That totally caught me off guard.

"Son, what's going on?" I placed my napkin on the table and stood up.

Demetri pushed Teddy in our direction. He stumbled, but didn't fall. "This nigga been talking to the police and we caught his ass. He been snorting up the product too. That's why he been short."

Hugo cracked his knuckles before delivering a hard punch to Teddy's gut. The junky doubled over in pain. "I'm sorry, man." His voice was winded.

"You been using my product and talking to the fucking pigs. Are you crazy? You must have a death wish."

"It's not like that. Let me explain." Teddy held his stomach, trying to reconcile.

Hugo forced him down in the chair and hit him again. "I don't want to hear no excuses. I'm running a profitable business, not a non-profit organization."

Teddy deserved more than an ass whooping. Quite frankly, I didn't want to hear any excuses. It wasn't the first time he was short. I only spared him because I knew his mother. Now he had taken it too far.

"Do you have proof?" My eyes were on Demetri and Omar.

Demetri huffed. "My eyes and ears. I heard them talking, so I placed my ear to the door and listened. He was planning on flipping because he caught a possession charge. And instead of going down like a man, he chose the bitch way out."

Hugo snatched him up by the collar, while breathing hard in his face. "When you came to my wife and me, you begged for a position in our organization. Reluctantly, we decided to give you a chance, and this is the way you repay us by snitching?" Hugo chuckled. "What part of the game is that?"

"I'm sorry. I can make this right. Just give me a chance." Teddy begged for his life. Honestly, it was making me nauseous. It was time to put an end to it.

"You're all out of chances, Teddy," I snapped.

"Please Miss V. You know me," he pleaded.

"That's like letting the same snake bite you twice." Removing my coat, I hung it on the back of the chair. "You have to pay for what you did."

"You heard my wife. I'll let her take care of you. Maybe she'll be a little more lenient than me." Hugo took a step back with his hands up. "Handle it, queen."

Demetri removed his gun from the waistband of his jeans and passed it to me. With the pistol clutched tightly in my hand, I slammed it against Teddy's temple. Blood gushed from the side of his head. "You stupid muthafucka! I put you in a position to make money and you'll bite my hand like that. You might as well spit in my face, you disrespectful snitch bitch."

Teddy's head bobbed up and down, as I pistol whipped him. Once his face was mangled and covered in blood, I took him out of his misery with a single gunshot to the forehead. *Boc!*

Brain matter splattered on the wall. Blood splashed onto my face from the blowback. Wiping my face with the napkin, I smiled. There was something about catching a body that gave me sheer pleasure. That was until I looked down at my bloodstained expensive blouse. Raising my foot, I kicked his corpse. "Made me waste a two thousand dollar blouse, you idiot."

Hugo chuckled. "That's replaceable, sweetheart."

"I know," I smirked. "Now get this trash out my kitchen and clean up this mess. I'm about to go shower. I have an errand to run."

No one in Tampa was fucking with the baddest bitch in the land. But it was always the crackheads that wanted to be made an example. Teddy got exactly what he deserved, and I didn't feel any remorse.

Chapter 15

Domestic

My brain constantly racked over Emilia's attempt to blackmail me. Over time she had become a lot bolder, and I wasn't sure what her motives were. All I could think about was, her ways had to have finally caught up with her. Emilia was known to use her badge as a way to get over on the drug dealers for years. Maybe someone was after the bitch, and she was trying to flee on my dime. Carlos promised to handle our little problem. Therefore, I would wait until he gave me the word.

On another note, I needed to smooth things over with my woman. It was time for us to have a clear understanding of our relationship and what I expected. A nigga was older and more mature than my last situation. There were a lot of things I wouldn't tolerate at all. Not then. Not now. My future wife needed to know that.

Foreign walked through the door, looking like a ray of sunshine. The soft colored, yellow dress complimented her beautiful skin. Her scent lingered in the air. It reminded me of a sweet, summer breeze. If the afternoon wasn't so busy, I would've made love to her at that very moment.

"Hey, beautiful," I greeted her cheerfully.

"Hey, baby." Foreign flashed the beautiful smile that captured me from day one.

Grabbing her waist, I planted a sweet kiss on her soft lips. "We need to talk."

"I agree."

Foreign allowed me to take her hand and whisk her to the seat in front of my desk. As the king, I took my seat on the throne and eyed my queen.

"This conversation is long overdue," I cleared my throat. "But there's no time like the present. Do you remember the first night we met?"

Foreign's eyes sparkled, as she glared passionately in my eyes. "I do."

"The night we met, I showed you my aggressive side. You loved that. That's who you fell in love with and that's who I am."

"I get that but—"

Raising my hand, I cut her off. "Let me finish." Foreign sat back and listened attentively. "Now, like I was saying, I showed you my aggressive side out the gate and you loved that. That's who you fell in love with—Domestic. Not Demerius. I feel like you keep trying to change me into some ole cream puff ass nigga. I'm not Aaron. I ain't the average nigga." Hitting my chest, I expressed my feelings. "I'm one of a kind, baby."

Foreign parted those sexy ass lips. "I'm not trying to change you. What part of that don't you understand? All I want is for you to respect me and not put your hands on me. I want the old you back."

There was a lot of sincerity in her voice, so I decided to keep my cool. "There's no old me. I'm still that same man. The only difference is our status. You're solely mine now. Before, I was letting you get away with that slick tongue. Now, things have changed and I won't accept anything less than the respect that I deserve as your man."

"And what about the respect I deserve as your woman? I've earned that from you."

"That's true." In agreement, I nodded. "We both know that your tongue gets a little flimsy at times. I need you to understand that I love you to death. The ground you walk on, I cherish that. At the same time, I don't need you."

"Excuse me?" Foreign scoffed in surprise.

"Let me clarify that before you blow it out of proportion. A want and a need are two separate things. Oxygen is what I need to live. I want you, but I won't die if you leave me."

"Is that right?" She smirked.

"I won't die, but you will." My statement wiped the grin off her face in a split second. Now I was the one smirking. "See how that works?"

Foreign's chest heaved up and down, but she didn't say a word.

Silence.

Now I had her attention.

"You think I'm crazy don't you?" I chuckled slightly. When she didn't offer a response, I continued. "Foreign, baby, when you chose me you chose forever. I'm not trying to scare you. I'm just letting you know that we are in it until we die."

To ease the tension in the room, I grabbed a hold of my baby and kissed her. "You know I love you, right?"

"Yes."

"And you know I'll do anything for you?"

"Yes."

"I'm not going to hurt you, okay?"

"Okay."

Gently, I kissed her forehead. "You have my heart and no one else. All I need is for you to know your place as my woman and everything will be smoother than silk." My hand found its way to her belly. "I'm going to take good care of you and my baby. You'll never have to worry about money or another woman. That's my promise to you. Just take care of our home and respect me. Can you do that?"

"Yes. I can do that."

"The next thing I need you to do is start planning our wedding. You can have whatever you like. No price is too big when it comes to you. I'll add you to one of my accounts and have a card issued to you."

"Okay." Her voice was a bit shaky, as she agreed to my terms.

Our eyes remained locked for several moments. There was an uncomfortable silence throughout the room. Then suddenly, all of that erupted when a familiar voice sent eerie chills over my body.

"Good evening, Demerius. How are you?"

Veronica's presence made me cringe the moment I looked up and saw her face. That was the last person on earth that I wanted to see. The bitch was just flat out evil. "Good evening," I replied softly.

Veronica adjusted the Louis Vuitton coat she was wearing. The jewels and bag she carried screamed money. Flashy was the way she preferred to dress on a daily basis. Her hair was jet-black with curls. It flowed down her back. Veronica's brown skin was flawless in her fifties. She hadn't aged one bit.

"I'm starting to think that you aren't happy to see me." The evil lady's smile was brighter than the sun.

"Um. I'm. I'm. Just a little surprised. That's all." Quickly I glanced in Foreign's direction. Her facial expression told me that she was curious. I needed her out of the office and fast. "Baby, can you leave so we can talk in private please?"

Foreign cut her eyes, but she stood up with no hesitation. "Sure."

"Demerius, that's rude. Aren't you going to introduce us?" Veronica stood there with her hands on her hips.

"Foreign, this is Veronica. Veronica, this is Foreign."

Veronica was now looking directly at Foreign. "Please forgive Demerius, he's forgotten his manners. I'm his mother."

"Mother?" Foreign's word slid off her tongue slowly.

"Yes. I'm his mother and apparently, he failed to mention me to you."

"I'm sorry. It's nice to meet you."

"It's okay, darling. My son has a tendency of being a little secretive when it comes down to me." Veronica never took her eyes off of Foreign. "You're pretty."

"So are you," Foreign said sweetly.

"Son, this is quite a step-up from Casey," she giggled.

One thing about my mother, she loved to put me on the spot every chance she got. I stood there in silence as my painful childhood flashed before my eyes.

"So, are you and my son dating?"

"Yes, ma'am."

"She's my fiancée and the mother of my child," I boasted proudly.

"Oh, congratulations. Hopefully, I'll get to see this grandchild." Veronica was steady taking shots at me. The embarrassing part was her doing it in front of my woman.

"Foreign, can you excuse us please?"

"No. Foreign, have a seat." Veronica insisted.

Foreign looked at me for confirmation.

"Oh, Demerius, you're doing it again, I see." Veronica placed her hand on Foreign's shoulder. "Have a seat, darling." Then she looked at me. "Demerius, sit your ass down, right now." Veronica's scream was loud enough to cause Foreign and I to jump.

There was no fight in me. I sat down immediately to see what she had to say. Veronica never showed up unless it was something urgent. The last time we were face to face was roughly four months ago, and that was the way I preferred things to be. Too bad it couldn't be longer. In fact, I would prefer not to see my mother until it was time for her funeral.

"Now, as you know, my birthday is coming up. Your father is sending me on a trip to Thailand for two weeks."

"Must be nice," I mumbled.

"Oh, Demerius, don't be salty."

"I'm not."

"Before I leave, I'm having a birthday dinner at the house. I would love for you and Foreign to attend."

"When is it? I might be busy."

Veronica's laugh was loud and sinister. "Oh, my sweet child," she waved her hand. "You thought I was asking. This is a request. A mandatory one at that. I'm going to send you the details. Go out and get yourself a nice, black tuxedo. This is a formal gathering and I won't settle for anything less than superior. Do you understand that?"

"Yeah."

Veronica tilted her head to the side. "Excuse me? What was that?"

"Yes, ma'am," I replied, removing the anger from my voice.

"You've never disrespected me in your life and you surely not about to start that shit today." Veronica bit her bottom lip and made a tight fist. "Please don't make me show out right now. You know I will do it."

"No. No ma—ma—ma'am. That's not necessary." With every passing minute in Veronica's presence, I was losing my manhood. Proper English was certainly out the window. My ass couldn't stop stuttering for shit. Foreign didn't need to see me like that. As far I was concerned, she would surely think she could talk to me with a reckless tongue.

"Good. Foreign doesn't need to see my bad side just yet." Veronica stood up and smiled at Foreign. "It was so nice to meet you."

"The pleasure was all mine," Foreign smiled back.

Veronica casually turned on her heels and headed towards the exit. Before she could walk through the door, she glanced at me. "Be on time."

"I—I will."

"As a matter of fact, I'll arrange a car to pick you up." Veronica's eyes bounced around my office. "Cute little office, son. When you get tired of working here, the family business will be waiting for you." Veronica's phone rang. She removed it from her handbag and quickly glanced at the screen. "I have to go, but I'll be in touch."

The relief I felt when she left was priceless. It was a shame that I felt uncomfortable in my own space. Veronica had me under her thumb my entire life. The leftover tension in the room was still lingering. A set of eyes were burning my soul. Foreign didn't blink once. Instead, she rose to her feet and walked out of my office.

Foreign...

Domestic hadn't said a word since we left the car wash two hours ago. His mother's impromptu visit wasn't welcome. Dinner was quiet. The only sound heard at the table were our forks tapping against the glass plate. We barely made eye contact. It was like we were two strangers eating in the cafeteria on the first day of school. There were so many questions running through my mind. It was so much I wanted to say. For the first time in our relationship, I witnessed Domestic lose his dominance to a woman. That man was like a five-year-old child in her presence. A scared little boy.

Finding courage within myself, I managed to use my words. He wasn't going to address the situation. Therefore, I needed to be the initiator.

"Domestic."

"Yeah," he replied dryly.

"Are we going to talk about what happened earlier?"

"I didn't plan on it."

"Well, I think it's only fair to do so. I mean, I was only in there with you."

"That's something I don't care to elaborate on. Now just drop it before you piss me off." Domestic snapped.

The attitude he was giving me was the one he should've had earlier. He let his mama treat him like a little boy and now he wanted to take it out on me. This dude was hilarious and I couldn't keep myself from giggling. Not that it was funny, but because he was straight up trying me.

"Do you think that's fair?" I wiped my mouth with the cloth napkin. "Keeping secrets from me."

"I think it's on a need to know basis."

Domestic didn't have to finish the statement. I knew the rest, but now I was agitated. "Why do you have all of this hostility towards me? I didn't do or say anything to you to warrant any of this. You must love to intimidate me?"

Domestic was staring down at his plate, but slowly he raised his head. His eyes were now in tiny, dark slits. Similar to snake eyes. "Intimidate you? Foreign, miss me with that shit. I'm starting to think you get aroused when I talk to you like this. See you," he pointed his finger in my direction. "You don't know when to close your fuckin' mouth. We just discussed what I expect from you. All that back talking won't be tolerated."

"Tuh," I mumbled. "It's funny that you say that, when I just watched you clam up like a five-year-old in front of your mother." My stare was just as hard. "I guess that's why you feel the need to control me."

On the outside looking in, Domestic was beyond pissed. His nostrils flared wide like a bull. Evil had taken over his soul, as he stood up and snatched the tablecloth. All of the food and kitchenware crashed to the floor. In a matter of seconds, Domestic snatched me from the table by my hair. Unable to keep my balance, I fell to the floor. Despite me being able to walk, he dragged me like a rag doll. I could feel broken glass scraping against my skin. My piercing screams went unanswered.

"I'm sorry. I'm sorry," I wailed.

"Not as sorry as you about to be," he shouted while slapping me across the face.

Suddenly, the tile felt slippery. When I looked down I could see blood. Instantly, I began to panic. "Stop! I'm bleeding. I'm bleeding."

Just as we reached the steps, Domestic stopped in his tracks and fell to his knees. Loud painful cries filled his lungs. Now, kneeling by my side, he held me in his arms. "I'm so sorry, baby. I don't know what's wrong with me."

To see Domestic breakdown and cry broke my heart. Regardless of the pain, he inflicted on me, I felt bad for him. I knew he needed me more than ever, so I put my personal feelings to the side. Right now, it was about his need. I wrapped my arms around his waist and cried with my man.

"I love you, baby, but I need you to control your anger. When you snap and lose it, not only do you hurt me physically, you damage me mentally."

"I love you so much. I just don't know how to love you properly."

To hear Domestic in a vulnerable state let me know that I could help him. All I had to do was be patient with him. He needed me to show him how to love me correctly.

"You have to let me help you. Stop pushing me away. I'm not trying to hurt you or be combative. I just need you to open up and tell me about the things in your past that's causing you to lash out at me."

Domestic's eyes were fire-red. His face was drenched in tears. The pain was evident. "I don't know where to start."

I took a deep breath. Silently, I prayed that he would open up to me without a fight. Domestic's actions were unpredictable and I didn't want to set him off again. "Start with your mother. She's the main source of your pain. I can see that."

Domestic and I sat on the floor, holding hands as he revisited the most traumatic moments of his childhood. Every word he spoke shattered my heart. A lot of the details were traumatic. No wonder he had a hard time loving a woman properly. He was never loved as a child. Veronica did a number on Domestic mentally.

Chapter 16

Casey

One week later

The news of Craig's death got the best of Shawn. For the past week, he'd been depressed. Most days he sat in silence and cried. His alcohol consumption picked up, and so did a new smoking habit. My baby was going through the motions, and I was doing my best to keep his head above water.

The drive back to Florida was quiet for the most part. Shawn only engaged in conversation when it was time to eat or take a restroom break. Since the murder occurred, Tim kept a low profile and searched for his brother's killer. No one knew anything. That was odd because the streets were always talking.

Tampa was my hometown, but to step back into the city gave me anxiety. Domestic had me on his radar, so I had to steer clear of him. DP still loved his dad. That alone made me feel guilty for creating a wedge in their relationship. All I ever wanted was for Domestic to change his controlling ways and commit to me. In my eyes that wasn't too much to ask for. We were past that stage now, and he hated me with a passion. It was okay because I was safe. Free from abuse and manipulation.

"Damn, it's hard coming home and not being able to see my brother," Shawn sighed, as he pulled into the driveway of his old home.

"I know, baby. I'm here to help you get through this. Once the funeral is over, we'll work on the healing process," I promised.

All three of us exited the rental car.

DP grabbed my arm. "Mom."

"Yes."

"I want to see my dad."

Fear embedded in my soul, but I couldn't show it. "I don't think that's a good idea."

"Why not? He's still my dad and I miss him."

"Let me think about it. We still have to get something to wear for the funeral, so let me see if we have time."

DP's shoulders slumped. "I'm sorry, but I'm not going to the funeral."

That was a surprise to me. "Why not?"

"I don't want to. I rather spend time with my dad while I'm here. It's bad enough I can't talk to him and I'm tired of being in the middle of y'all feud. That's not fair to me."

For a moment, I just stood there. His words sunk deep into my brain and he was right. But at the same time, he had no idea of the type of man his father truly was. DP towered over me in height, but he was still my baby.

"DP, listen to me," I placed my hand on his forearm. "I'm sorry that I put you in the middle of this situation with your father. Please understand that my intentions are not to take you away from him. It was only to protect myself from him. You're my son. My only child, and I can't maneuver through life without you. I know that things are different without him around, but they will get better. I promise you that."

"Then you understand that I have to see him."

My mouth wanted to scream no, but my heart was on a different accord. "Yes."

"Don't worry, I won't tell him where I'm at. I'll just go to him."

"I would appreciate that. He doesn't need to know where we're staying."

"I won't tell him. I promise."

"Okay."

Inside the house, Tim and Shawn were sitting on the sofa smoking a blunt and talking about Craig. Tim looked towards the door when we walked in. His eyes were sunken, and it looked as if he hadn't eaten anything in days.

"How are you holding up?" I hugged him tightly.

"Shit rough right now. They took my best friend from me." Tim shook his head and wiped the tears from his eyes. "Whoever did this shit gon' pay. I swear to God."

"You fuckin' right they gon' pay," Shawn added.

That was out of Shawn's character. He wasn't in the street life with his brothers. I've never heard him speak in that manner, and neither did my son.

"DP, go in the room, baby, and let me talk to them in private— please." DP walked away without saying a word.

I knelt in front of Shawn and grabbed his hands. "Baby, this is not like you and I can't lose you to these streets. I chose you because you live a quiet lifestyle."

"Damn sis, what you trying to say?" Tim leaned forward in his seat.

"I got this, bruh," Shawn replied.

127

"No. I can speak for myself." I cut him off. "All I'm saying is that I want my man to stay safe. You know he's not built like you and Craig. Both of you shielded him his whole life and you know it."

"We may have shielded him, but that thug shit runs deep in our blood. Ain't no changing that." Tim was determined to make me understand the logic behind Shawn getting involved in a beef that had nothing to do with him.

"He's right," Shawn agreed. "They only kept me out the streets because one of us had to make it in life. You know, do something positive. But now that shit has changed. A fuck nigga came for my brother and I'm not turning my back on him. I'm riding with my nigga. I want all the smoke. On God!"

"What am I supposed to do if something happens to you?" My voice was whiny, but I needed to get my point across.

"You'll survive."

"Shawn, I need you," I pleaded.

"Bae, relax. I'm not going anywhere, but if I do, continue to live your life to the fullest."

"Wow! That's how you feel?"

"Right now my brother needs me. I can't do this with you. Just chill out and let me mourn."

"Okay." His response wasn't what I wanted to hear, but I decided to leave it alone. "I'm going to the mall. I'll be back later on."

University Mall wasn't packed at all. I was able to go in and grab a nice black dress for the funeral. Shawn hadn't called me once since I left. I understood the loss of his brother was hard, but that didn't mean he should throw his life away. Craig and Tim lived by the gun. Therefore the old saying, *you live by the gun, you die by the gun*, applied to their situation. Two hours passed since I left the house, and I was in no hurry to get back. Once I made it back to the car, I called my best friend—Tiffany. She was also DP's Godmother. Months passed since I last saw her, and we needed to catch up.

"What's up, bitch?" Tiffany shouted through the phone. "I ain't heard from you in a month of Sundays."

"Girl, I know. Shit has been rough lately. What you got going on over there?"

"Shit. Just listening to music while I do my laundry."

"You have liquor over there?"

"You know I do."

"Good. My ass needs a drink and a listening ear."

"You know I got you, boo. Come through."

"I'm leaving University Mall, so I'll be there in a few."

"I'll be waiting."

"Okay."

After I hung up, I pulled out of the parking lot and made the twenty-minute drive to Tiffany's house. Traffic was nice and breezy. I was able to think and reevaluate my last conversation with Shawn. It hurt to know that he would risk his relationship for the streets, but I had to truly grasp the fact that he wanted street justice for his brother. Truthfully, I thought he should allow the cops to handle it, but with Tim in his ear, that was highly unlikely.

Tiffany opened the door and greeted me with a smile. "Damn, I missed my best bitch. How the fuck you just up and leave a bitch with no warning?" She locked the door behind us.

"You know I had to get away from my crazy ass baby daddy. I needed something new. A fresh start to a better life."

"Bitch, please, you had a great life with that nigga."

"Yeah, if you like ass whoopings in the process." I removed my jacket and sat down on the brown leather sofa.

"That's 'cause you hard-headed, bitch. If I was in your shoes, that nigga wouldn't have to ask me to do shit. His dinner would be ready, a hot bath and head on deck," she laughed. "This pussy would be like Little Caesars, hot and ready."

"If only it was that simple. Domestic has control issues and I couldn't do it anymore."

"So do broke niggas. At least he pays the cost to be the boss. Bitch, you had nothing to worry about. You sleep."

"Yeah, I would be sleep, if I stayed. Permanently at that," I assured her.

"Well, tell me all about it while we sip this good drink."

Tiffany had a bottle of Patron, lime juice, and ice sitting on the table.

"I'm glad you ready for me," I giggled. "I've been going through the wringer for weeks now. Domestic wants to beat my ass for the stunt I pulled with Shawn and for taking DP away from him."

"Can you blame him? Nothing on earth made him happier than you giving birth to his son. That man loves his child more than life itself or any female for that matter."

"He does love his son. I can't deny that."

"As long as you know." Tiffany poured up two drinks and passed me one. "I heard he has a baby on the way from some chick."

"What?" That news hit me like a baseball upside the head. "A new baby? I know like hell he doesn't. The nigga told me he didn't want more kids."

Tiffany smirked. "You sound salty, sis. I know you not mad about that?"

"I'm not mad, but he acts like he so in love with that girl."

"Well, he is. You know my cousin Tracy works up there and she can't hold water for shit. That's how I found out she's pregnant." Tiffany sipped her drink. "They're engaged too."

Now, that was the straw that broke the camel's back. The nigga had the nerve to propose after knowing the bitch for five minutes. I was heartbroken all over again. "Wow! He put me through hell and back about Shawn, while he was living his best life. And he wonders why I hate his guts. All he did was use and abuse me."

Domestic's affairs fucked me up so bad, that I downed the entire drink. "Fix me another one."

"Damn, you didn't know?"

"No." The second Tiffany passed me another drink, I downed that one too. "Fix me another one."

"You better slow down, girl."

"I can't." Tears started to slide slowly from my eyes. "I've put up with so much shit from Domestic, and he has the nerve to just move on like I didn't mean shit to him."

"I'm sorry, Casey. If I knew you didn't know, I would've never said a word."

"It's not your fault. I was destined to find out, anyway." The Patron felt good as I consumed it. My life was still a mess, although I moved on. "It's crazy because I met her."

"Oh, really?" Tiffany crossed her legs. "Spill the tea, sis."

To relive the moment in his office was painful, but I needed to get it out. "While I was still living in the house, I popped up at his job. I had suspicions of him sleeping with another woman, but DP confirmed that for me. When I arrived to talk to him, the bitch was in the office with him. He made her leave, so he could put his hands on me."

"Damn, for real?" Tiffany seemed shocked at the news.

She had always rooted for Domestic. Even when he was doing me dirty in the streets. Tiffany claimed that a man would always cheat, but as long as he took care of our home, that was all that mattered. However, I begged to differ. I wanted a commitment. A ring. That never happened. Domestic dragged me along until I was tired of being mistreated.

"Yep. She witnessed the shit too. When it was over, she ran to my car to check on me. I warned her that the same thing would happen to her."

"What did she say?"

"Not too much. Their relationship was still early, but I'm sure she sees what I was talking about now."

"Maybe. Maybe not. Again, your ass is hard-headed. Shit, she might be that submissive bitch he needs."

"I guess."

Tiffany and I discussed my problems as we knocked down several cups of liquor. The bitch wouldn't stay out of her phone for some reason. "Who the hell you keep texting?"

"This dude I met. His ass trying to come over and get a piece of this snapper," she giggled.

"Tell that nigga you busy."

"I did."

"Good." Another drink added to the roster, and I was slumped on the sofa. Sleep was calling my name loud from the mountaintop, so I answered. The next time I opened my eyes, all I could see was darkness, and I couldn't open my mouth.

Shawn...

Tim stood in the middle of the living room floor with his hands in his pockets. "Did you talk to her?"

"Nah. She not answering the phone. I guess she mad at me." I called Casey four times and every call went unanswered.

"What you wanna do? 'Cause I'm not trying to cause problems between you and your lady."

"Shiidd, she'll be alright. This my brother we talking about. If she can't understand that then I don't know what to tell her." I stood up and slid my phone into my back pocket.

"You sure about that?"

"Positive. Now let's roll out."

Casey was my heart, but my brothers and I shared the same blood. They were the same ones that helped release the chains Domestic had on her.

"DP, come here," I shouted throughout the house.

"What's up?" He entered the area with his AirPods in his ear and iPhone clutched in his hand.

131

"We headed out. Don't answer the door for anybody."

"You leaving me here?"

"Yeah. I have some business to go and handle. I'll be back a little later."

"Okay."

"You good?" I had to make sure he was okay.

"Yeah."

"A'ight. We'll be back." Tim and I walked out the door.

Two bloodthirsty vampires were lurking in the dark of the Tampa streets. No one was safe. No one was going to stop us. For years I kept to myself and walked a straight path, while my brothers pursued the street life. Some fuck nigga had officially forced me into the game, and I wanted all the smoke. Both of my brothers had my word. I was not leaving Florida until the shooter was dead.

Chapter 17

Domestic

One hour ago

For weeks I racked my brain trying to find my son to no avail. DP's absence fucked me up mentally. All the frustration I developed behind Casey caused me to damage the most precious woman I've encountered throughout my thirty-five years on earth. Between my childhood trauma and the hate I had for Casey, Foreign didn't stand a chance at true happiness with me. If I didn't change my ways, I was going to lose her forever.

As I sat out on the porch, a slight breeze caressed my face. It was the only place where I could think in peace. The neighborhood I lived in was upscale. A person needed money to reside here. At the place I was in life, I should be happy. I owned three lucrative businesses, luxury cars, and two homes. There wasn't anything I lacked financially, but behind my success, I was a broken man.

Loud chirping from my cellphone stopped me from daydreaming. It was a text message. One that I had been waiting on. My mood automatically shifted, and a smile was present on my face. Fully charged, I ran into the house to get my keys, backpack, and a firearm. Just when I thought my life was falling apart, the universe proved me wrong.

My Bentley slid through the streets like the batmobile. I wasn't about to fight no damn crime, but someone was about to get buried in the dirt. That adrenaline rush was a motherfucker.

Once I pulled up to the spot, I couldn't get out of the car fast enough. This meet up was long overdue. All of the pain that I'd endured bubbled long enough, finally coming to a head. Instead of knocking, I sent a text message saying I was outside. Seconds later, the door opened and Tiffany stepped onto the porch.

"Damn, how many red lights did you run to get here so fast?" she asked with her arms folded across her chest.

"You already know how I drive. Where is she?"

"In the living room passed out."

"You sure about that?"

"Yep. She's white girl wasted."

"Good. I appreciate your help." Just as I started to walk inside, Tiffany placed her hand on my chest.

"Hold up. Not so fast. Where is my money?"

"God forbid I forget that." I reached into my pocket and pulled out a stack of folded bills. Tiffany watched closely as I peeled off five one-hundred dollar bills.

"Thanks," she smiled. Now you can enter and make sure she doesn't find out about this."

Tiffany insulted me like I was a snitch. "Stop acting like you don't know me. Snitching has never been in my blood. No matter the time I face or circumstances."

She held her hands up. "You right. Let me be quiet."

Casey was laid out on the sofa without a care in the world. Little did she know her nightmare had just begun. Before I lifted her from the chair, I restrained her wrists and covered her mouth and eyes with duct tape. Casey was about to regret crossing me for another nigga and taking my son.

Present time

Back at the old house where Casey and my son resided, I took her into the shed. It was dark and warm enough to make her sweat. That bitch didn't deserve to be kept inside the house. Especially since she moved out and stole my shit.

Casey wiggled on the futon. I watched as she struggled. First, I snatched the duct tape from her mouth. I wanted to hear that bitch scream. Next, I snatched it from her eyes. Casey's scream was horrific. It was the worst when she saw my face.

"I hope I snatched your eyelashes off, bitch."

"Domestic," she cried. "Please don't hurt me."

"We begging now," I chuckled. That shit was hilarious. "Nah, what happened to the big bad wolf that I been talking to for the past several weeks? The one who cursed me out like she ain't have no sense."

Casey's body shook violently, as she cried. I wasn't fazed

"Baby mama, don't get quiet on me now. Let me hear that bear again. Talk shit to me like you been doing."

"Don't do this. I'll do whatever you want me to do." The look of terror on her face was a pleasant sight to see.

"Where the fuck is my son?"

"DP doesn't want to see you. After he heard you curse me out, he's been upset with you."

"That's a lie." Casey couldn't tell me shit about my son. DP texted me a few days ago and told me that he missed me. But he wouldn't tell me where he was out of fear that I would hurt his punk ass mother. "I spoke to my son a few days ago."

"I'm not lying."

Fed up with her bullshit, I drew the gun from my waistband and pressed it against her temple. "I'm not fucking around with you. Now, tell me where the fuck my son is. Is he here?"

"Yes."

"Where?" I yelled in her face.

"I can't tell you."

Casey's eyes grew wider when she heard the bullet slide in the chamber. "Come again," I stated.

"He's at his friend's house." She finally admitted.

Taking my cellphone from my pocket, I dialed his number. He picked up on the second ring. "What's up, dad?"

"Hey, son. Where are you?"

"Shawn's brother's house."

"I'm about to call Foreign and have her to pick you up."

"Have her to meet me. It's not a good idea for her to come here."

"Who said that? Your mother."

"Yeah. She told me not to tell you where we were staying."

"Is that right?

"Yes, but don't say anything to her."

"It's all good. I promise."

"Okay."

"I'll be home after I handle this business. See you later." As soon as we hung up the phone, I called Foreign.

"Hello."

"Baby, I need you to go and pick up DP for me."

"From where?"

"Call him. I'm about to send you his number."

"What time are you coming home?" she asked sweetly.

"In a few hours. I have some business to take care of, but I won't be too long."

"Okay."

"I love you."

"I love you too," she replied with no hesitation. We hung up.

Foreign had to love me unconditionally. She was still there throughout all of my bullshit. I've snapped, laid hands on her on more than one occasion, and revealed my past. My baby was still by my side. Foreign was every man's dream.

Putting my phone away, I stepped closer to Casey and slapped the shit out of her. *Whap! Whap!*

"You are one lying ass bitch. Do you really think I was going to let you take my son and not look for him? You must be smoking on a glass dick if you thought that."

"Domestic," she whined.

"Stop calling my fuckin' name."

"I only took him away so I could protect myself from you. It was time for me to go, but you and I both know that you weren't going to let that happen."

The broad was funny as fuck. "Casey, do you think I would've given a fuck if you wanted to be with that lame ass nigga? No. You just wasn't about to be laid up with that nigga in my house. All you had to do was move in with that nigga and leave my son. I have moved on. You could've done the same. Trust me, I would not be mad."

"I wish you would have said that back then." Her reply was a bit sassy.

"Oh, really?"

"Yeah."

Next thing I knew—I was leaning over Casey, pounding her face with a closed fist. Somehow, I blacked out. Her screams became silent. By the time I stopped raining blows on her face, my fists were covered with her blood. Casey was crying and holding her face.

"Bitch, don't you ever talk to me like that again."

DP started to call my phone in the middle of me beating on his mammy's ass. "What's up, son?" My breathing was slightly heavy, so was my heart rate.

"Foreign just picked me up."

"Good. Y'all on the way to the house?"

"We going to get something to eat first. Do you want something?" He politely asked.

"Nah. I'm good. I'll be there soon."

"Okay."

"I love you, son."

"I love you too, dad."

To hear my son express his love for me melted my heart. I couldn't wait to get home and have a man-to-man talk with him. As for Casey, I chained that bitch to the bed like the dog that she was. On the way out, I locked the shed and whistled all the way to my car.

In the driveway at my house, I made a mad dash to the door and gained entry to the inside. To my surprise, Foreign and DP were sitting in the living room talking and laughing. That showed me they were getting along just fine. It was something I needed to see since they hadn't spent any alone time together.

"Hey, what's going on in here?" I kissed Foreign and joined them in the living room.

"Hey, baby." Foreign smiled pleasantly. "DP and I are just sitting here talking."

"My favorite girl and main man," I laughed. "I like what I'm seeing. What's up, son?" I hugged DP.

"Just chillin', pops. I missed you."

"Man, you don't know how much I missed you. Your absence fucked my whole world up." Our emotional reunion had me teary-eyed. "I never want to lose you."

"You will never lose me. You're my dad and I love you."

"I love you too."

DP and I sat down on the sofa beside one another.

"Congratulations on the baby."

"You ready to be a big brother?"

"No doubt," he smiled, flashing those twenty-four-carat gold braces. "I've always wanted a sister or brother. This is my chance."

Those words put a bigger smile on my face. "I'm happy you feel that way. So, does that mean you'll be here to see your sister or brother?" DP had a saddened look on his face. Something was wrong, and I knew it.

"Yes."

"You're here to stay?"

"Yeah. Can I?" His question was filled with innocence. That confirmed what I already knew. Casey filled his head with a bunch of bullshit to get him to leave.

"That's not a question. I never wanted you to leave in the first place."

Foreign stood up. "I'm going to leave you two alone to talk."

"No. You can stay. We're a family now. I don't want any secrets between us." I assured her.

"DP, is that okay with you?" Foreign said with sincerity.

"Yeah. It's cool."

Foreign sat back down.

"Why the change of heart? Did something happen?" If that was the case, more blood was about to be shed.

"No."

"Are you sure?"

"I promise. Nothing happened. I just miss being home with you and my friends. Tennessee is not for me."

The answers I'd been looking for had finally come out. That bitch was hiding my son in another state. Far away at that. "So, that's where she's been keeping you all this time?"

"Yeah. I don't want to go back."

"You don't have to."

"You promise."

"I promise." I hugged my son once more. "You don't have to worry about me losing you again."

"All my stuff is in Tennessee." He shrugged.

"Don't worry about that. I'll get you new stuff tomorrow. Whatever you need, you know I got you."

DP was quiet for a moment. If I knew my son, I knew he was about to ask another question. "Can I use the car?"

I looked at the gold timepiece on my wrist. "Where are you trying to go?"

"Cheyenne's house."

Cheyenne was his girlfriend. I should've known that was where he wanted to go. "Sure, man. Go ahead." I passed him the keys.

"I'll be back later."

"A'ight. Be safe."

"I will." DP was gone in a matter of seconds. Foreign and I retired to the bedroom for the remainder of the night.

Chapter 18

Emilia

Forty-eight hours had come and gone. Domestic hadn't reached out to me about my request. It was time for me to put pressure on him. Several times I tried his number and there was no answer.

"This motherfucker trying me like I can't destroy his ass."

To put Domestic on blast about his wrongdoings would ruin my reputation. It would certainly implicate me in a few crimes that could land me in prison. Out of options, I decided to pay him one last visit. This was going to determine my final move. It was early in the day, and I was on my second cup of Vodka. The loss of my job had me depressed as fuck. I gulped down my drink. "Oh well, it's five o'clock somewhere."

Upstairs, I slipped on a two-piece workout set. It's been a minute since I hit the gym, but I was still fine. My flawless skin glowed in the mirror. I pulled my hair up into a messy bun and put on some lip gloss. Now, I was ready to go.

It was a little windy outside. The sun beamed bright enough for me to put on a pair of shades. Slipping them on, I climbed inside my Infiniti coupé, which was reserved for the weekend. Without a job and my police cruiser, it quickly became my everyday vehicle. On my way to the wash, I reflected on my time with the police force. Over the years, my team had become my family. They completed me, and now I was all alone. If I could turn back the hands of time, I would've kept my ethics training on the frontline. Greed caused me to lose everything I loved, and I didn't know what to do.

Domestic was my last hope at a fresh start. I needed to go where no one knew me and start over. A recommendation from the captain was highly unlikely. There was no way he would vouch for me after all the shit I did. To my surprise, my ringing phone lit up the car speakers. On the screen was Domestic's name.

"What a pleasant surprise," I mumbled, as I answered his call. "Hello."

"Aye, where you at?" he asked. "I need you to come by the office."

"Coincidently, I'm on my way to you."

"Good. That's why I was calling."

"I'll be there in ten minutes."

"I'll be waiting."

"Okay."

Receiving that call from Domestic was like a breath of fresh air. All wasn't lost after all. He didn't have to say a word. I knew why he was calling. It was to give me the money. Now, I could finally begin to make plans for my new life.

Domestic was sitting in his office looking dapper as usual with his fine ass. If he would've given me the chance, I would've been Mrs. Payne by now with a few babies. Without being told, I closed the door and sat in the leather chair.

"How are you, Emilia?"

"I'm good. How are you?"

"Life is great." He flashed a million-dollar smile.

"That's good to hear." Small talk wasn't why I was there, so I decided to get straight to the point. "Did you call me here for some good news?"

"Of course I did, but before I elaborate on that I have a question for you."

"What's that?"

Domestic folded his hands and leaned forward. "The last time you were here you threatened me. You know I don't take threats too lightly."

"I do." I nodded.

"That was dumb on your part. Do you have any idea how much dirt I have on you?"

"I do."

"Now, this shit about killing Aaron—where did you get that from? What makes you think that I had anything to do with that?"

"I have my suspicions." Domestic was different that day. He didn't perform his normal routine check. "Aren't you going to search me for a wire?"

Domestic's laugh was menacing. "That's not necessary."

"Why is that?" He had me curious.

"Oh, my dear Emilia. You don't have a clue."

"About what?"

"See, just like you, I make it my business to do research. I know that you were fired. Is that why you trying to blackmail me? To get your old job back."

This chance encounter could not go wrong. "Domestic, I'm not trying to blackmail you. The only reason I said that is so you would help me." Full of emotion, I managed to muster up some tears. My voice cracked as I spoke. "I'm sorry for what I said, but I need you to help me. Please. I'm begging."

Domestic scratched his head and coughed. "Listen, this is what I'm going to do. I'm going to give you some money for the last time. After this, do not call, text, email, or stop by my damn shop."

"That's fair."

"I know it is. I'll call you in a few days once I collect all the money and you can pick it up."

That was music to my ears. Domestic made me a very happy woman. I was so ecstatic that I couldn't hear any other words that rolled off Domestic's tongue.

Foreign...

Since DP's return, Domestic had quickly turned back into the man I fell in love with. There was no arguing or fighting. That had me sitting on my high horse. As long as DP was in his life, I could see things getting better between us. In all honesty, the beatings didn't start until Casey left.

Domestic had me in a good mood since last night. He took care of me mentally and physically. To feel his warm body against my frame made me melt. To feel him inside of me, stroking me to death, was food to my soul. It was something I wanted and needed. For weeks I'd felt unloved and undesired, but now his actions proved me wrong.

That morning I was able to get up and make breakfast for me and DP. I whipped up some salmon patties, grits, eggs, and biscuits. My unborn child had me hungry as hell. Against Domestic's wishes, I consumed a cup of coffee. It's been a while since I had caffeine and after I drank it, the baby was doing somersaults.

"Calm down, little one." I smiled while rubbing my stomach. "I knew that sugar would have you doing flips."

Motherhood was always something I craved. It was such a joy to have a life growing inside of me. Domestic granted one of my lifelong wishes. All he had to do now was, control his temper. When I decided to be in a relationship with him, ass whoopings were not what I signed up for. Aaron wasn't perfect by a longshot, but he never put his hands on me. The beatings Domestic gave me were far worse than cheating in my eyes. Aaron's jersey that I wore made me teary-eyed when I stared at it. The team was releasing balloons at the cemetery, and I would be in attendance.

Breakfast was done, so I dried my eyes and went up to DP's room. It was about to be a long, sad day and I needed to prepare myself. The last thing I wanted to do was stress out my baby. Loud music was coming from DP's room. I knocked, but there was no answer. So, I took it upon myself to just walk in.

"Hey, I made—"

Midsentence, I stopped dead in my tracks. The view caught me off guard completely. DP had some girl bent over the bed doggy-style. She was moaning and gripping the sheets. My presence startled him.

"Oh shit!" DP pulled out and tried to cover his goods with both hands.

The last thing I wanted to see was DP naked with socks on. That part was funny. Quickly, I turned on my heels and rushed out of his bedroom. Distraught, I ran back downstairs and tried to shake the image of my stepson in action. He was certainly well-endowed like his father.

"That was why the music was up so damn loud," I mumbled. "I can't believe what I just saw."

A few minutes later DP entered the kitchen fully clothed. He stood across from me. "Foreign, I am so sorry you had to see that. I thought I locked the door."

With my head down, I acknowledged him. It was hard to give eye contact. "It's okay. I shouldn't have barged in the way I did."

"Oh, my gosh! I am so embarrassed." The female voice caught my attention. It was the first time I gave full eye contact.

"This is Cheyenne. My girlfriend."

"I'm so sorry." Cheyenne was fully-clothed also.

"It's okay." I couldn't help but notice her beauty.

"Are you going to tell my dad what you saw?" DP asked curiously.

"No. I'm not. We can keep this between us."

"Thanks."

"Sure. I was coming to tell you that I made breakfast, so help yourself."

"Thanks."

"You're welcome. I'm about to head out. I'll see you later."

"Okay."

The cemetery was packed with Aaron's teammates. Everyone in attendance wore his jersey. To my surprise, his parents were not present, but Lexi was there hugged up with Calvin. He was comforting her and drying the tears from her face. Periodically, she would glance in my direction, then look away. That made me feel like she wanted to talk. It was an emotional event, and my tears started to fall. Unlike Lexi, I was there alone. There was no one to wipe my tears.

Aaron's coach stood in the middle of the crowd and gave a heartfelt speech.

"The loss of our brother Aaron has been a reoccurring nightmare. It's like a bad dream I can't wake up from. Over the years I have grown to love Aaron like a son. He was an outgoing man, husband, son, and brother to many of you that are in attendance right now. My heart goes out to his wife—Foreign Young and his twin sister—Alexis. There are no words that I can say to either of you to ease the pain that you are feeling. On behalf of Aaron and the greatness he brought to his team, we will be retiring his jersey. Foreign and Alexis, if there is anything that you need, please do not hesitate to reach out to me or the other teammates personally. You will forever be a part of the Buccaneer family. We love you, Aaron."

One of Aaron's teammates passed the coach three balloons. He took them and continued to speak. "On the count of three, I need everyone to release their balloons. One, two, three."

Everyone let the red balloons fly. "Long live Aaron," the crowd shouted.

The coach waited for everyone to settle down. "In honor of Aaron, we would like to present these two framed jerseys to Foreign and Alexis." Since the funeral, this was the first time Alexis and I shared the same space. We both thanked the coach and separated.

Out of the blue, raindrops began to fall. A few splashed onto my face. Within a matter of seconds, the rain came down harder. One thing about Florida weather: it could be sunny one minute, pour down raining for five minutes and stop. Careful not to fall, I moved quickly across the grass and shuffled to the car as fast as I could. From a distance, I could see Lexi. On my way over, I was hopeful that we could have a conversation since she'd been avoiding my call. There was no way she could ignore a face-to-face. Thanks to the rain, that plan was out of the question. It was okay. Lexi and I would be seeing each other soon enough. In the meantime, it was time for me to go home. My energy was off, and I was tired.

Chapter 19

Domestic

The ordeal with Emilia was finally coming to an end. In a matter of days, she would be out of my life for good. That was one greedy bitch I was sick of. If Emilia would've spent less time preying and fucking on young NFL players, she wouldn't need to flee the state of Florida. Some women insisted on fucking up their lives behind dick.

Back focused on my daily tasks, I logged the receipts for the previous week. Foreign hadn't been helping out in the office, and I fell behind documenting my finances. Our relationship had been rocky for a while, but things had finally cooled down a bit. With DP back in my life, my stress level had been damn near non-existent. He was my one and only child until the arrival of my new baby. We shared a bond unlike no other, and Casey did her best to ruin that.

"Sorry to interrupt."

When I looked up, Tracy was standing at the door. "What's going on?"

"I'm sorry to do this to you, but I need the rest of the day off. The school just called me to pick up my son. He's sick."

"No problem. Do you need to borrow my car?" Tracy wasn't the type to lie about the well-being of her children. She was a very good mother. Therefore, I had no issue with her leaving early or driving my car when in need.

"I appreciate the offer, but my sister is on her way."

"Okay."

"Thanks."

Tracy was about to walk away, but I stopped her. "Wait."

"Yeah," she replied.

"I want to apologize to you about the other day and the way I spoke to you. I was going through some heavy shit and you received some of that backlash."

For the first time in days, Tracy smiled. "It's okay. I understand."

"No. It's not okay. I shouldn't have spoken to you that way."

"You right. You shouldn't have. It's all good."

"We good?" I needed to be sure.

"Of course we are," she laughed. "I know you can be a grumpy old man at times."

"This old man has a lot of stamina too," I chuckled.

146

"I guess, chile. Bye!" Tracy laughed as she walked away.

"See you tomorrow."

Now I had to get ready and run the front for a few hours. It was cool, though. The day was going to be breezy. I locked my computer and closed the office door. "Alright, time to get to work."

Tracy's area was well-kept. Photos of her kids were present. Her presence was certainly there in her absence. If that motivated Tracy to keep her job, that was fine by me. The door opened and in walked a regular customer of mine.

"Hey, Demerius."

"Hey, Ms. Pam. How are you?" Pam was a seasoned woman in her late fifties that came in often for her weekly wash. Her body looked better than some of the young shit that slid through here. If I wasn't too young in her eyes, she could get it.

"I'm doing good. I can't complain. How about you?"

"Same ole. Just working to take care of the family."

"I hear that. Tracy has you working today, I see."

"She did a half-day."

"Oh, okay."

"What did you get? The usual."

"Yes. I had my backseat cleaned also. My grandson left his gum behind."

"You let him eat that in your car?" I knew how much she took pride in her brand new Cadillac.

"His badass snuck and ate it while I was driving." Pamela laughed. "Don't worry, his daddy paying for this. How much do I owe you?"

"Forty-five." Pam handed me a fifty-dollar bill. "Let me get your change."

"No. Keep it."

"Who washed it so I can give the tip to him?"

"I gave Tony a tip already."

"Okay. I'll just leave it for Tracy."

"Tell her I asked about her."

"Will do. Have a good day."

"You too."

The flat screen television displayed breaking news on channel 8. Neighborhood crime wasn't a shocker in some Tampa Bay areas, but the scene unfolding before my eyes angered me. Clear as day, I watched Foreign shedding tears, as she accepted Aaron's framed jersey from his coach.

"This bitch," I mumbled.

It was a slap in the face to see Foreign crying on national television once again. For the life of me, I couldn't understand why she felt like she could try me once again. Nodding, I cracked my knuckles. This bitch was gon' pay for embarrassing me. In my eyes, it was like she didn't consider my feelings at all. I was so mad that I couldn't stay at work another second.

The tires on the Bentley screeched, as I pulled out of the parking lot. My blood was boiling. I was ready to put my foot all up in her ass. A week hadn't passed since I explained my expectations, and she was already spitting in my face. Foreign was about to learn today. It didn't take a rocket scientist to realize she was acting out on behalf of my mother's visit. Foreign needed to know she could never disrespect me like that and get away with it. That was the last bitch I needed her to see. Veronica managed to cause strife in my family with a brief five-minute visit.

After entering my home, I immediately made my way to DP's bedroom. We hadn't spoken all day, so I needed to check on him. Instead of busting in his room, I decided to knock. "DP."

"It's open."

DP and Cheyenne were lying on the bed playing the PS4. Based on their laughter, the couple was enjoying themselves. It was cute.

"What's up, pops?" DP never took his eyes off the game.

"Hey, pops." Cheyenne smiled, but her attention was elsewhere too.

"Tired as hell. What y'all ate?"

"Foreign cooked breakfast earlier. We only had junk food after that."

Slipping my hand into my pocket, I pulled out the fifteen-hundred dollars I separated earlier, and waved it in his face. Instantly, I had his attention. All I could see were the gold train tracks in his mouth. "Take this and go to the mall and dinner."

DP dropped the controller on the bed. "I get the Bentley too?" he asked with sheer excitement in his voice. My son missed his life of privilege. That was something Casey couldn't spoil him with, and she knew that.

"Yeah." I tossed him the keys. "Enjoy."

"We will, Pops." DP stood up. "Come on, bae. Let's go. I can beat you later," he laughed.

"You wish." Cheyenne dropped her controller and crawled from the bed. "Watch how I spank you when we get back."

"We'll see about that."

"Come on 'cause I'm starving." Cheyenne led the way.

Their young love was a reminder of me and Casey at that age. We truly thought we were in love. No one could tell us shit.

From upstairs, I could hear the door close. That was my cue to handle my business. Foreign was asleep when I entered the bedroom. There was some snoring, but not too loud.

"Ya ass must be tired from lying to me and being disobedient," I mumbled while closing the door.

Sitting down on the side of the bed, I stroked her face gently. The love I had for this woman was crazy. It made me feel demented at times. Every wrong move she made had me wanting to snap. Granted, I didn't enjoy it. I just needed her to understand that we were together *forever*, and the only way out was death. Nobody was going to love and cherish Foreign the way I did. They could try, but that would result in a nasty death for whoever. No matter who it was.

Slowly, I pulled the comforter down. The sight of Aaron's jersey took me out of my body. Filled with rage, I wrapped my hands around her throat and squeezed.

"Wake yo' ass up," I shouted.

Foreign snapped out of her dream and gasped. Her hands were now on top of mine. She was trying to move my hands. Fear was evident in her eyes, so were misty tears.

"See, this is what you make me do to you. Why the fuck you wearing this nigga jersey? Do I look like a fuck nigga to you? You think you can do what you want?" Foreign shook her head, by way of saying no, repeatedly. I could feel her nails seep into my flesh. That shit stung, but I wasn't letting go.

"Why do you keep doing this to me? Do you love to see me act out?" Slightly, I eased my grip so she could respond. "Answer me."

"Just let me go," she panted.

"Answer me."

"Domestic, please," she panted. "You promised not to hurt me anymore. I'm going to lose the baby if you don't stop." I listened to her beg repeatedly for me to stop.

Foreign was trying to persuade me by using reverse psychology to keep me off of her ass. Miraculously, it worked. The thought of hurting my unborn child made me release the grip I had on her neck. Foreign turned on her side and exhaled loudly. She was relieved.

The sight in front of me still had me disgusted. "Take that off."

Foreign squinted, displaying a slight frown. "Take what off?"

"Don't play dumb with me." I couldn't stand for a person to play on my intelligence.

"I'm not. What are you talking about?"

"Girl," I rubbed the top of my head in a circle and yelled. "Take off that fuckin' jersey and now!"

"You're mad about a jersey?"

"You goddamn right. That's disrespectful as fuck."

"Domestic, that's stupid. I went to his balloon release. What is the problem?"

"Oh, I can name a few problems. You didn't ask permission to go. Nor did you stop and think how that would make me feel, as your man. Then you have the nerve to parade around in his jersey like it's all good. It's like you rubbing it in my face."

"Domestic, all of that is crazy. I'm an adult. I don't need permission to go anywhere. And I'm entitled to grieve. I don't see what the problem is. I was with that man since high school."

"That's funny. You didn't feel that way when he was out here fucking everything moving and ramming bitches in they pussies with cucumbers."

"Wow! That was low. Even for you," she hissed.

Foreign tried to walk away from me, but I snatched her by that whack ass jersey she was wearing. I was surprised when she spun around and slapped me in the face with the palm of her hand. Roughly, I pushed her onto the bed and straddled her legs. Foreign took swings at me. That was her first time fighting back. Maybe she was getting tired.

Forcefully, I grabbed the bottom of the jersey to remove it physically. The fight continued. Foreign fought desperately to stop me. She was no match compared to my strength, as it slid over her head.

"You wanna be disrespectful. I'll show you the ultimate disrespect." I walked into the bathroom and retrieved the metal garbage can. Standing at the door, I set fire to the jersey and tossed it in the trash.

Foreign sat on the bed and cried, like I gave a fuck!

Foreign...

Domestic was the epitome of *evil* in my eyes. He didn't love me. All he wanted was control, and to make me feel bad for grieving my husband. On so many levels it was my fault. Out the gate, this man showed me who he was. Not once did he hide it. My fading marriage caused me to become blind and vulnerable. One of my biggest regrets was, trying to get back at Aaron by dealing with Domestic. I should've followed my heart and taken time out for myself to figure out what I truly wanted. Now I was stuck with this deranged, psychopathic, and controlling human. I felt trapped.

To see him smile, as he burned Aaron's jersey, broke my heart. Domestic was cruel and heartless. He was not the man I thought he was. I was fooled.

"Don't leave this house." Crazy ass left the room with the trash can in his hand after putting out the fire. Then I heard the door slam.

Jumping to my feet, I ran and locked the door. I didn't want him anywhere near me. Here I was, stuck in this hell hole with no one to talk to. It was a shot in the dark, but I grabbed my phone and called Lexi. She was the only person I talked to. Our bond was too strong for it to be over indefinitely. My heart sunk to the pit of my stomach when I heard the voicemail.

There was no one to run to. Lexi and I were so content with each other that we only hung with each other. Back then, all I needed was Aaron and Lexi, outside of my family.

My closest family members resided in Fort Lauderdale, but we weren't close at all. They lived a completely different lifestyle from what I was used to. My father kept me away from his side of the family because his daughters and nephew was into the street life too heavy and didn't want me exposed. Funny how things were playing out right now. If I would've hung with them more, I would have the strength to handle Domestic on my own.

Now, for the first time since a child, I felt like an outcast. A black sheep. Life was sad at that moment, and I didn't know how I was going to deal with this shit alone. My overly sensitive ass just sat there and cried, while scrolling through my phone at people I couldn't depend on. Determined not to give up, I called Lexi back and left her a voicemail message.

Chapter 20

Lexi

"Oh my goodness," I snapped. "Why does this bitch keep calling me. Like damn, I legit don't fuck with you no more, so stop it already."

This bitch was pissing me off. I swear I wanted to pull up and fight her. The shit she did to my brother was unforgivable. I was cool with her getting outside dick. She could've divorced him too because that was her right. Aaron did shit to her that I would've never forgiven my man for. Therefore, I understood her pain.

Foreign first crossed the line when she was laid up with that nigga in my brother's house, but I forgave her because he did the same thing before they got married. The stunt that put the nail in the coffin on our sisterhood was her bringing that buff ass bastard to my brother's funeral. It was the ultimate disrespect. I just couldn't forgive her for that. It made me feel like my twin was run off that road purposely.

Calvin walked into the room with no shirt on with his sweaty, sexy ass. "What the hell you in here hooting and hollering for girl?"

"First of all," I laughed. "What the hell is *hooting and hollering*? I've heard that most of my life and as an adult, I don't know what the hell that means."

"Shit, me either. My granny used to say that shot all the time." He flopped down on the bed.

"Eww, get your sweaty ass up. I don't want to sleep on no musty ass sheets." I pushed him away.

Calvin made his chest jump. "I look good, don't I?"

"You still musty."

"Whateva! So who you cursing out?"

"Foreign. She keeps calling and now she done left a message on my voicemail. This shit aggravating. I'm about to block her number. That will put an end to all of this shit."

Calvin snatched the phone out of my hand. "Don't do that."

"Why not? We're not friends anymore," I spat.

"That's because y'all relationship is deeper than that. You and that girl are like sisters. I've never seen a bond so tight between females with no beef involved. I know you miss her."

No lies were detected, but I was mad and hurt. "Okay, I'll admit it. I do love Foreign like a sister, but my loyalty lies with my brother."

Calvin grabbed my hand. "Listen, bae, I get that, but you need to stop acting so stubborn and bullheaded. Aaron is gone. He's never coming back. Your brother caused that rift between him and Foreign. No matter what she did to keep him happy, he still cheated on her and did that girl dirty. We both know that, so stop being so hard on her."

This nigga was fucking with my emotions big time. Thoughts of Aaron surfaced in my mind, and I started to drown in my tears. Calvin held me tight. "I miss my brother so much. Life is not fair, man. I swear it ain't."

"You have me. Like I told you before, we'll get through this together and I mean that. I know you didn't want a relationship, but we're in one. There's no ifs, ands, or buts about it. Do you understand that?"

In between my sobs, I managed to reply. "Calvin, you're a male whore just like Aaron. I'll be crazy to think that you'll be faithful to me. You and my brother ran together, so I know what time it is when it comes to these thirsty ass groupies. This is not to be a rerun of Aaron and Foreign's story."

"I'm not going to do anything to hurt you and I promised Aaron that I would always take care of you. I've had my share of women and to be honest, I'm tired. I just want one woman and that's you. See the difference with us is that we had an understanding. You let me do me and I let you do you."

"Oh, really?"

"Real shit. I know all about your hookups with Twan. It didn't faze me because I knew where we stood. But now all of that shit is out of my system and yours too."

"How do you know?" There was so much sarcasm in my tone. He needed to tell me how he knew I was done playing the field with these no good ass NFL players.

"You moved in with me. The old Lexi would've never done that. You have money and can easily buy a house, condo, or penthouse, but you're here with me. That speaks volumes to me."

Look at this nigga trying to break me down like a fraction. Truth be told, I had a lot of love for Calvin. He always treated me with respect. Although we were fuck buddies, he never disrespected me in my face. Calvin kept his composure with the random thots whenever I was in the same vicinity as him.

"Aww, this nigga has a heart."

Calvin pushed me away. "See, you play too much, ole big head ass," he laughed. "I'm trying to be serious right now."

"I know. I'm just fucking with you."

"On a serious note, I'm not going to do anything to hurt you and I promised Aaron that I would always take care of you. My whorish ways are behind me. I swear. Can I get the chance to prove that to you?"

Nodding, I agreed. "Yes. And I'm telling you now, don't fucking play with me. I'll make your ass disappear, and the bitch you cheat with." There wasn't a single smile on my face. I was dead ass serious.

Calvin covered his mouth while he laughed hysterically. "I swear you don't have to worry about that. I'm done fucking these random hoes. All they want to do is extort a nigga and blow up his spot. I need a solid woman on my team, and that's you."

"Okay. We'll see." There was some heavy shit laying on my heart, and I needed to address it. I took a deep breath and looked into Calvin's eyes. "I need to be honest with you about something and I need you to take me serious about it."

"What is it?"

"The reason I can't forgive Foreign is that I think—" The words wouldn't leave my mouth. Maybe it was because I didn't believe what I was about to say. I sat there quietly.

Calvin hit me with that infamous side eye. "What?"

"What if Foreign had something to do with his death?" It sounded crazy once I said it.

It had to sound crazy in Calvin's ears. His eyebrows were now slanted. "You can't be serious right now."

"I am."

"Come on, Lex, you know she's not like that. Foreign loved Aaron to death. That girl wouldn't do no shit like that."

"That's true, but her new boyfriend is some thug ass nigga. That's not her type. What if he put her up to it."

"Do you know how crazy that sounds? I'm not about to believe she had anything to do with that. Besides, his death was an accident." Calvin refused to agree with me. "Before he died, Aaron told me that Foreign decided to work on the marriage."

That was new to me. I wasn't aware of that. "Okay," I hesitated. "If that's the case, what if he was aware of that and wanted Foreign to himself? But the only way to have her was to get rid of my brother?"

"Baby, that sounds crazy. You have to stop watching that crazy murder mystery shit on T.V."

This man wasn't taking me seriously at all. "You think I'm crazy, don't you?"

"No. I think you're overly obsessive with your brother's death. You don't want to accept that it was fate. Aaron's time on earth was up. He succeeded in everything and now it's time for him to rest."

Pouting, I folded my arms and sucked my teeth. "I'm not about to believe that a random car forced my brother off the road."

"Who said it was forced? It was an accident. Again, you watch too many murder shows."

"I'll prove it. Just watch." It didn't matter what I had to do, but I wasn't about to rest until I found the answer to this mysterious accident. My brother needed to rest in peace. That wasn't going to happen until his killer was brought to justice. And that included his wife too.

Calvin left me alone in the room. I played back the message Foreign left on my voicemail.

"Lexi, I know you're upset with me and I'm sorry for the way things went down between us. You have to know that I loved Aaron. I still do and I miss him so much. Before he died, I took him back so we could work on our marriage. A few days later, he was dead. Another thing you should know is that I didn't invite him to Aaron's funeral. I told him it was a bad idea for him to show up, but he didn't care. It's like he had this weird obsession with Aaron."

I could hear her crying.

"Things are really bad and I need you. This man is crazy and abusive. He just burned Aaron's jersey right in my face. Lexi, you're my only friend. Please call me back."

After listening to her message, all I could do was sit and stare at the wall. I guess the grass wasn't greener on the other side. If she knew like I knew, she'll pack up and leave that nigga. I drove past Aaron's house and she hadn't been staying there at all. The grass was unkempt, and that wasn't normal. She would've never let that happen if she still resided there.

Domestic…

Devious thoughts ran through my mind, as I raced through the streets with no destination sought out. In the passenger seat was someone I could depend on: Hennessey. This bitch never let me down under any circumstances.

Imagine giving someone everything they needed just for them to give their ass to kiss in return. That was the way I felt about the woman I shared my bed with. Foreign hurt me, and now it was time to return the favor. With a new mission on my mind, I made my way to the wash.

When I pulled up, I spotted a car parked in front of the door. Then I realized whoever was there was on the inside. The lobby lights were on. I parked behind the car and grabbed my heat.

"I see somebody wanna die tonight."

With my ratchet aimed at arm's length, I walked inside. At first, I didn't see anyone, so I walked down the hall, towards the bathroom. The door opened. I kept my gun pointed, prepared to pull the trigger on the perpetrator. Tracy stepped out. Her eyes were wide and her hands were up.

"Domestic, it's just me. Put that thing away."

I lowered my arm. "What the hell you doing in here this time of night?"

"Me and my baby daddy got into a fight and I left the house. I needed someplace to crash for the night, so I came here." She wasn't lying 'cause the bruise on her face was evident.

"You came here because you thought this was the hotel?"

"No. I don't have money for a hotel." Tracy was whining and I wasn't in the mood to scold her about the actions she took.

"It's late and I'm not going to get into all the reasons why this is wrong on so many levels. Instead, I'm going to give you the money so you can get a good night's sleep and a proper shower."

"You would do that for me?"

"Haven't I helped you before?"

"Yeah." Tracy exhaled and rubbed the top of her head. "Thanks. I appreciate you for this."

"You need to get rid of that nigga."

"I'm trying to, but he won't leave."

"I can help you with that."

"Let me think about that and get back to you."

"You do that." I pulled two hundred dollars from my pocket and held them up for Tracy to see. "In the meantime, you know what you have to do for this money."

Tracy took the gum out of her mouth and dropped to her knees. She opened my zipper and freed my semi-limp member. My dick reached its full length as soon as I felt the inside of her warm mouth. Sloppy toppy was just what I needed after the day I had. With my back against the wall, I closed my eyes and allowed Tracy to erase those upsetting memories.

Our little rendezvous came to an end and I was pleased, to say the least. Tracy had the suction like a vacuum cleaner, so it didn't take that long for me to bust. I zipped up my pants and gave Tracy the two hundred dollars. "What time will you be in tomorrow?"

"I'll be here at nine since I left early today."

"Alright."

Once I escorted Tracy out the door, I went into the storage room and took out a gas can, along with a box of matches. It was half full, so I didn't need to go to the gas station. On my way out the door, I set the alarm and locked up the business.

Foreign thought she saw evil today, but it was nothing compared to the fire that I was about to start. In deep thought, I cruised the streets, doing thirty-five miles per hour. For one, I didn't want the gasoline to spill in my fine, foreign whip. Secondly, I wasn't in a rush to get it done. And thirdly, I didn't need to be stopped by the police.

While sipping from my cup, I bopped my head to JT Money's album, *Return of the Bitchizer*. That shit was a classic. It took me back to my early days of hustling. A nigga or a bitch couldn't tell me shit. I was the man in the streets. The mob stood behind me, so the beef was non-existent. That meant I was untouchable.

"I used to be a nigga every day out on da block, socks full of rocks dogging da muthafuckin cops. Now I was just a jit, but I was down wit' da set. Used da have da fattest shit so dem basers used ta sweat."

My car shifted into the right lane, so I could make the turn into my destination. It was dark as hell, but it didn't affect my vision. Determination had me ready to finish my mission. With the gas can in my hand and matches in the other, I shuffled through the grass until I found the spot I was looking for. I sat the can down at my feet and smiled.

"What's up, pussy nigga? Your old wife is my new wife and she carrying my child. That was something you could never pull off. I hope the maggots tearing your ass up. While you down there rotting away, I'll be up here fucking the air outta Foreign and making her forget all about you."

The rest of the world was grieving Aaron, but not me. I hated that nigga with a passion, in life and death. Standing over his grave, I whipped my dick out and pissed all over it. "This how I feel about yo' low down ass. These muthafuckas act like you were a saint or some shit. Not me, I always saw you as a lame-ass nigga that couldn't keep his wife satisfied."

Now that I was done relieving myself, I picked up the gas can and poured gasoline on his grave. Taking a step back, I lit a match and dropped it. That blaze was fierce and aggressive. "Goodnight, bitch."

Feeling good, I walked off smiling. Just call me the fireman because of the way I just got shit started. "I'm the Fireman, Fire, Fireman, I got that fire, I'm hollin', I got that fire, come and try me, and you can spark it up and I'ma put you out. You can spark it up and I'ma put you out."

Cars drove past the cemetery as I exited the premises. No one paid the fire any attention. Hopefully, it stayed that way for a little while longer. Before I went home I decided to swing by and check on Casey. She had been there for two days, so I was certain she was thirsty by now.

Chapter 21

Foreign

It was two in the morning when I heard Domestic jiggling the knob on the door. That demon spawn was the last thing I wanted to see, let alone share a bed with. For five minutes, I listened to him struggle until he finally got inside the room. Earlier, I placed a knife underneath the pillow just in case he tried to fight me again. This was not the life I wanted for me or my child. Therefore, I had to make plans to get away from Domestic. If not, he was going to end up killing me.

When I was a small child, my cousins and I would play dead during a game of cops and robbers. I was damn good at it, so that came in handy. The door closed and I could hear the shower running. Prayers were needed for myself and Domestic. I prayed he didn't kill me and I didn't kill him. Ass whoopings weren't something I was used to receiving.

A few minutes later, Domestic crawled into the bed. Once again, I prayed that he didn't touch me. That prayer went unanswered. There was a lot of movement behind me. His hand inched slowly up the nightgown I was wearing. It made my skin crawl. But I wasn't about to stop him, so I remained silent as if I was sleeping.

Sex was the furthest thing from my mind, but much closer in Domestic's brain. Despite me being uncooperative at rolling onto my back, Domestic found a way to creep into my insides. Disappointed he was getting his way, I laid on my side and made faces in the dark. Lazy side booty was all he was getting.

After a few minutes, Domestic climbed on top of me and kept going. Feverishly, he pumped in and out of my semi-dry vagina. It was uncomfortable as hell. Not one moan escaped my lips. All I wanted was for him to hurry up and catch his nut so I could go to bed.

Domestic leaned closer to me and kissed my face. Then he used his tongue to lick my neck before sucking on it. My juices started to flow. Now he was able to glide freely. That pissed me the fuck off. I just wanted him to stop. Crying and complaining wasn't going to solve the problem, so I closed my eyes and pretended I was somewhere else. Finally, he stopped. When I looked at the clock it was a quarter after three.

"I love you baby, both of y'all."

Domestic cuddled up beside me with his hand resting on my stomach. "I just want us to be a happy family. Is that too much to ask?"

160

"No."

That was the only thing Domestic said before falling asleep with me in his arms. Oh boy, this was about to be a long-ass night. No, I didn't want to cuddle. I just wanted to be left alone completely.

The following morning, I woke up with a better state of mind. I had all night to think and come up with a solution to my happiness. The shower was running, so I made my way into the bathroom. Quickly, I removed my clothes and stepped inside.

Domestic smiled and put his arm around my waist. "I see someone is in a good mood today."

"I am." I rested my head upon his chest. "I'm tired of arguing and fighting, baby. I just want to be happy. Is that too much to ask for?" My ass hit him with the same line he hit me with just hours ago.

"No. That's all I want to do."

"Well, do that and stop making my life a living hell. I'm carrying your baby. You should be more concerned about our well-being."

"You're right. I'm sorry." Domestic raised my chin so I could look into his eyes. "Will you please forgive me?"

"Yes, but you have to change."

"I will," he promised.

The look in his eyes said he was sincere, but I've been with him long enough to know better. However, I agreed. "Okay." Slowly, I leaned towards Domestic and kissed his lips. Careful not to slip, I got down on my knees to please him.

For one hour, I had mind-blowing, passionate sex with Domestic. It reminded me of the very first night he and I fucked in his office when I was on that drunk shit. On my part, all of the theatrics were included. He needed to know that he had me fully and that I wanted and needed him for satisfaction and happiness. When it was all over, we both got dressed.

"Where are you going?" he asked with a raised brow.

"First, I'm going to check out some baby furniture. Then I'm making a stop by the bridal shop. It's time that I check out some wedding colors."

"It's about time. I was starting to think you didn't want to be my wife."

"Of course not." My smile was bright and wide as the sun. "I just felt we needed to talk first and we did. Now we can move forward."

There was a knock on the door.

"Come in," he answered.

DP walked into the room. Something was wrong. He had a serious look on his face. Maybe scared for that matter. "I can't find my mom. I've been calling and her phone is going straight to the voicemail."

"She hasn't called me. I'm sure she's with her boyfriend."

"He's been trying to call her too. He hasn't seen her in three days." DP grew more frantic by the second. "You have to find her, dad, please."

Watching that boy plead for his mama broke my heart. He truly loved her. Domestic hugged his son. "I'll find her. I promise."

Fifteen minutes later, I was out of the house and ready to get in the streets. It felt so good to get out of that place. Domestic made me feel like a damn prisoner. This dude thought he was slicker than oil, but I outslicked his ass that day. I gave that nigga some TLC and he freed me. Silly me, I should've been thought of that shit. Inside the car, I fired up my engine and let it run while punching in the address. According to the map, I was forty-five minutes away.

Prepared for my next move, I backed out of the driveway and turned on the radio. Radio stations reminded me of a church. They loved to play sad music that fucked with your mental state. Out of all songs, they chose "Missing You" by Mary J. Blige. I was in my feelings immediately. All I could think about was Aaron. At the time of his passing, I was upset because of all of the shit Emilia revealed to me. I was grateful for our great conversation and bomb-ass lovemaking before he perished. Aaron was on one that night 'cause he had me stretched the fuck out. Reliving that moment made me smile. We had a lot of good memories, but we also had many bad ones. More than I would like to count.

Tired of being in my feelings, I switched up the flow. Trap music was up next. I had to stop feeling sorry for myself behind the foolish choices that I'd made. Not getting to know Domestic was my biggest mistake. To make matters worse, I ignored the warning from Casey. Sis tried to tell me that things would get worse. My ass was too hooked on the dick to see straight. That was my fault. I could own that. Hell, I'm human.

As I drove into the secluded neighborhood, I realized it was an area I had never seen before. The last road on the street took me to a long stretch of a gravel road. At the end of the road, a cabin-like home sat all alone.

"This looks like a scary house from *Jeepers Creepers*." A nervous ball of fear invaded my stomach. Ignoring it, I got out of the car and knocked on the door.

A tall and chocolate dude stepped into the frame, flashing those beautiful white teeth. "Wow! I never thought I would hear from the charismatic woman that caught my attention months ago."

"Neither did I. Thanks for not ignoring me."

"Ignoring you is not possible." Maurice stepped to the side and extended his arm. "Come on in."

Over time, I had forgotten how fine this man was. That was a thing of the past. Although I didn't know him, it felt good to be accepted by someone. I was hopeful that Maurice was the solution to my problems. Fingers crossed!

Shawn...

"Bruh, I been calling this girl for the longest and her phone keeps going to the damn voicemail." I punched the steering wheel.

"Chill, bruh! Maybe she just needed some time to cool off. You already know how she feels about you being in the streets with me." Tim fired up the blunt and passed it to me.

"Nah, I'm good on that."

"Fine with me," he laughed. "Ion like sharing my shit anyway. A nigga was just trying to be courteous and shit."

Bro was buggin'. I couldn't do shit but laugh. "You stupid dawg."

"Real shit, bro. You eat pussy and probably ass too. I don't need none of that shit on my lips. Real spill in the battlefield."

"Man, shut up, bro. You eat the same shit I eat."

Tim bobbed his head up and down while pulling on the blunt. "True, but this my shit tho'. I can leave all that shit behind."

"You a nasty nigga. Mama and daddy must've found you by the garbage can."

"That's cool 'cause yo' ass adopted."

"Whatever, nigga," I laughed and pulled out of the gas station.

"On the real tho'. Do you think she with that fifty-cent looking nigga?"

"Nah. She can't stand that nigga."

"I think that—" Tim paused and stared at the traffic ahead of us.

"You think what?" He didn't respond, so I repeated my question once more. "You think what?"

"I think that's the nigga that killed Craig. Follow that Mustang, bro and don't lose him."

Without taking a second look at traffic, I pulled out in front of the on-coming cars. I wasn't worried about an accident. My concern was catching my brother's killer. Pushing seventy miles per hour, I zipped through traffic and caught up to the vehicle. The sound of the motor could be heard growling.

"That's the car, bro. I'm telling you."

"I'm on his ass, don't worry." I was determined to catch the nigga responsible for breaking up my family.

The engine growled louder as the Mustang accelerated on the gas, zipping between cars. That didn't deter or cause me to lose him. Less than one hundred yards away from the intersection, the light turned red and the Mustang came to a complete stop. And so did I.

We sat still for a good three minutes before taking off and hooking a quick right beside the gas station. Careful not to be seen, I followed him but kept my distance. The Mustang pulled up to a house and got out. Tim climbed over the back seat and rolled down the window. Just as the shooter was walking up to the porch, he stopped and turned towards the road, wielding a gun. Tim let off multiple rounds, so did the shooter. It was an all-out gun battle. A few bullets could be heard slamming against the car frame.

"Go, bruh! Pull off," Tim shouted in a panic. And I did just that, tires screeching and all.

Casey...

Domestic had me locked inside this damn shed for days, and I was over being tied up like a damn dog. It was dark and hot. Thank God no bugs or rodents were running around. Last night he brought his trifling ass in and gave me some water. My life with him had gone from bad to worse. All I kept thinking about was my son. I wasn't ready to die just yet, but somehow I had a feeling that Domestic wasn't about to let me go. In the event he did, I was going straight to Tiffany's house. She had some explaining to do. That was my last location before I woke up in captivity.

Tears started to stream down my face. I missed Shawn so much. This was the longest we'd been apart in months. Every night, I prayed that he would find me. It made me wonder if he bothered to look for me. Unless he felt that I left because I was mad at him.

"God please get me out of here," I sobbed. "I don't want to die."

No sooner had I stopped praying than the door opened and in walked Domestic. He had a scary smirk on his face. "What's up, BM? How you doing?"

"Better if you would let me go."

"Humph! That would be your request." He closed the door behind him.

"Domestic, why are you keeping me here?"

"Why did you take my son away from me?" He walked up to me and grabbed me by the neck. "You know my son is my reason for living and doing the right thing."

"Kidnapping his mother is doing the right thing?" Domestic backhanded me. *Whap!*

"Shut the fuck up!" he barked.

A strong tingling sensation filled my face. It stung like hell. "I know you're mad at me, but you can't do this. If you kill me, who's going to take care of our son?"

"Who said I'm getting caught?" Domestic leaned closer to my face. "I'm going to bury you so deep that they'll never find your body."

Fear pierced my heart. I knew he meant every word. It wouldn't be the first time he murdered someone and got away with it. "Domestic, please don't do this." My bottom lip quivered, as I begged for my life. "I still love you. I always will. Just forgive me for everything I've done."

"Casey, save that shit for judgment day. I'm sure God will listen when you talk. I'm not listening."

I cried harder when he ignored my pleas.

Domestic's phone rang. He looked at the screen and pulled his gun out. Aimed at me, he spoke harshly. "Say one word and I'll blow your mutha-fuckin head off."

"Hello," he answered almost right away. Based on the content of the phone call, I knew it was DP. The next sentence was confirmation. "I'm going to find her, I promise."

Domestic hung up the phone and put his gun away. "Good girl."

Seconds later, he untied me. "Are you letting me go?"

"Our son just saved your life." He sounded like he was disappointed, but I didn't care.

A bitch was relieved to hear he was setting me free. I just knew I was going to be on Cold Case Files. The Lord answered my prayers, and I was forever grateful. Domestic snatched me up by the collar and breathed heavily in my face.

"I'm letting you live for now. Try me one more time and your ass is dead."

"I won't," I promised.

"After you leave here I don't give a fuck where you go. Just know that my son is not going. You and Shawn can ride off into the sunset, or to the depths of hell, but my son is staying here with me. You got that?"

"Yes." I nodded.

"Good. Let's go."

Domestic drove me to the nearest shopping plaza and put me out of the car. The location didn't matter to me. My ass was just happy to be alive. Quickly, I dialed Shawn's number so he could pick me up. There was a new sense of urgency. We needed to get out of dodge as soon as the funeral was over.

Chapter 22

Domestic

Saturday rolled around fairly quickly. It was a night that I dreaded for so long. Being around Veronica was the last thing I wanted to do on earth. I would rather rip my toenails off one by one and end up with a nasty, painful fungus. Veronica could be a very irrational woman. That was the reason I chose to suck it up and attend her birthday party. Fortunate for me, I had Foreign to keep me company.

"Babe, you almost ready?" I stood in the mirror brushing my waves. My cut was fresh, and the kid was looking mighty dapper.

"Not yet," Foreign yelled from the bedroom.

Women were the slowest creatures in the human race. No matter how much of a head start they receive, they'll never beat a man getting dressed.

Foreign was struggling to fix her dress when I entered the frame leading into the bedroom. It was funny, so I had to laugh. "You okay over there?"

"I need you to help me zip up this dress."

"I got you, baby, turn around." The long, sleek black dress clung to her hips and waist. Pregnant or not, she was fine as hell. I loved the way the baby was filling her out in all the right places.

Foreign's skin glowed. She was flawless without any make-up. I couldn't keep my hands off of her. Placing my lips on her neck, I kissed her gently. "I'm tempted to snatch this dress off of you right now."

"I'm tempted to let you do it, but we have to go."

"Yeah. We have to be on time. Veronica is a certified bitch when it comes to promptness. Bad enough I don't want to go in the first place."

"Then why are we going?"

"If I don't go, she'll keep popping up in my life and I don't need that. It's best if I just suck up being present for a few hours. After this circus is over, I can go on about my business."

"Well, I'm here to support you."

"About that," I paused and rubbed my temple. "Steer clear of Veronica. She's nothing like you and honestly, I don't want y'all communicating."

"So, I'm supposed to ignore her?"

There was a little sarcasm in her response, but I let that slide.

"No. Just keep the conversation simple. That's it. You and Veronica are not about to be the best of friends. I don't want you around that woman.

We've already discussed my relationship with her and it's not a good one. You witnessed that with your very own pretty eyes."

"Yeah, I know. Got it. Keep my distance and smile for the camera." Foreign sat down on the bed and slipped on her heels.

"Thank you. That's all I require from you tonight."

Foreign stood up and smiled. "Okay."

I kissed her on the cheek and escorted her out of the room. On our way out, I stopped by DP's room to inform him that we were leaving.

Being the distinguished gentleman that I was, I opened the door for my love. Chivalry wasn't dead at all in my books. Foreign put on her seatbelt and I closed the door. Climbing inside, I put on some nineties R&B music. My baby sat pretty in the passenger seat and sang so sweetly. Once three songs played, I had to interrupt her. I turned down the music and glanced in her direction.

"How are you feeling these days?"

"I'm fine."

"Would you say that things are good between us?"

Foreign hesitated before responding. "In this present moment, we're okay. Things between us can be a lot better, but that's going to take some hard work."

"Before or after the wedding?"

"That needs to happen before we do that. I've been down that road before and I think we should tackle the problem before we walk down anyone's aisle. There are things that you've gone through that need to be addressed."

Foreign's comment threw me for a loop. Just the other day she went by the bridal shop. Now, it seemed as if she was having second thoughts. "So what you're saying is you don't want to get married?"

"I'm saying I want you to get help first. The grudge you have against your mother is affecting the way you treat me."

"So you're diagnosing me with mommy issues?"

"All I'm saying is, you need to talk to someone. You were abused as a child and you've conflicted that same pain onto Casey and now me. You have to break that curse if you want our relationship to flourish. If not, our relationship doesn't stand a chance."

The truth hurt like a million paper cuts. No one ever called me out on my shit until now. One thing I could say about Foreign, she was going to voice her opinion no matter what the consequences were. I nodded. "I hear you."

"You hear me or do you understand me?"

"I hear you."

"Okay." Foreign turned the volume up on the radio and glanced out the window.

Foreign...

Domestic was the biggest jackass I've met in my entire life. He didn't take anything I said into consideration. Nor did he take my words seriously. It was going to take my absence to make him see the light. The first step to recovery was admitting he had a problem. Domestic couldn't see that with a magnifying glass.

To keep him from flying off the handle, I ended the conversation. There was nothing left to discuss. For the remainder of the ride, I stared out the window and thought back to the time I spent with Maurice. Talking to him was like a breath of fresh air. He allowed me to vent without judgment. As I thought back to the night we met, he was probably the one I should've chosen versus the mental patient I was with.

Domestic pulled up to a massive mansion. It was breathtaking. I didn't know what his mother did for a living, but she had real money. The valet approached the car and opened both doors.

"Good evening, ma'am."

"Good evening." He took my hand and escorted me out to the walkway. Domestic stood beside me and grabbed my hand. "I hope you're ready."

"Ready or not, we're here." We held hands and walked through the double glass doors.

The inside of the house was exquisite. The outside did no justice to what I was looking at. Veronica had great taste when it came down to the décor. Expensive paintings clung to the walls, along with the crystal chandeliers. However, there wasn't a single family photo in sight. That was pretty strange to me, but oh well. I like to mind my own business.

"This house is stunning," I beamed with a smile. "What does your mom do for a living?"

"She married rich," he said dryly.

"Oh, really?"

"Her husband is a very powerful man."

"I see." It was obvious that Domestic didn't want to answer any questions, so I left it alone.

As we maneuvered through the crowd, Domestic hugged and pop-kissed women on the cheek. It didn't bother me, not one bit. In the middle of the crowd, we bumped into his mother. The infamous Veronica. I was so intrigued by this woman's power. She had me low key hating on how she controlled Domestic with no effort. Damn, I wished I had it like that!

Veronica kissed me on both cheeks. "Good evening, gorgeous."

"Good evening," I smiled.

"Son, I'm glad you decided to show up and bring my daughter-in-law along." Veronica grabbed my hand. "Come on, sweetheart. Let me introduce you to some people."

Domestic wore a tight frown. He warned me, but I didn't care. If he thought I was going to ignore his mother, he was crazier than I thought.

Veronica had friends of multiple shades and ethnicities. She even had Mister and Missis Chung in the building. They were such a nice couple. Last but not least, I was introduced to the man of the hour, her husband. If I had to say so myself, he was very handsome. That man gave me sugar daddy vibes. He could've easily been my type. I kept my inappropriate thoughts to myself and smiled.

"Foreign, this is my husband Hugo. Babe, this Foreign, Demerius' fiancée."

"Aren't you quite the catch," he smiled and kissed my hand. "You look really familiar. Have we met somewhere before?"

My first response in my head was, *If we met, I wouldn't be with your son*. I kept those thoughts to myself. "No. I probably just have one of those faces."

"I've seen you somewhere. One thing about me is, I don't forget faces. Especially one as beautiful as you."

Veronica slapped him on the arm. "Stop it before you make our daughter-in-law uncomfortable."

A slight giggle escaped from my lips. "It's okay. I'm not offended."

"Good. He loves to uplift women, if you know what I mean."

"I do." Truthfully, I didn't. Had it been Aaron acting like Hugo just now, he would've caught a smooth ass beat down by now for being too damn friendly. Veronica wasn't fazed by Hugo's mannerism, so why should I be. Damn, I missed my cheating ass husband.

A slender male approached us dressed in all black. "Hey, Hugo. Can I steal you away for a moment?"

"Well, I guess that's my cue to leave. It was nice meeting you, Foreign."

"Likewise," I smiled.

171

"Foreign? As in Foreign Young?" The slender man shouted with sheer excitement.

The tall and slender dude threw me for a loop. He wasn't familiar at all, and I was stumped as to how he knew my damn name. "Yes."

"Oh my! First, let me start by giving you my condolences. I am so sorry for your loss."

That was when it hit me. He must've known Aaron.

"I was a very big fan of your husband."

"Thank you."

"I knew you looked familiar," Hugo added. "We used to go to a majority of the home games. During the super bowl, we sat in the skybox. That's where I saw you at."

"Yes. I was there."

"I never forget a face. Aaron was headed to the hall of fame. He was a man of many talents. You have my condolences. I know this is very hard on you."

"It has been, but I'm getting through it." As quickly as the night started, I was ready for it to be over.

Veronica was no longer smiling. Instead, there was a disappointing stare. Hugo walked away and Veronica leaned closer to me. "Come with me."

"Okay."

Veronica led me through the home until she found Domestic. Grabbing him by the arm, she whisked us away into an empty room. She slammed the door hard. "Would you care to explain to me how you're engaged to a married woman?"

Domestic sighed hard and rubbed the top of his head. "She's not married."

"Like hell, she ain't." Veronica was pissed and she wasn't afraid to let it be known. "This woman's husband just passed away recently. Are you that desperate for a woman? Or you just couldn't find a single one?"

"I have no problem getting women."

"Oh, you just prefer to commit adultery, huh?"

"Maybe." Domestic shrugged. "I'm going to hell anyway."

Out of nowhere, Veronica raised her hand and slapped the spit out of Domestic's mouth. "You goddamn right. You going straight to hell in a hand basket. This man hasn't been dead a month, you talking about the two of you are engaged."

Now I understood why I should've kept my distance and stayed low-key. It felt like I was being scolded for stepping out on my marriage.

Domestic opened his mouth to say something, but Veronica slapped him again. "Don't you say a goddamn word. Get out of my house now, demon, and take your jezebel with you."

Once again, I witnessed that frightened five-year-old boy again. Domestic snatched me by the arm and stormed out of the room. The night had gone terribly wrong, and all because one of Aaron's fans recognized me. I just wanted to disappear. My fate for the night had been sealed. There was no way he was going to keep a cool head about the chain of events that transpired.

The valet pulled the car around, and I hopped inside. My heart was beating hard and fast. I was terrified. Domestic waited until we pulled out of the driveway to address me. "What did you tell her?"

"I didn't tell her anything."

Domestic raised his hand and it made me flinch. The look in my eyes had to be what stopped him from hitting me. It was nothing but fear. "Don't lie to me. What did you tell her?"

"Nothing. I swear. One of Aaron's fans spotted me and offered his condolences. She heard everything."

Domestic didn't utter another word. He simply hit the gas and flushed it out of the neighborhood. When we arrived home, he went straight to the kitchen and came into the bedroom with a bottle of Johnny Walker. That whiskey was about to put him on his ass for the rest of the night.

Flopping down on the bed, Domestic turned the bottle up to his lips. I was already lying down. Dealing with him and his mommy issues were not on my list of things to do. Something came over his spirit because we didn't fight. Normally, he was quick to take all of his frustrations out on me, but tonight it was different.

"I'm sorry about tonight. This was all my fault. I should've followed my first mind and kept my distance. If that bitch wasn't my mother or a mob wife, I'll kill that hoe."

Mob wife, I thought. This nigga had to be drunk. He would never willingly come out and tell me what they did for a living. Now it all made sense as to why there was so much security. Who the hell did I get myself caught up with? That information made me realize I didn't know Domestic at all, or his background for that matter.

"You don't mean that. You're just talking."

"Nah." He took another gulp from the bottle. "I'm dead ass serious. I'll tie that bitch up, whip my dick out and piss all over her face." Domestic started to laugh hysterically. It was quite disturbing. "Then I'll shoot her right between the eyes."

"Don't talk like that. At the end of the day, she's still your mother. No matter how crazy she acts."

"Yeah, okay," he smirked. "Just because she gave birth to me don't make her a mother. I've watched a dog have puppies and do a better job than the mutt that had me."

Damn! Talk about a low blow. Pure hatred lived in his heart for Veronica. To me, a loving and caring relationship was something Domestic couldn't give me even if he wanted to. His words just confirmed it.

Destiny Skai

Chapter 23

Casey

Craig's funeral was set to start in five hours. That left me plenty of time to run a quick errand. Shawn was sitting on the bed smoking a blunt and nursing a cup of Remy.

"Don't you think it's a little too early to be drinking and smoking?"

"It's five o'clock somewhere and besides, my brother is being laid to rest. I'm not ready to say goodbye."

Standing in front of him, I rubbed his shoulders. "I know you're not, but I'm going to be right there with you. This is something you won't have to face alone. We're not related by blood, but Craig was like a brother to me also."

"Thanks, bae, I appreciate you being here."

"You don't have to thank me. I'm here because I want to be."

Shawn grabbed my hand and kissed it. "That's why I love you the way I do. Despite everything you just went through, you're here worrying about me."

"I'm going to be okay."

Shawn gently touched the bruise on my face. "That nigga gon' feel me for what he did to you."

"Just leave it alone, please. You have enough to worry about. Domestic won't be bothering me again. He's going to pay for what he did to me on my terms. I got this. Just promise me that we'll leave after this funeral is over."

"I can do that."

"Good." I popped-kissed him on the lips. "That breath is kicking, baby. It smells like you've been smoking, drinking, and eating pussy all night."

Shawn laughed. "I have."

"That's another reason we need to leave." Sitting down beside him, I put on a pair of Nikes. "You're starting to engage in too many vices."

"Where are you going?"

"I need to run a quick errand."

"I don't want you going anywhere by yourself."

"I promise I'll be okay." I opened up my purse and pulled out the .380 handgun I got from Tim. "See. I'll be just fine and I won't be afraid to shoot it."

"Where did you get that from?"

"Tim gave it to me, just in case I needed it."

"Okay. Well, be safe and I'll see you when you get back."

"Take a nap please, and put the weed and liquor down." I was about to walk away, but I stopped. "As a matter of fact, let me hit that blunt before I go." Shawn handed it over quickly.

Some time had passed since the last time I smoked weed. It was a blessing not to be on crack while dealing with Domestic. His rages would have a weak bitch on free-base.

Speaking of the devil, my mind shifted to his poor, naïve young girl. I was willing to bet my last dollar that her happy days with Domestic were long gone. Although I didn't know Foreign, I tried to warn her about his wicked ways. By now I was certain he was able to trick her into thinking it was my fault he laid hands on me. The bastard was charming, to say the least. He could make a woman drop her panties on the first night and fall in love before the month was out. Hell, he got me.

In the beginning, it was like a fairytale. Once the honeymoon phase was over, the magic disappeared. A first-class trip to hell was up next. See, Domestic had a long list of problems that started with his bat shit crazy mama. I swear, that witch was two steps from becoming a permanent resident at the insane asylum.

"You gon' pass the blunt over, bae?" Shawn brought me back from my daydream.

"Damn bae, my bad. I was about to kill your shit," I giggled.

"Hell yeah."

"Okay. I'm about to head out now. I'll see you in about an hour."

"Be safe," he repeated, as if I didn't hear him the first time.

"I will." Once more I kissed his lips before I left.

Checking my surroundings, I scurried to the rental car and unlocked the doors. The shooting and now the kidnapping had me paranoid. On the driver's side in the passenger seat, I spotted a bullet hole.

"What the hell?" I mumbled.

This was the main reason I wanted to get out of dodge quickly. If we stayed too long, there was a possibility that I could lose Shawn to the streets or prison. Either one was too much to bear. My first thought was to go back inside and question him, but I had my very own situation to handle.

My first stop was Tiffany's house. She was the last person to see me before my short disappearance. I was going to call her, but I decided to do a popup visit instead. To my surprise, she was just pulling into her driveway. I was right on time. Pulling in behind her, I parked and got out. Tiffany's stunned expression proved she wasn't expecting me.

"Well, don't look so happy to see me."

'No. It's not that. I'm just surprised to see you, that's all."

"I need to talk to you."

"About what?" she asked.

"Girl, stop acting all weird and shit so I can come in."

Tiffany unlocked the door, but she didn't say anything. She didn't have to because I was about to do all of the talking. "You know why I'm here, right?"

"Not really, but please enlighten me." Tiffany stood beside the sofa with her arms folded.

"The night we were here drinking, what happened? And how the hell did I end up with Domestic?"

"He showed up and forced his way inside. I didn't have any control over what happened to you that night."

"How did he know I was here?" That was the puzzling part. Domestic didn't know where I was, and I was careful to make sure I was not being followed. That shit was oddly strange.

"He had to have followed you here."

"I don't believe you."

Tiffany rocked on the ball of her feet. "Casey, I swear I didn't know he was coming here. I had nothing to do with that. After you passed out on the sofa, he just showed up."

"So you just let him take me? Do you know that man was going to kill me?"

"Okay," she huffed with her hands down at her side. "Okay then, so what you thought he was gon' do to me if I didn't let him in?"

"You right. I know Domestic and I know what he's capable of doing. However, you just let that fool kidnap me and you didn't bother to say anything." Tiffany and I had been close for years, so it hurt to know that she did nothing to protect me.

"I'm sorry. If I could've done something I would've." Tiffany's eyes were glassy, but she didn't cry.

This bitch had to be the biggest idiot if she thought I believed that bogus ass story. Her explanation didn't hold any weight in my eyes. "Okay, I'm not going to go deep into that, but I do have a question for you."

"What's that?" Tiffany acted as if I was the one who let her get kidnapped.

"For two days I was missing. If you were so concerned about me, why don't I have not one missing call or text message from you?" Tiffany started to cry. That was the guilt fucking with her lying ass.

"I'm so sorry, Casey," she sobbed.

"Sorry for setting me up!" I snapped. "That's fucked up. How could you do something like that to me?"

"You got it all wrong," she screamed hysterically. "He made me do it. I didn't want to."

Furious after her confession, I rushed Tiffany and rained blows onto her face. "Bitch, you almost got me killed."

Tiffany grabbed my hair and uppercut me in the chest. But that didn't stop me from trying to beat that bitch face in. The brawl grew wild. We bumped into the edge of the table and crashed to the floor. Tiffany weighed more than me, so she used her weight to try and keep me down. Somehow, I managed to use my strength and straddle her body. Angrily, I mushed her head against the floor. Then I banged it twice. Tiffany gave up and laid on the floor with her hand covering her head. If I was about that life, she would've been dead, but that's not in my nature. I'm a lover, not a fighter. She just pushed me over the edge. Thank the Lord for that because I can't go to prison.

"Don't ever talk to me again in life. You dead to me."

I walked outside and slammed the door behind me. DP had already stated he didn't want to attend the funeral, but I needed to ask one more time for confirmation. He picked up on the third ring.

"Hey, Ma."

"Hey, baby. How are you doing?"

"I'm good and you?"

"I'm fine. I was calling to see if you changed your mind about coming to the funeral?"

"No. I'm hanging out with Cheyenne today."

"Okay. Well, I'll talk to you later."

"Love you, Ma."

"I love you more, son." I ended the call and headed back to the house.

Chapter 24

Carlos

"Babe, we need to talk." Angie walked into the room, holding our three-year-old son.

"About what?"

"You. Us. Our family. The way you live."

"Come on, Angie, don't start that shit. We already talked about this shit last night. You knew what I was into, but you steady trying to change me. This is who I am."

"Carlos, you keep saying that, but don't you think it's time you put us first?"

"Man, what you talking about? I do put y'all first and as a man, I provide for my family. Damn, cut me some slack!"

"Cut you some slack!" The second she screamed, my son started to cry. He hated loud noises, and she knew that shit.

"Are you happy now?" I took my son from her arms and rocked him. "It's going to be okay, son."

"That's just a warm-up. There will be a lot more crying if you don't leave this criminal lifestyle in the past. 'Cause your ass is going to end up dead or in jail. And I'm telling you now, I'm not doing no damn bid with you. Leave me out here alone and I'm leaving you in there alone."

Bad enough I had to deal with beef in the streets, but to deal with it at home was *un-fucking-believable*. This was not what I signed up for when I got us a place to share and raise our children. Angie could miss me with the bullshit.

"That's cool. I don't expect you to ride with me. I'll be okay, no matter the circumstances. You can throw me to the wolves and I guarantee, I'll come back leading the pack."

Angie stood there in silence. Her eyes became glassy as they expanded to the size of golfballs. It was like she had seen a ghost. Then she grabbed my hand and sniffled. "Do you want to die? Do you want our children to grow up without a father? Think about your answer before you respond."

Angie meant the world to me, and so did my kids, but all I knew was the streets. The street gangs raised me. My involvement in criminal activity was my specialty. It was what I was good at. I didn't know how to do anything else. By all means, I never had any intentions of hurting her. Nor did I want her to leave me. There was no future without the mother of my kids.

I wanted them to have what I didn't have. A strong family foundation. Pulling Angie into my arms, I kissed her forehead.

"You know I don't want to die and I'm not going to. I'll always be here for you and my kids. I love y'all more than I love myself."

Angie laid her head on my chest. "I love you too and I don't want to leave you, but I will. If you don't change your life around."

That wasn't a promise I wanted to make, but if I wanted to keep my family together. I had no choice. "Angie baby, I want to spend the rest of my life with you. I want to grow old with you. There's no one else that I'd rather be with than you. Step-parents aren't in my vocabulary."

"Then change. For us, please," she begged.

"I don't know what I'd do next."

"We can start a business together."

"Okay," I sighed. "We can do that. Think of some ideas and run them by me when I get back."

Angie lifted her head and stepped back. "Where are you going?"

"I have one last business move to make, and I'm done."

"I don't believe you," she pouted.

"I swear, baby. After today, it's over. I've already been paid for this job and I have to do it. When I'm done, I'm coming straight home."

"You promise?"

Holding my right hand up, I replied. "I do. Damn, those words sound good."

"Well, we can say them once you deliver on your promise."

"That's a bet." I kissed my son on top of his head and passed him back to Angie. "I'll be back soon."

"Okay."

On my way out the door, I grabbed my gun and tucked it in my waistband. Then I called Domestic.

"What's up, bro?"

"I'm about to go handle that business."

"Cool, bro. Let me know when it's done."

"I gotchu, bro."

Stepping out of the street life wasn't something I planned. Hopefully, I could find my niche so I wouldn't have to return to my bad behaviors. I would lose it if I lost my family to another man. I hopped in the Mustang and peeled out. It didn't take me long to reach my destination. When I pulled up, I spotted a USPS truck in front of the house.

181

Emilia...

Today was about to be a wonderful day. I put my house up for sale and my clothes were packed. Domestic was coming to drop off the money, and I was on the first thing smoking out of Florida. The road ahead of me was going to be unpredictable. That's what a fresh start was all about. With Aaron being gone, I had no reason to stay. All Domestic had to do was, get Foreign out the way and leave Aaron alone. Not once did I say, kill him. He took that upon himself to take matters into his own hands. Domestic wouldn't admit it to me, but I knew he did it. The evidence didn't lie. People did, but facts were facts. His ass was guilty as sin. There wasn't a shadow of a doubt in my mind.

"Yassss!" I shouted while sipping my wine and doing a two-step to some jazz music. "All this shit is about to be over. California, here I come."

A hard knock on the door interrupted my celebration. "Damn, who is this fucking up my groove."

With my glass clutched tightly in my hand, I walked to the door and peeped through the peephole. "Who is it?"

"USPS."

When I opened the door, the driver was standing there in his doo-doo brown uniform. He was cute with his little bit of facial hair. I knew he was young and just my type. "Hello."

"Hi!" He smiled. "I'm here for a pickup."

"Oh yes! Hold on one second, let me go and grab the package."

"Okay."

I scurried towards the kitchen and retrieved my package. That was my last task before I boarded my flight later on that night. Now, I was officially set to make my exit. When that package landed at its final destination, there was going to be a lot of chaos. It didn't matter to me because I was going to be long gone. No one would be able to find me.

"Here you go."

"Alright, have a good day."

"You too."

As the driver walked away, I stood on the porch and took in the breeze. I'd purchased my home during my second year on the force. I had plans to retire and pass the house along to my child. That was a bittersweet memory due to the unfortunate miscarriage I suffered a while ago. Loud pipes from the road grabbed my attention. The first thing I spotted was the Mustang.

"Humph! What is he doing here?" I stood on the porch with my hands on my hips.

Carlos got out of the car and slipped his hoodie over his head. His ass looked like he was up to no good. From what I knew, that was always the case. As he walked up onto the porch, I spotted the gun on his hip, and he had a killer's look in his eyes. I had no idea what he had going on, and I didn't like it.

"What are you doing here?"

"I need to talk to you."

"I'm listening."

"Not out here, inside."

Turning on my heels, I walked back into the house with Carlos on my heels. We both sat down on the sofa, but across from each other. I was not in the mood for his shit. "What's going on, Carlos? What have you gotten yourself into now?"

Carlos…

One thing about Emilia: she didn't hold any punches. She had a slick ass mouth for as long as I can remember. Sometimes she made me want to knock her ass out. That was God's honest truth. "Damn, that's how you greet your baby brother?" I removed my gun and set it down beside me.

"When you show up out the blue, yes. I know you did something so you might as well tell me now and not wait until your ass is arrested."

My mind was racing. After all that shit Domestic put in my head, I knew it would be a matter of time before they realized Aaron's death wasn't an accident. I couldn't risk going to prison for life and miss out on the growth of my kids. No one was about to gamble with my life like that. By all means, she had to be dealt with. He asked me to handle her, so that's exactly what I came to do.

"You right. I am in some shit."

Emilia rolled her eyes and exhaled. "Tell me something I don't know."

Her nasty ass attitude was getting on my fucking nerves. Emilia was two seconds from getting knocked the fuck out. Sister or no sister! "Fuck is yo' problem? I'm trying to talk to you and you catching an attitude and shit."

"I get tired of bailing you out. And the only time I hear from you is when you need my help."

Ignoring her comment, I changed the subject. "What's going on between you and Domestic?"

Emilia's tone and demeanor changed. "What do you mean?"

"Exactly what it sounds like. What's up?"

"Nothing."

"You sure you wanna do this?"

"Do what?" she huffed.

"Lie to me."

"I'm not lying to you."

"So you're not trying to pin Aaron's murder on him?"

Emilia seemed surprised. She sat up straight and tilted her head to the side. "What! Why would you say that?"

"You know why."

"Did he tell you that?"

The twenty questions were starting to aggravate me. "Just answer the damn question."

"He did it and I can prove it."

"How?" It was something I needed to know.

"Now you know I can't reveal any details about an open case." Emilia leaned forward. "Do you know something? What did he tell you?"

"He didn't tell me shit because he didn't do it."

"And how do you know that?"

One thing I could bank on was Emilia not turning me into authorities. "Because I did it."

"What?" Emilia's face instantly turned beet-red. "Why the fuck would you kill him?"

"I have my reasons. Just know that I'm the one that ran him off the road."

"Why are you telling me this?" she stammered.

Folding my hands, I rested my elbows on my thighs. My voice was low and vicious. I meant business. "You need to sit this one out and relocate as planned. Because if I go down, we all going down. And that's not a threat. It's a promise. Don't think I don't know about the plan you hatched with Domestic. I know everything."

"Wow!" she nodded her head. "You're threatening me."

"I'm telling you to let this one go. Don't think that I didn't find out about you being fired. I know everything."

"It's not a secret."

"Okay then. Let it go, and stop reaching. I can't afford to go to prison."

"You need to stop doing things that will land you there."

"I am. I'm going straight now. No more criminal activity. It's time for me to put my family first. My kids need me."

"Good." She sat back and exhaled. "We all need to start with a clean slate. That's what I'm doing."

"That means you're going to let it go?"

"Yes."

Grabbing my gun, I stood to my feet and looked into her eyes one last time. "I hope you stand by your word. This could get really bad if you don't. I'll see you later."

"I'm leaving tonight."

"Where are you going?"

"The Midwest."

"A'ight. Well, I guess I'll see you at the wedding."

"I'll be there," she smiled.

Emilia...

The second Carlos walked out of my house, I ran to the door and locked it. Sliding my back against the door, I took a deep breath. I was terrified. My brother was a loose cannon. Blood or no blood, he would kill me without batting an eye and cry at my funeral. I don't know where my father went wrong. Carlos had been a problem since elementary school. The military camp he attended was no help at all.

All I kept thinking about was, fleeing Tampa in a hurry. Domestic needed to bring that money so I could get the fuck out of dodge. I had two days at the most before my plan exploded in my face. My ass was sweating bullets because there was nothing that I could do to stop it. Or was there?

Quickly, I scrambled from the floor and searched for my cellphone. Once I found it, I *Googled* the number to USPS and called them. While waiting for a customer service representative, I poured myself another drink. With so much stress bubbling on my brain, I took that shot to the head.

"Emilia, what the fuck did you do?" I hit the wall. "Fuck!"

Four minutes later, an agent picked up the phone. "Thank you for having called USPS. How may I assist you?"

"Yes. Hi. I have a question."

"Sure. I'll be more than happy to assist you with that," she replied pleasantly.

"Is there any way to stop a package from being delivered?"

"Yes. There would be a fee to do that. Do you have the tracking number?"

"Um. Hang on one second and let me check my email real quick."

"No problem. Take your time."

Happy to hear that news, I opened my email to find the label I printed from my computer. Disappointed, I realized I sent the package as a first-class package and a tracking number wasn't provided.

"Shit," I blurted out into the phone.

"Ma'am."

"I'm sorry. I don't have a tracking number. It was sent as first-class."

"I'm sorry ma'am. Unfortunately, we're unable to do that without that tracking number. Once the package has been collected there is nothing else that we can do. Your only option at this point is to intercept the package on the delivery date."

"Okay. Thanks anyway."

"Is there anything else that I can assist you with?"

"No."

"Well, it's been my pleasure to assist you today. Thank you for calling USPS. Have a nice day."

I was so fucking pissed that I couldn't do shit but hang up the phone. "Damn! Kiss my ass."

Chapter 25

Domestic

The bikini wash was jammed packed when I pulled up. Every spot was taken except for my personal space. I made sure they knew that was off-limits. Foreign whips and candy painted cars were posted wall to wall. Loud music blared through the speakers. One of my homies was a rapper and wanted to use the wash for his video shoot.

It was so many fine hoes on set. Of course, they hissed and shouted, trying to get my attention, but I kept it moving. I had little interest in women dressed in little to nothing. A real king needed a queen and I had that at home. On the flipside, if being a video vixen didn't work out for them, they had a fasho spot at the wash. That was on the big man upstairs.

My homie J.Digg was posted in front of the building with a bad bitch on each side. As I rolled up on him, I grinned. "Muthafuckin J. Digg." We G-hugged. "What it do fam?" Foolie was rocking a big ass Cuban link. His platinum grill with diamonds shined bright as the sun.

"Shit! Just coolin', fam. A nigga 'preciate you letting me do my video at your spot."

"It's all love, fam." I rubbed my hands together and smiled. "I see you brought the city out." The publicity would be great for business. Especially when his video hit the internet, social media, and the television screens.

"These niggas live for a nigga just like these bitches," he chuckled.

"Shiidd, they see who got the money," I joked.

J.Digg chuckled and touched his chin. "Shiidd, I'm trying to stack my bread like you. You got this shit on lock."

"I'm a businessman."

"As jits, me and my boys looked up to you. Still do. It's good to see you put those millions to use."

"Thanks, man," I replied. My phone vibrated in my pocket. When I pulled it out, I grew irritated on the spot. "Check it, fam. I gotta go handle some business, but I'ma slide back through if you still here."

"A'ight, fam. Be easy."

"You too, fam."

Mary—the supervisor—was standing behind the counter, talking to a customer when I stepped into the lobby. "How's it going, Mary?"

"Hey, Domestic, everything is good. It's very busy, but that's a good thing."

"I agree."

"How long you staying?" she asked while handing the customer her change.

"Not long. I'm in and out."

"Okay."

I walked into the office and closed the door. Then I called Emilia back. Her money hungry ass wouldn't stop calling. She picked up on the first ring. I didn't give her a chance to say hello.

"What do you want?"

"I was just calling to see when we were going to meet up. My flight leaves in a few hours."

"I'm picking up the money right now. I'll be there in a few."

"To my house?" she asked.

"Yeah. Give me like thirty minutes and I'll be there."

"I can just meet you," she insisted.

"Do you want it or not? I don't have time for these games you trying to play."

"I'll be here."

There was no need for me to respond, so I hung up and sat the phone on the desk. "This the last time you'll ever call me, bitch!"

Opening the closet, I pulled out a black duffle bag. I loaded it up with all of the money from out of the safe. Once I was done, I locked the safe and left. Normally, I was dressed in business attire, but today I chose an urban look. Hell, I looked like a rapper myself.

Once I arrived at Emilia's house, I backed into the driveway and got out. The bag was slightly heavy from a large number of bills inside. I banged on the door a few times. Emilia opened the door and held out her hand.

"Girl, let me in here." I pushed past her and walked inside.

Emilia was dressed in a tracksuit. It hugged her thighs and ass just right. Being the man that I am, I had to feel her up. "You know I'm hitting this one last time."

"Oh, really?"

"Don't play crazy."

"Is that the money?"

"What you think?" I asked sarcastically. To ease her mind, I slid the zipper down so she could see.

Emilia smiled. "Thanks."

"Don't thank me just yet." I slid my hand inside her pants. She wasn't wearing any panties. Gently, I caressed her plump lips. Emilia moaned and placed her hand on the back of my neck. Scooping her up into my arms, I made my way to her bedroom.

Emilia stripped naked and climbed up on the bed. I removed my clothes and stroked my dick with my right hand. "You know you gotta slob on the knob."

Emilia hopped down feet first and took every inch into her mouth. Hungrily, she sucked and slurped, making loud noises. That was the best head job she ever gave me. It was funny how money motivated her throat skills.

Using my left hand, I grabbed a hand full of her hair and massaged her scalp. The tip of my dick hit the ball in the back of her throat like a punching bag. Emilia gagged a little, but she didn't stop deep throating my shit.

"Fuck! Eat that dick just like that," I grunted.

Emilia's head moved rapidly while clenching her jaws tightly together. She was trying to suck the life out of me. That wasn't going to be an easy task. Gripping her hair tighter, I thrust my hips and fucked her mouth. Those gag reflexes were a motherfucker. It sounded like she had the hiccups. Emilia was a certified head doctor. After another five minutes of deep throating, I could no longer hold my nut. Holding my head back, I grunted as I ejaculated in her mouth. Thick, white cum covered her lips.

"Swallow it," I demanded. And just like that, she did it. "Get up on the bed." Emilia crawled onto the bed and laid on her back. "Let me see you play with it." Emilia put her hand between her legs and rubbed on her clit.

My eyes were stuck on her, and my hand was back on my dick. Slowly, I jacked off until I was hard again. Crawling between her legs, I launched my missile into her dark, warm galaxy. Emilia placed both hands on the side of my waist.

"Domestic! Domestic," she moaned loudly.

"You better enjoy it 'cause this your last time," I promised.

For approximately ten minutes I pinned her legs to the headboard and tried to knock her cervix loose. Emilia could barely release those high pitched screams. Placing her legs on my shoulders, I slammed into her pussy aggressively.

"Ouuu! Shit! Fuck! You killing me," she screamed.

"That's what I'm trying to do," I breathed heavily.

Those words were my cue. While continuing to bang her relentlessly, I placed my hands around her throat. Using every ounce of my strength, I choked her.

"Domes—" She tried to say my name, but my grip was too tight.

"Shut up, hoe," I spat. "I'm gon' kill yo' ass today. If you thought I was gone let you threaten me and give you a hundred stacks, you dumber than I thought."

Emilia tried to fight, but she was no match for me. The pressure in my hands increased. I was trying to break the bone in that hoe neck. "Now, in the next life, you can think about how stupid you were to try a nigga like me. If I killed that young nigga and his innocent bitch about my money, you knew I wouldn't bow down so easily."

I watched the life fade from Emilia's body slowly. Her eyes started to flicker. "This dick is to die for, ain't it?" I laughed.

A few moments passed, and Emilia's eyes rolled to the back of her head. Finally, that bitch was dead. I pulled out of her and put on my clothes. Using the comforter on her bed, I wrapped her body with it and dragged her into the living room.

Outside, I peeped the scene to make sure there were no witnesses that could identify me. The coast was clear, so I backed my car up to the front door and placed her body in the trunk. Careful not to leave any evidence, I wiped down the doorknobs, grabbed my duffle bag, her purse, travel bag, and fled the scene. No one would be looking for her since she had planned on leaving the state. This would be the perfect murder.

After riding around searching for a desolate place to bury her body, I ended up at Torreya State Park. The area was deserted. Not a single car in sight. I pulled alongside some trees and popped the trunk. Then I pulled out my shovel and walked a half of a mile into the wooded area. It didn't take long for me to dig a deep enough hole so she couldn't be found.

Using quick strides, I made my way back to my car. Before removing her body, I looked east and west to make sure no cars were traveling. Emilia's corpse was a lot heavier than it was when she was alive. I dropped her body into the hole and proceeded to cover her body with dirt. Carefully, I blended the sand, to make sure the ground didn't look disturbed. Emilia was buried with all of her items.

"Rest in peace, Emilia." I did a four-point motion, making a cross in front of my chest. Then I left. During my ride, I blasted Hezekiah Walker's song, "Every Praise." Some may call me a devil, but the Lord knew my heart and that I'd let the devil use me. And for that, I needed his forgiveness. God was my savior and healer. He was the only one that could help me and wash away my sins.

On my way home, I swung back by the wash to grab my cellphone. To my surprise, the crowd was gone and Mary was closing up for the evening. Foreign was in the kitchen cooking dinner when I arrived. I slid behind her and wrapped my hands around her waist.

"Hey, my love. What's on the menu?"

"Beef ribs, macaroni and cheese, and baked beans."

"Mm. That sounds good." Seductively, I kissed the side of her neck and caressed her backside. Despite my encounter with Emilia, making love to the woman I was in love with was the only thing on my mind at that time.

"Go wash up. It's almost time for dinner."

"I'm about to hop in the shower. I've been out in the sun all day. You know the video shoot was today."

"Yeah. I can tell."

"I smell like the sun."

"That's fine." She inhaled deeply. "As long as you don't smell like pussy."

"Never that," I lied. "Your pussy is the only scent I need on me."

"I know that's right."

"Where's DP? In the room?"

"No. Him and Cheyenne went to the bowling alley."

"Oh, you dropped them off?"

"I let him drive my car," she replied nonchalantly.

"You let him drive your car?" I had to ask again because I couldn't believe what I was hearing.

"Yes." Foreign turned to face me and placed her hands on my chest. "It's just a car. A material thing. Besides, you let him drive your Maserati all the time."

"Okay."

"I'm not worried about that car. If he messes it up, that's what insurance is for and whatever they don't cover, his father will." She smiled and kissed me on the cheek.

"I knew it was a catch."

Foreign laughed. "Don't worry. He's going to drive safely."

"That's because I taught him how to drive." I smacked her on the ass and walked off. "I'll be right back."

Dinner was fabulous. Foreign and I sat and talked like best friends. It had been a while since we got along so well. Our conversation was as friendly as the first day we met. The love I had for her was unexplainable.

My past traumas just kept getting in the way. But I was doing my best to keep that anger under wraps. Hopefully, the anger I unleashed on Emilia would lighten the load and calm me down. I was a killer by nature and for some odd reason, it made me feel good.

"Baby, you put your foot in this." I wiped my mouth with a napkin.

"Thank you, baby. I'm glad you enjoyed it."

"I'm ready for dessert now." I licked my lips so she'll know exactly what I was referring to.

"I bet you are," she smiled. "I think we—" Foreign rubbed her stomach. "Are ready for dessert as well."

"I've been thinking about you all day."

"Well, let me clean up this mess and I'll be right up."

"Nah!" I retorted. "I'll handle the kitchen later. Right now I need you to save all your energy for me."

The front door slammed and I knew it was DP coming in. A few seconds later, he walked into the kitchen with Cheyenne right behind him. They both had stale looks on their faces. Foreign and I looked at each other, then at the young couple.

"Why y'all looking crazy? You done fucked up Foreign's car?" For some reason, I knew that's what he was about to say. Now, I had a new bill on my hands. It was no pressure. I would get it fixed. More than likely, I would probably just buy her another car, depending on the damages.

"I need to talk to you." DP's voice was lower than usual.

"What's up, son?"

The room went silent. DP looked at Cheyenne, then back to me. "Cheyenne is pregnant."

All I could hear was silverware falling onto a plate and Foreign clearing her voice. "What?" That was not what I was expecting to hear at all. "How do y'all know that? Did she take a test?" I spoke as if she wasn't in the room.

"She took a pregnancy test earlier today. It was positive."

Placing my elbows on the table, I rubbed my face. Not only did I have a baby on the way, so did my son. This damn boy just created another bill. I would've preferred that he fucked up Foreign's car. A baby bill was eighteen years at the minimum. I could've bought a luxury car cash and came out cheaper.

"Baby, are you okay?" Foreign asked softly. My silence answered that question for me.

"I'm sorry, dad. Are you mad at me?"

To say that I was mad was a tad bit unfair since I knew they were having sex. Disappointment described exactly how I was feeling. "No. I'm not mad. Just surprised." Finally, I was able to look up at them. "Cheyenne, does your mother know about this?"

Cheyenne had her hands folded in front of her, as she rocked on her heels. "Not yet."

"Okay," I sighed. "I need a little time to process this and we'll handle this tomorrow."

"Mr. Payne, I'm sorry. We didn't mean for this to happen."

"Yeah, I know." I turned my attention back to Foreign. "Baby, can you fix me a strong drink please?"

"Yes." Foreign stood up and went into the kitchen.

DP and Cheyenne went upstairs while I sat and waited on my drink. Foreign returned and sat the glass in front of me. "Are you okay?"

"Yeah. I'm just surprised by the news that's all. I was not expecting this."

"Oh, I'm sure. So, what do you want her to do, have an abortion?"

"Honestly, babe, I don't believe in that. We had DP at a young age and no one forced us to have an abortion. I'm not going to do that. Whatever they decide, I'll back it. Just be ready to raise two kids."

"I've always wanted a house full of kids. As you can see, that never happened."

Foreign looked sad when those words left her mouth. As bad as I wanted to say something, I held my tongue. That was a sensitive subject for her, so I left it alone. "Don't worry, daddy will swell you up as many times as you'd like." I downed my drink. "Daddy ready for dessert. Come on." It was time to relieve some of this added stress my son just applied.

Chapter 26

Foreign

Two days later

My morning started better than usual. Domestic had a warm bath going for me in the Jacuzzi tub with candles, bubbles, and rose petals. "Now, what could I have possibly done to deserve such wonderful treatment? Is it because I did that thing you like a little while ago," I joked.

"Maybe." Domestic laughed with me. "Nah, babe. I'm joking. I know you deserve so much more than this."

"I'm glad you know that."

Domestic caressed the back of my neck. "I do and I want you to know that I appreciate you for having patience with me. You have stuck by my side when the average woman would've walked away. The faith you have in me is greater than I could ever imagine, and I appreciate your every being for it."

A few tears surfaced, clogging my vision. Somehow, I became a sucker for love and a happy ending. I felt horrible about Domestic's upbringing.

It made me want to stand by his side and not abandon him. "I know how it feels to want someone so bad, but your past gets in the way. Ever since I was a little girl, I've always dreamed about being a mother. I wanted to have a marriage like my parents and live happily ever after with a house full of kids.

Taken by surprise, I looked into Domestic's eyes and watched the tears fall. It took no time for him to become emotional.

"I want to give you all those things, but I'm afraid I'm going to lose you. I love you so much, but I don't know how to love you properly. All my life I've witnessed abuse and it made me feel like it was love. She convinced me that as human beings we would always hurt the ones we love. My mother would beat my ass, then tell me that she loved me."

My tears started to fall. "I love you too and I want us to have that happy ending. That's the only reason I'm still here. As long as you keep your hands to yourself and communicate with me, we can get through this together."

"I'm trying so hard to do that—Just help me get through it," he pleaded.

"I will," I promised.

Domestic bathed me gently. He took his time and caressed every inch of my body. After my bath, my baby massaged my body with baby oil. It was exactly what the doctor ordered. I drifted off into some deep, emotional thoughts. Flashbacks of Domestic abusing me hit me hard. In all of my twenty-four years on the planet, I've never worn an ass-whooping. Not by a male or female. That didn't happen until I climbed into bed with danger. The warnings were there. God always sent a warning before destruction. Unfortunately, I'd managed to ignore every sign. I was too blinded by the attention and mind-blowing sex he showered me with. It was something Aaron failed to give me at home.

During the massage, I'd fallen asleep. Time slipped away, and I was awakened to great pleasure stimulating between my thighs. When I looked down, Domestic was munching down on my coochie. The orgasm was heavy and intoxicating. My legs were shaking and a warm, wet puddle was underneath my ass.

After being cooped up in the room for hours, it was time for me to get out of the house. Domestic had a few errands, so I made it my business to find something to do. I ended up going to my house. It was no longer home because Aaron wasn't there. No matter how much pain he'd caused me over the years, I missed him terribly.

The eerie silence in the house was crazy. It was funny how I could hear his laughter. When I looked up at the staircase, it reminded me of the time I threw objects at him during one of our spats. That made me laugh. We had a lot of good memories. Those were the ones I held on to the most.

Walking throughout the house, I ended up in the kitchen. The refrigerator was filled with old food. "I guess I can clean up while I'm here."

For an hour, I emptied the fridge and filled two trash bags. With both bags occupying my hands, I took them to the side of the house and dumped them in the large garbage pail. Walking to the front yard, I spotted the mailman approaching the door.

"Hey, Mrs. Young. How are you?"

"I'm good, Matt. How about you?"

"Just earning a living. I haven't seen you in a while."

"Yeah. It's hard to sleep in this empty house by myself."

Matt nodded. "I'm so sorry for your loss. I can only imagine the pain you're going through."

"It's been rough. I'm just taking it one day at a time."

"That's all you can do. I'll be sure to keep you in my prayers."

"I would appreciate that." It was hard to smile, but I'd managed to keep my tears at bay.

Matt handed me the mail, along with a small package. "Have a good day, Mrs. Young."

"Thanks, Matt, you do the same."

Matt had been our mailman for years. I could remember the first time he met Aaron, he was so excited. Tampa Bay was his favorite NFL team.

Flopping down on the sofa, I opened the package first. It didn't have a return address on it, so it made me wonder if it was another scandal. "God please do not let this be another scandal for money. My heart can't take any more drama."

Inside the box were pictures from Aaron's accident. Tears fell from my eyes instantly. I had never seen the damage up close and personal. Then there was a USB. I plugged it into the smart T.V and let it play. A woman was sitting on a sofa. That woman was none other than Emilia. Someone I hated with a passion.

"By the time you get this video, I'll be long gone. I know I'm the last person that you want to hear from, but there's something that I must get off my chest before it's too late. Domestic is not the man you think he is. When the two of you met, it was by some string of luck on his behalf. See, Domestic and I had a meeting. I told him to get close to you so that I could be with Aaron. He and I met when y'all were having problems after your miscarriage. We were together for a month and I fell deeply in love with him. But he didn't want to be with me. You're the only woman he wanted a future with. It hurt me because I felt like he used me." Emilia wiped her tears away and continued to tell her story.

"I purposely got pregnant by his teammate and tried to convince him that it was his baby. That didn't work either. Instead of giving up, I took another avenue and enlisted Domestic for his help. His job was to make you fall in love with him so that you would leave Aaron. Things still didn't go as planned. No matter what I did, Aaron still didn't want me. I'm telling you this so that you can get away from Domestic. He's dangerous and possessive. A while back Domestic beat and raped me at the car wash one night. All because he thought I was wearing a wire. Get away from him before he kills you. That man killed Aaron so that the two of you could be together, and I have proof of that. If I end up dead, just know that it was by the hands of Domestic. I know you hate me. Hell, I would hate me too. But I'm telling the truth. If you don't believe me, check inside Domestic's wallet and you'll see a picture of you. I gave him that so he could find and seduce you. Be careful, Foreign, and I'm sorry for everything I've done to ruin your marriage and lose your husband."

When the video came to an end I was bawling. My heart broke all over again. Then I thought back to that photo I found in his wallet. Emilia had to be telling the truth. It made me wonder: *Was our relationship a sham all of this time?* Whatever the case may be, I was now convinced that Domestic was responsible for my husband's murder. My only question was *how?*

The news was so painful. It made me feel like I was somehow responsible for Aaron's death. Revenge led me into the arms and bed of another man. Now, I was a widow because of my irrational thinking. If I could go back in time, I would've never slept with Domestic. As I laid in our bed, I cuddled with Aaron's pillow and wept. "I'm so sorry, Aaron. All of this is my fault. I brought that man into our lives and now you're gone."

Alexis was right all along. I didn't know what to do with this information. And if Emilia knew that Domestic was guilty, why didn't she have him arrested. If Emilia loved Aaron the way she claimed she did, her ass should want justice.

Unable to fall asleep, I removed myself from the bed and left the house in a hurry. For thirty minutes, I drove around aimlessly. There was only one person that I cared to see, and that was where I went. Maurice opened the door and, as always, he was smiling.

"Wow! I'm surprised to see you here."

"I'm sorry for just dropping by unannounced, but I had no place else to go." My voice was shaky.

"It's okay. Come on in."

Maurice escorted me to the sofa. The first thing I noticed was a travel bag. "Are you going somewhere?"

"I am. I'm investigating a high profile case and I need to interview a witness. He's locked up in the Broward County Jail, so that's where I'm headed."

"Oh yeah, I forgot you're some sort of agent or detective. How long will you be away?"

"Not long. Just a day."

I didn't want to be a burden, so I stood to my feet. "I should leave. I'm not trying to be in your way."

Maurice grabbed my hand. "What if I want you in the way? Sort of like a good distraction."

This felt like déjà vu from when I first met Domestic. Repeating the cycle was negative. I was not going back down that road again. Before I moved on, I needed to close the door on Domestic. It was clear that he would kill for what he wanted.

"I'm flattered, but I'm pregnant and my life is a mess."

"I like a little mess sometimes," he laughed. "We're not perfect. My life tends to get a little messy at times, but it's nothing I can't handle."

My phone rang. The sound of the ringtone sent frightening chills all over my body. I closed my eyes and took a deep breath. He was the last person I wanted to talk to. Strangely, my legs started to feel like noodles.

Maurice grabbed me at the waist. "Are you okay?"

"Yes. I'm fine."

"Is that him calling?" During my first visit with Maurice, I gave him a little intel on my relationship with Domestic.

"Yes."

"Did he do something to you?"

"No." I paused.

Maurice looked me in my eyes, and I could see the concern in them. "Are you telling me the truth?"

"I am. He hasn't touched me."

"Okay," he exhaled deeply. Maurice hugged me and I allowed it. After all of the shit I just witnessed, I needed a damn hug.

"I just don't understand why all of this is happening to me." Out of the blue, I became an emotional mess.

"What's going on with you?"

Unable to contain my true feelings, I admitted the unthinkable out loud. "I think he killed my husband."

"What?" he seemed surprised. "Why do you think that? Has he said something to you?"

"He hasn't admitted it to me if that's what you're asking. He's just so insensitive and never has a good thing to say about Aaron. It's like he hates him, but he doesn't have a reason."

"He may not have a reason in your eyes, but in his case Domestic hates Aaron because of the things you told him. The fact that the two of you were married made it worse."

"I'm afraid of him," I sobbed. "What if I'm right?"

"How about this? Why don't you come with me? You can visit your family, while I interview my witness."

I agreed.

We arrived in Fort Lauderdale a little after nine o'clock that night. Throughout the drive, I dozed off here and there. When I was awake, we shared deep conversations about life. As we drove through the city, it brought back a lot of old memories. Once I left for college, I never returned. Now, I was back and unhappy.

"Are you nervous?" Maurice glanced at me once we stopped at a red light.

"A little. I still don't know how you were able to get her address for me."

"That's easy," he smiled. "I work for the federal government. No one can hide from me."

"Okay."

We pulled up to an immaculate mini-mansion in Plantation Acres. My nerves were all over the place, and I became sweaty underneath my breasts. "Whew! Calm down, girl. It's going to be okay."

Maurice opened the door and helped me out. "Come on, big girl."

"Gee, thanks."

"It's okay. You still look as good as the day we met."

"Flattery will get you everywhere." The way he dropped compliments made me smile. Maurice was an absolute gentleman and very sweet.

"I hope so."

"Can you stay right here until I come back? I don't want to show up on her steps with an extra guest."

"Sure."

I took a deep breath and walked up to the house. From the door, I could hear children playing. That was the way I wanted my house to sound. My hands shook as I pressed down on the doorbell. A moment later the door swung open. Needless to say, this woman was not happy to see me.

"I know damn well you not on my porch." Blacque Barbee stood there with her hands on her hips. "You might as well take whatever fourteen-carat gold horse and carriage you rode on and get the fuck off my property?"

"Please, I need your help."

"No, the hell you don't," she snapped.

Corey must've heard the commotion. He hit the corner with a gun in his hand. "Bae, who you talking to?"

"Nobody. She was just leaving." Blacque Barbee folded her arms and huffed.

"Foreign?" Corey squinted. "Is that you?"

"Yes."

"Bae, why won't you let her in?" Corey slipped his gun into his pocket.

"Miss Sadity is not welcomed here. That's why."

Putting my pride to the side, I pleaded my case. "Please B, don't do this to me. I have no one else to turn to and if I go back home, I'm going to die."

"Not my problem, goodbye." Blacque Barbee pushed the door, but Corey caught it.

"Bae, stop. This is your family."

"I don't know her."

"What's going on?" Corey asked. I could see a great deal of genuine concern in his eyes.

"He's going to kill me," I cried.

To Be Continued...
The Price You Pay for Love 3
Coming Soon

Submission Guideline

Submit the first three chapters of your completed manuscript to ldpsubmissions@gmail.com, subject line: Your book's title. The manuscript must be in a .doc file and sent as an attachment. Document should be in Times New Roman, double spaced and in size 12 font. Also, provide your synopsis and full contact information. If sending multiple submissions, they must each be in a separate email.

Have a story but no way to send it electronically? You can still submit to LDP/Ca$h Presents. Send in the first three chapters, written or typed, of your completed manuscript to:

LDP: Submissions Dept
Po Box 944
Stockbridge, Ga 30281

DO NOT send original manuscript. Must be a duplicate.

Provide your synopsis and a cover letter containing your full contact information.

Thanks for considering LDP and Ca$h Presents.

BOW DOWN TO MY GANGSTA

By **Ca$h**

TORN BETWEEN TWO

By **Coffee**

THE STREETS STAINED MY SOUL **II**

By **Marcellus Allen**

BLOOD OF A BOSS **VI**

SHADOWS OF THE GAME II

By **Askari**

LOYAL TO THE GAME **IV**

By **T.J. & Jelissa**

IF LOVING YOU IS WRONG... **III**

By **Jelissa**

TRUE SAVAGE **VIII**

MIDNIGHT CARTEL IV

DOPE BOY MAGIC IV

CITY OF KINGZ II

By **Chris Green**

BLAST FOR ME **III**

A SAVAGE DOPEBOY III

CUTTHROAT MAFIA III

DUFFLE BAG CARTEL VI

HEARTLESS GOON VI

By **Ghost**

A HUSTLER'S DECEIT III

KILL ZONE **II**

BAE BELONGS TO ME III

A DOPE BOY'S QUEEN III

By **Aryanna**

COKE KINGS V

KING OF THE TRAP II

By **T.J. Edwards**

GORILLAZ IN THE BAY V

3X KRAZY III

De'Kari

THE STREETS ARE CALLING II

Duquie Wilson

KINGPIN KILLAZ IV

STREET KINGS III

PAID IN BLOOD III

CARTEL KILLAZ IV

DOPE GODS III

Hood Rich

SINS OF A HUSTLA II

ASAD

KINGZ OF THE GAME VI

Playa Ray

SLAUGHTER GANG IV

RUTHLESS HEART IV

By Willie Slaughter

THE HEART OF A SAVAGE III

By Jibril Williams

FUK SHYT II

By Blakk Diamond

TRAP QUEEN

By Troublesome

YAYO V

GHOST MOB II

Stilloan Robinson

KINGPIN DREAMS III

By Paper Boi Rari

CREAM II

The Price You Pay For Love 2

By Yolanda Moore

SON OF A DOPE FIEND III

By Renta

FOREVER GANGSTA II

GLOCKS ON SATIN SHEETS III

By Adrian Dulan

LOYALTY AIN'T PROMISED III

By Keith Williams

THE PRICE YOU PAY FOR LOVE III

By Destiny Skai

I'M NOTHING WITHOUT HIS LOVE II

SINS OF A THUG II

By Monet Dragun

LIFE OF A SAVAGE IV

MURDA SEASON IV

GANGLAND CARTEL III

CHI'RAQ GANGSTAS III

By **Romell Tukes**

QUIET MONEY IV

EXTENDED CLIP II

By **Trai'Quan**

THE STREETS MADE ME III

By **Larry D. Wright**

IF YOU CROSS ME ONCE II

ANGEL III

By **Anthony Fields**

FRIEND OR FOE III

By **Mimi**

SAVAGE STORMS III

By **Meesha**

BLOOD ON THE MONEY III

By **J-Blunt**

206

Destiny Skai

THE STREETS WILL NEVER CLOSE II

By K'ajji

NIGHTMARES OF A HUSTLA III

By King Dream

THE WIFEY I USED TO BE II

By Nicole Goosby

IN THE ARM OF HIS BOSS

By Jamila

MONEY, MURDER & MEMORIES II

Malik D. Rice

CONCRETE KILLAZ II

By Kingpen

HARD AND RUTHLESS II

By Von Wiley Hall

LEVELS TO THIS SHYT II

By Ah'Million

MOB TIES II

By SayNoMore

<u>Available Now</u>

RESTRAINING ORDER **I & II**

By **CA$H & Coffee**

LOVE KNOWS NO BOUNDARIES **I II & III**

By **Coffee**

RAISED AS A GOON I, II, III & IV

BRED BY THE SLUMS I, II, III

BLAST FOR ME I & II

ROTTEN TO THE CORE I II III

A BRONX TALE I, II, III

DUFFLE BAG CARTEL I II III IV V

HEARTLESS GOON I II III IV V

A SAVAGE DOPEBOY I II

DRUG LORDS I II III

CUTTHROAT MAFIA I II

By **Ghost**

LAY IT DOWN **I & II**

LAST OF A DYING BREED I II

BLOOD STAINS OF A SHOTTA I & II III

By **Jamaica**

LOYAL TO THE GAME I II III

LIFE OF SIN I, II III

By **TJ & Jelissa**

BLOODY COMMAS I & II

SKI MASK CARTEL I II & III

KING OF NEW YORK I II,III IV V

RISE TO POWER I II III

COKE KINGS I II III IV

BORN HEARTLESS I II III IV

KING OF THE TRAP

By **T.J. Edwards**

IF LOVING HIM IS WRONG…I & II

LOVE ME EVEN WHEN IT HURTS I II III

By **Jelissa**

WHEN THE STREETS CLAP BACK I & II III

THE HEART OF A SAVAGE I II

By **Jibril Williams**

A DISTINGUISHED THUG STOLE MY HEART I II & III

LOVE SHOULDN'T HURT I II III IV

RENEGADE BOYS I II III IV

PAID IN KARMA I II III

SAVAGE STORMS I II

By **Meesha**

Destiny Skai

A GANGSTER'S CODE I &, II III

A GANGSTER'S SYN I II III

THE SAVAGE LIFE I II III

CHAINED TO THE STREETS I II III

BLOOD ON THE MONEY I II

By J-Blunt

PUSH IT TO THE LIMIT

By **Bre' Hayes**

BLOOD OF A BOSS **I, II, III, IV, V**

SHADOWS OF THE GAME

By **Askari**

THE STREETS BLEED MURDER **I, II & III**

THE HEART OF A GANGSTA I II& III

By **Jerry Jackson**

CUM FOR ME I II III IV V VI

An **LDP Erotica Collaboration**

BRIDE OF A HUSTLA **I II & II**

THE FETTI GIRLS **I, II& III**

CORRUPTED BY A GANGSTA I, II III, IV

BLINDED BY HIS LOVE

THE PRICE YOU PAY FOR LOVE I II

DOPE GIRL MAGIC I II III

By **Destiny Skai**

WHEN A GOOD GIRL GOES BAD

By **Adrienne**

THE COST OF LOYALTY I II III

By Kweli

A GANGSTER'S REVENGE **I II III & IV**

THE BOSS MAN'S DAUGHTERS I II III IV V

A SAVAGE LOVE **I & II**

BAE BELONGS TO ME I II

A HUSTLER'S DECEIT I, II, III

WHAT BAD BITCHES DO I, II, III

SOUL OF A MONSTER I II III

KILL ZONE

A DOPE BOY'S QUEEN I II

By **Aryanna**

A KINGPIN'S AMBITON

A KINGPIN'S AMBITION **II**

I MURDER FOR THE DOUGH

By **Ambitious**

TRUE SAVAGE I II III IV V VI VII

DOPE BOY MAGIC I, II, III

MIDNIGHT CARTEL I II III

CITY OF KINGZ

By **Chris Green**

A DOPEBOY'S PRAYER

By **Eddie "Wolf" Lee**

THE KING CARTEL **I, II & III**

By **Frank Gresham**

THESE NIGGAS AIN'T LOYAL **I, II & III**

By **Nikki Tee**

GANGSTA SHYT **I II &III**

By **CATO**

THE ULTIMATE BETRAYAL

By **Phoenix**

BOSS'N UP **I , II & III**

By **Royal Nicole**

I LOVE YOU TO DEATH

By Destiny J

I RIDE FOR MY HITTA

I STILL RIDE FOR MY HITTA

By **Misty Holt**

LOVE & CHASIN' PAPER

Destiny Skai

By **Qay Crockett**

TO DIE IN VAIN

SINS OF A HUSTLA

By **ASAD**

BROOKLYN HUSTLAZ

By **Boogsy Morina**

BROOKLYN ON LOCK I & II

By **Sonovia**

GANGSTA CITY

By **Teddy Duke**

A DRUG KING AND HIS DIAMOND I & II III

A DOPEMAN'S RICHES

HER MAN, MINE'S TOO I, II

CASH MONEY HO'S

THE WIFEY I USED TO BE

By Nicole Goosby

TRAPHOUSE KING **I II & III**

KINGPIN KILLAZ I II III

STREET KINGS I II

PAID IN BLOOD **I II**

CARTEL KILLAZ I II III

DOPE GODS I II

By **Hood Rich**

LIPSTICK KILLAH **I, II, III**

CRIME OF PASSION I II & III

FRIEND OR FOE I II

By **Mimi**

STEADY MOBBN' **I, II, III**

THE STREETS STAINED MY SOUL

By **Marcellus Allen**

WHO SHOT YA **I, II, III**

SON OF A DOPE FIEND I II

Renta

GORILLAZ IN THE BAY **I II III IV**

TEARS OF A GANGSTA I II

3X KRAZY I II

DE'KARI

TRIGGADALE I II III

Elijah R. Freeman

GOD BLESS THE TRAPPERS I, II, III

THESE SCANDALOUS STREETS I, II, III

FEAR MY GANGSTA I, II, III IV, V

THESE STREETS DON'T LOVE NOBODY I, II

BURY ME A G I, II, III, IV, V

A GANGSTA'S EMPIRE I, II, III, IV

THE DOPEMAN'S BODYGAURD I II

THE REALEST KILLAZ I II III

Tranay Adams

THE STREETS ARE CALLING

Duquie Wilson

MARRIED TO A BOSS… I II III

By Destiny Skai & Chris Green

KINGZ OF THE GAME I II III IV V

Playa Ray

SLAUGHTER GANG I II III

RUTHLESS HEART I II III

By Willie Slaughter

FUK SHYT

By Blakk Diamond

DON'T F#CK WITH MY HEART I II

By Linnea

ADDICTED TO THE DRAMA I II III

IN THE ARM OF HIS BOSS II

By Jamila

Destiny Skai

YAYO I II III IV

A SHOOTER'S AMBITION I II

By S. Allen

TRAP GOD I II III

By Troublesome

FOREVER GANGSTA

GLOCKS ON SATIN SHEETS I II

By Adrian Dulan

TOE TAGZ I II III

LEVELS TO THIS SHYT

By Ah'Million

KINGPIN DREAMS I II

By Paper Boi Rari

CONFESSIONS OF A GANGSTA I II III

By Nicholas Lock

I'M NOTHING WITHOUT HIS LOVE

SINS OF A THUG

By Monet Dragun

CAUGHT UP IN THE LIFE I II III

By Robert Baptiste

NEW TO MONEY, MURDER & MEMORIES

THE GAME I II III

By **Malik D. Rice**

LIFE OF A SAVAGE I II III

A GANGSTA'S QUR'AN I II III

MURDA SEASON I II III

GANGLAND CARTEL I II

CHI'RAQ GANGSTAS I II

By **Romell Tukes**

LOYALTY AIN'T PROMISED I II

By Keith Williams

QUIET MONEY I II III

THUG LIFE I II

EXTENDED CLIP

By **Trai'Quan**

THE STREETS MADE ME I II

By **Larry D. Wright**

THE ULTIMATE SACRIFICE I, II, III, IV, V, VI

KHADIFI

IF YOU CROSS ME ONCE

ANGEL I II

By **Anthony Fields**

THE LIFE OF A HOOD STAR

By Ca$h & Rashia Wilson

THE STREETS WILL NEVER CLOSE

By K'ajji

CREAM

By Yolanda Moore

NIGHTMARES OF A HUSTLA I II

By King Dream

CONCRETE KILLAZ

By Kingpen

HARD AND RUTHLESS

By Von Wiley Hall

GHOST MOB II

Stilloan Robinson

MOB TIES

By SayNoMore

Destiny Skai

BOOKS BY LDP'S CEO, CA$H

TRUST IN NO MAN

TRUST IN NO MAN 2

TRUST IN NO MAN 3

BONDED BY BLOOD

SHORTY GOT A THUG

THUGS CRY

THUGS CRY 2

THUGS CRY 3

TRUST NO BITCH

TRUST NO BITCH 2

TRUST NO BITCH 3

TIL MY CASKET DROPS

RESTRAINING ORDER

RESTRAINING ORDER 2

IN LOVE WITH A CONVICT

LIFE OF A HOOD STAR